KINGDOMTIDE

KINGDOMTIDE

RYE CURTIS

Little, Brown and Company
New York Boston London

The characters and events in this book are fictitious. Any similarity to real persons, living or dead, is coincidental and not intended by the author.

Little, Brown and Company
Hachette Book Group
1290 Avenue of the Americas, New York, NY 10104
littlebrown.com

First Edition: January 2020

Little, Brown and Company is a division of Hachette Book Group, Inc. The Little, Brown name and logo are trademarks of Hachette Book Group, Inc.

The publisher is not responsible for websites (or their content) that are not owned by the publisher.

The Hachette Speakers Bureau provides a wide range of authors for speaking events. To find out more, go to hachettespeakersbureau.com or call (866) 376-6591.

ISBN 978-0-316-42010-5
LCCN 2019946515

10 9 8 7 6 5 4 3 2 1

LSC-C

Printed in the United States of America

For Mimi

KINGDOMTIDE

I

I no longer pass judgment on any man nor woman. People are people, and I do not believe there is much more to be said on the matter. Twenty years ago I might have been of a different mind about that, but I was a different Cloris Waldrip back then. I might have gone on being that same Cloris Waldrip, the one I had been for seventy-two years, had I not fallen out of the sky in that little airplane on Sunday, August 31, 1986. It does amaze that a woman can reach the tail end of her life and find that she hardly knows herself at all.

I sat by the window and my dear husband, Mr. Waldrip, sat on my right. He had his hands busy fiddling with a ragged cuticle. My husband was a kind, bird-faced man and he wore strong glasses. He was born in Amarillo, Texas, to an awning salesman and a midwife. I first ever laid eyes on him in the summer of 1927 at a county dance in the town hall. This was after his family had moved the some sixty miles east from the big noisy boomtown of Amarillo to little ole Clarendon, where I was born and raised. He was a terribly handsome boy, tall and dark-haired. However he wore a little blue cap that made him look mighty silly. We were both only kids. I had just turned thirteen. He gave me a pitifully wilted rose he had stolen from Mrs. Mckee's garden.

On that morning in August of 1986 he had a dab of jalapeño jelly on his chin. It had been there since our complimentary breakfast at the Big Sky Motel in Missoula, Montana. I was going to tell him to use the handkerchief I had embroidered with his initials and given him some many Christmases before, but he had already begun for the pilot a monologue on rainfall. Such was his custom with men he had just met.

Mr. Waldrip had arranged for us to take a scenic flight to an airfield near a cabin we had rented in the Bitterroot National Forest. The pilot he had hired was a strong, well-groomed young man by the name of Terry Squime. Terry was not a hair over thirty and was newly wed. He showed us a photograph of his bride. She was pretty and resembled Catherine Drewer, a rude and frustrating brunette woman I knew from our church, First Methodist, only Mrs. Squime was quite some years younger and had a jaw less like a shoehorn and a nose less like an old mushroom. When I would later come to know Mrs. Squime, whom I have cautioned against reading certain passages of this account, I would find her to be a pleasant and selfless young woman, and to be very little like Catherine Drewer at all.

Mr. Waldrip carried on about rainfall and the nuisance of beavers and I returned to looking out my little window. The Cessna 340 is a little twin-propeller airplane of six seats, and ours had taken off from an airfield outside of Missoula and was flying south over the Bitterroot Mountains. I mean to tell you these are mountains, the kind that remind a person, no matter how old they are, that they are infinitely young to the earth. These mountains are edged and scalloped like gigantic kin to the arrowheads my little brother, Davy, God rest his tiny soul, unearthed in Palo Duro Canyon when we were small. I had lived seventy-two years in the Texas Panhandle and mountains are not a geological feature you will find in that country. The land is as flat as flat can be, level with what is level in the constitution and spirit of the people who walk it. We plains folk are a grounded people and rarely see a mountain. But having seen what I have now seen of them, when I say these were mountains, you would be right to believe me.

I was then fifty-four years married to Mr. Waldrip. We lived in a little brick ranch house in the orbital shade of a municipal water tower that serviced the some two thousand thirsty souls in Clarendon. Only the day before we had locked up the front door and had taken the truck to the airport in Amarillo, where we had then flown, with a quick stop in Denver, to Missoula on a jet airplane. We did not often venture far from our little house, and this was to be the first trip we had taken in a good long while. We had spent the first night of it under a full moon in the Big Sky Motel, off I-90, an establishment with damp carpets and laminate wood. Mr. Waldrip was not a poor man, but neither was he an extravagant man. I had come to terms with this early on in our marriage.

Mr. Waldrip hesitated half a second on the subject of rain gauges and Terry took the opportunity to ask how long we were planning to stay in Montana.

Just a few days, Mr. Waldrip said. Our pastor and his wife had the best time up here. Figured we'd get ourselves a cabin, do some fishin and kick back. But we sure need to get back this comin Thursday.

Mr. Waldrip likes to pretend he is not retired, I said.

Terry looked back. What kind of work did you do, sir?

I bought a cattle ranch in '45. We sold it a year ago September.

Well, I bet you two will have a great time up here, Terry said.

We're countin on it, Mr. Waldrip said, and he pulled the cuticle from his thumb. A point of blood rose on the nail and he stanched it on his blue jeans.

Doing Mr. Waldrip's laundry, you might come across several pairs of blue jeans peppered with blood like that. If you did not know him, you could mistake him for a fighting man. But the only physical altercation I ever recall him having was with a mean old possum that had got itself snagged on a nail under our porch. Mr. Waldrip had his small ways of fidgeting. I suppose it was the result of his mind always being a few steps ahead of the rest of him, quick as he was, and it made him nervous trying to catch up.

Did you work, Mrs. Waldrip? Terry asked.

I had taught English in elementary school and was the librarian for forty-four years, and I told him so. I retired two years ago, I said.

Now we only got time for relaxin, said Mr. Waldrip, patting my knee.

Any kids? Terry said.

Never did get around to it, Mr. Waldrip said.

I turned back to my little window. The blue sky and the pane gave back my reflection. It reminded me of the oval portrait of my great-grandmother June Polyander which had hung over her bed until she passed away in her nineties. I fixed my hair. I wore it like many of the ladies at First Methodist. Permed up, we called it. When I was a young woman it had been the color of lovegrass in winter and I had worn it longer then. It started going gray in my forties. The grayer and whiter it went, the more Mr. Waldrip said I looked like a dandelion going to seed.

I have never been a great beauty—my nose is too much like a man's to earn that appellation—but I have always done my best to be presentable. A spiky-haired woman named Lucille Carver came to church often as not looking like she had been fired there out of a cannon. I never could understand why she would let herself out of the house like that. I had always supposed it had to do with a disrespect for worship and a disregard for femininity, but now I am not so sure. That warm Sunday in August I wore a pleated tan skirt and a white blouse, and I was carrying my nice leather purse. I am mighty glad now that I was also wearing my most comfortable pair of walking shoes.

I suppose women like me are a phenomenon of the past. In Dallas

I saw a young woman with long, screwy unwashed hair hold a restaurant door open for a man. I thought at the time that this young woman was without a sense of decorum and propriety. However I think now she was a sign of the times. Maybe something good and new of the future.

I spent my entire life with women to whom I felt akin, sitting in the fourth pew from the front at First Methodist. I know that each of them have had their hardships and have suffered one way or another. Mary Martha had been born with an odd-shaped kidney that did not work the way it ought to and caused her much pain and turned the whites in her eyes the color of egg yolk. Sara Mae lost her little boy in an accident involving a tire swing, and Mabry Cartwright never married, being that her teeth might as well have been woodchips and her breath the wind over a feedlot. I do not know how my trials and tribulations tally against those of any of these women. We do not know anyone's suffering but our own. However I do sometimes wonder if any of them could have survived the Bitterroot.

Forgot to make sure the pantry light was off, Mr. Waldrip said, looking past me out the window.

I told him that I believed it was.

I took a sweet from my purse and unwrapped it. I was partial to caramels then but I do not eat them now. I have lost the taste for them. Sleep had not come easy in the Big Sky Motel the night prior for the proximity of the highway and I was tired. I ate the caramel and I laid my head back against the seat. Mountains skirted the window and I dozed off listening to Mr. Waldrip talk of center-pivot irrigation.

I woke to Mr. Waldrip's hand on my knee. The little airplane was shuddering something terrible and he leaned forward to try and see into the cockpit. I was nervous to begin with up in the air like we were. Other than the jet airplane that had flown us to Missoula, I had only ever been on an airplane once before. It was June 1954 and I had just had my fortieth birthday and we flew to Florida to visit Mr. Waldrip's ailing brother, Samuel Waldrip. We also saw the beach.

Mr. Waldrip took his hand from my knee and said, I'm pretty sure now I left the pantry light on.

I wondered then why he woke me up to tell me something so silly, but I did not say so. I think now he wanted my company. That dab of jelly was still there on his chin. I opened my purse for a tissue and suddenly the airplane lurched. My stomach rose against the buckle of my seatbelt. I leaned over and looked into the cockpit. Terry's arm was jerking at the controls, his elbow held out high and jittering. The airplane leveled and I leaned back.

Mr. Waldrip asked Terry if something was wrong. Terry did not answer. He was face-forward like the last thing he had a mind to do was look back at us. I fixed my eyes on the back of his head. I recall being mighty afraid of the expression that might be on the other side of it.

The little airplane lurched again. I did not want to, but I looked out the window anyway. A range of fearsome mountains reached for us like an open claw meaning to snatch us out of the sky. The airplane leveled out again. Sun glared off the wing like it does off a seep pond and I covered my eyes. Mr. Waldrip put his hand back on my knee. I looked at him.

It's okay, Clory, he said. It's just some bumps, same as the road you dislike.

What road?

The road you complain about in the east pasture.

I told him I did not think I would complain about a road.

The little airplane whined and out my window the propeller had slowed such that I could make out each blade. It occurred to me that I did not know how an airplane stays in the air at all, and I made up my mind that we were all of us idiots for ever setting foot in one. The nose tilted downward and I could tell that we were descending because my arms were light and all my insides seemed to float. The back of Terry's head frightened me even more now, such like it was the flat featureless haired face of Satan himself.

I got ahold of Mr. Waldrip's hand and I turned to him. He would not look at me. Neither of the men would look at me. I imagine they dared not see their own fears confirmed in the wild horror laid out on a woman's face. Mr. Waldrip put his eyes ahead.

Out the window I saw the mountains rise up around us. The airplane shuddered and my seat vibrated.

Our hands were clammy together now, and I looked back to Mr. Waldrip.

Still he faced forward and said to no one in particular: What is it?

Terry did not answer him.

I did not answer him.

I have always been powerfully baffled that I did not pray then. Instead, I took Mr. Waldrip's face in my hands and pushed his cheeks together. He looked mighty scared and ashamed like a little boy and scarcely like himself at all. Never in all our years of marriage had I known he had in him an expression like that. I let go of his face and put my head on his chest. Gracious, how embarrassed we would be if this came to nothing!

I heard inside Mr. Waldrip that same old heartbeat going quicker and quicker, and then his voice in his chest muffled and big, like the way our pastor, Bill Dow, preached into his new microphone. Suddenly it was unfamiliar as if it had originated from some awful dimension in which I did not hold any belief.

He gasped and said that I was a wife. I like to believe he meant to say that I was a *good* wife, but before he could correct himself, the little airplane hit.

The noise was too much for ears. I do not know how noise like that comes about. Perhaps the impact had fractured all known sound into pieces I could no longer recognize on their own. Terry wailed out a thing horrible and unmanly and I recall being awed by the way people show their fear of God in such times. We all of us then did not behave as we had for nearly all of our lives. I can still only describe the noises Terry made as a turkey endeavoring to gobble in English. I believe to this day he said *God save Mrs. Custard* but I still do not have the faintest notion what he might have meant by it.

Mr. Waldrip did not make a peep and was torn from me, and all that I glimpsed were the scuffed-up soles of the alligator-skin boots I had given him years before on an occasion I cannot now recall. An object knocked the wind from me and came to rest on my shoulder. I do not recall when I realized that we had stopped moving, only that the caramel I had eaten had worked its way back up my throat.

Forest Ranger Debra Lewis, a thermos of merlot between her thighs and a .44 revolver at her hip, drove the sunbleached dirt road to Egyptian Point, an overlook up the mountain where teenagers from the foothills drugged and drank and had sex. A bowlegged Shoshone woman named Silk Foot Maggie lived adjacent in a mobile home and had radioed into the station about a bonfire and curse words and phantoms in the woods. Lewis had tossed a can of bear spray into the backseat of the green and tan 1978 Jeep Wagoneer in case the kids were belligerent.

She came upon two pickup trucks parked at the trailhead. The noonday sun knotted black shadows under them and there slept two pale bulldogs chained to the hitches. Lewis pulled over and fixed in the rearview mirror the campaign hat she wore over feathered brown hair shorn just at her shoulders in the cut of a schoolboy. She took a sleeve of her uniform to a row of winestained teeth and buffed them.

She hiked the trail up to Egyptian Point, the can of bear spray in one hand and the thermos in the other, until she came to the place. Voices carried on the wind and a coat sleeve disappeared into a mott of white pine. She clipped the thermos to her belt and wedged the bear spray into a coat pocket. Monoliths of granite encircled the clearing. Smoke unspooled from a smoldering pit of busted lawn chairs and a torn plastic bag. Blackened beer cans twitched at the foot of a disfigured drugstore mannequin adorned with a crown of used condoms. Curse words and Christian names lay coupled and carved and painted over rock faces and trees. From behind a bank of spruce and granite came whispers and pairs of eyes spun there in the shade.

Now you honyockers listen up like all your lives depended on it, Lewis said. Cause I just might decide that they do.

She stumbled around in a circle, crossing her legs like a dancer. She touched the revolver at her hip.

You can't do what you're goddamn doin up here, she said. You can't drink alcohol or smoke whatever it is you're smokin here. This's a protected region. Past that old sign back there it's the wilderness. I'm the goddamn law out here. I'm the adult here. Go on home, goddamn it, go on home.

No response came.

If I don't see you goofballs comin down in a hurry, I swear to God I won't be happy. I got the license plates on those outfits down there.

She faced about to leave and saw crouched in an alcove between two pornographically defaced boulders a teenaged girl with white hair and an overbite. The girl wore nothing save a brassiere and did not blink. She watched Lewis and palmed her small breasts, her bony ribs working fast. Her face was dirty and her forehead marked in soot like that of a supplicant on Ash Wednesday. Lewis was thirty-seven and figured the girl for at least twenty years younger than her. She looked once in the girl's eyes and returned to the trailhead where she sat in the Wagoneer and drank from the thermos of merlot until the lithe figures of cackling teenagers swept two by two from the woods like mythical waifs and left in their pickups as the sun fell behind distant peaks.

Lewis drove back in the direction of the small pinewood cabin she had lived in for the past eleven years. It sat off a mountain road in an alpine forest near vacation homes left vacant. She drank again from the thermos and listened to the only clear radio broadcast to reach up the mountain.

You're listening to *Ask Dr. Howe How*, I'm Dr. Howe, and it's time for our last caller until I'm back on tonight. Thank you for joining us today. What can I do for you, Sam?

A tired and dolorous voice belonging neither distinctly to a man nor a woman asked how it was that people could so resolutely misunderstand one another.

Before Dr. Howe could respond, Lewis swerved out of respect to miss a roadkill and spilled the thermos over her uniform. She took the Lord's name in vain and the radio signal went to static and Dr. Howe's answer was lost.

All was quiet. Then I heard a whistle that could have been a kettle. I opened my eyes. I am not certain that I was ever unconscious, but it is my understanding that it is often hard to know about that sort of thing. A bright red suitcase, not one I recognized, pinned my shoulder. My guess was that it was Terry's. I heaved it off. Where my window had been there was now a wide gash in the fuselage, as if someone had pried open a can of peas. I undid my seatbelt.

I had come to the end of a world in that little airplane, and in such a terrible calm I climbed through that gash and was born again into another. The airplane had stopped on an escarpment of granite up near the peak of a high rocky mountain, the nose not three yards from the edge where a jungle of tall conifers rose from below, nodding. All about were mountains. Two big ones flanked ours and farther out a snow-capped range repeated into the blue distance like all there were and all there had ever been in the history of the world were mountains.

I touched my forehead. Blood. My face was covered with it and in a piece of broken glass I saw that I had a small cut over my eyebrow. I looked like an Indian brave in warpaint. I hollered for Richard loud as I could. I only ever used Mr. Waldrip's Christian name when addressing him directly, a habit I learned from Mother.

The sun was out and the day was warm. It is a strange thing that such a pleasant and beautiful place can seem so mean-spirited. The mountain was high up, but no snow was on the ground and all about hairy plants with mighty pretty scarlet flowers grew from the rock. I later learned they are called mountainside paintbrushes. The airplane had been halved down the middle. The tail of it was gone.

I looked back at Mr. Waldrip's empty seat. I hollered for him again. My eyes returned to the treetops below the escarpment. One of Mr. Waldrip's alligator-skin boots was right side up at the edge. I started for it. As I went I looked back at the little airplane and saw the nose of the cockpit had been shorn away. Most of the flight controls were gone and Terry sat there in the open air still in his seatbelt. He was slumped over. I was sure he had passed.

When I reached the edge of the escarpment Mr. Waldrip was some half a dozen yards down, splayed out prone across the top of a large spruce. He was mighty high up off the ground. I hollered at him if he was all right but I ought to have already had the answer to that. He did not move and I could see blood was welling in the seat of his blue jeans. I hollered his name again. I worried he was hung there paralyzed and could not answer me. There was not a thing in the world I could do. I could not reach him, and if I had been able to reach him, what good would it have done? That was when it first occurred to me to pray. I knelt down at the edge of that escarpment and looked out over an immense valley and I prayed: Our Father, who art in heaven, Mr. Waldrip is down there in a tree, and he is badly hurt. Please help us, please help us, please save us, Lord... Mine eyes are ever toward the Lord, for he shall pluck my feet from out the net.

I prayed that way for some time until Mr. Waldrip's blue jeans had gone plum-colored. I doubtless would still be knelt there in prayer had it not been that behind me there was such a scream like I had never heard before. It was a high-pitched sort of cry, very wet and moronic. Best way I know to describe it, and it is a distasteful notion for which I hope to be forgiven, is that it was how I imagine a simple person would holler if they were immolated.

Well, I hollered too and threw my hands up over my face. Finally I turned and lowered my fingers. My dear! Terry had come to and was chewing the blood in his mouth, screeching that awful way in repeat. One of the residents in my building here at River Bend Assisted Living in Brattleboro, Vermont, has a son, Jacob, who is in a wheelchair and cannot move his body, not even his eyelids. It is awful. His eyes must be shut at night and opened come morning by a caretaker, who is a stout large-headed woman in white with a little squirt bottle of saline on her belt that she uses to mist his eyeballs at two-minute intervals throughout the day. Jacob might not blink, but he sure can scream. That is about all he can do. When I hear him in the halls I am reminded of Terry.

I took some steps forward. Terry was not in a good way at all. He had spit up a segment of his jaw which yet held several of his teeth in it and it had dropped into his shirt collar. One of his blue eyes was black entirely. He did not act like he could see out of either of them. He kept up his crazed screaming, and I matched each one. My hands shook and my heart jumped like a jackrabbit. There we were, just hollering at each other. In some better world the whole performance might have been comical.

Terry was upright some several feet off the ground, belted in his chair, exalted like a terrible overseer of terrible doings. I stood before him, continuing to holler myself silly, without the wildest notion as to what to do. I could just have about reached his shins to comfort him, but I did not want to touch him, and I sure felt bad about that. My whole family were Methodists and I was taught to keep charity and compassion in my heart, but there was not a thing in the world I could have done for that man.

After an awful spell, like a baby he calmed on his own accord and was cooing. He raised up his arm such as to issue an edict and said sweet as can be: Is it over?

Pardon? I said.

Excuse me, I've always been honest with my dentist. Am I at the dentist? Just a minute. Are we dead yet?

My husband is in a tree, I said, pointing behind.

Good for him, Terry said. He was always climbing that tree.

After that he said the word *waitress* some twenty times and soiled himself. Then he bawled and asked for his mailman so that he could post a letter to a relative for whom he had forgotten the name and address. He was carrying on like he believed he was having a tooth pulled on gas at his dentist's office. I took a notion to ask him what we ought to do but decided against it. Poor man.

He said: Waitress, bathtime, waitress, bathtime for Samantha. I've carried a torch for my mailman for years, but it was never going to work out. He's late. Late. Pull the tooth already, this gas is making me sick. I want to go home.

The rest of the day I sat bewildered with my back to a wall of limestone and my legs stretched out in a place of sun, turning my wedding ring on my finger. Mr. Waldrip's grandmother Sarah Louise Waldrip had bequeathed him the ring, and she used to tell a mighty tall story about how her husband had traded it off a gypsy for a sack of flour and a flintlock pistol. The story goes that the gypsy came back in the night and shot to death the sheepdog they had and stole every other single thing in the house, even the curtains, but left the ring. If I had been a superstitious person I might have been worried some about that.

I was not injured in any serious way far as I could tell. I had the cut on my forehead and the arthritis in my knees was acting up. I had wet myself and was mighty embarrassed about that, but this account should tell the whole of the story, even the unpleasant parts I would rather leave out. Perhaps especially the unpleasant parts. I could not see Terry from where I sat behind the little airplane, but bless you, I listened to him holler and jabber all day about people I did not know doing things I could not reconcile with logic. Often I looked down the escarpment at Mr. Waldrip's boot. I endeavored to will myself back to the edge where his body lay in the treetop below, but I could not.

How did I not shed a single tear then? I do not know. It is funny the way our minds put themselves at ease in times of distress. I do not recall having a complete thought for some time. Different physicians have offered the same opinion that I was in shock. They may be right. Could be I still am.

When the mountains began to go dark I appealed to the heavens. Dear Lord, I said, please do not let me die on this mountain in the dark. Please save me, Lord.

Gracious, was there ever a more selfish woman born?

Then Terry lowered his voice and said, You? Yes! A boy? I don't think so. There are two of me in every bathtub. Pardon me, excuse me, I'm sorry. I didn't want you to find out. Are you finished, Dr. Kessler? This gas is scary. I can't move. I'm tripping that I'm on a mountain.

I went to the airplane and kept around the side so I would not have to look at Terry. I could only see his legs dangling from the seat and I could smell him. I asked him how he was feeling.

Grown up, he said. I'm feeling grown up. I'm too big for my britches.

Good, I said. I spoke calmly so he would not holler anymore. I asked him what we should do.

My head hurts, he said. Do I have cavities? Bathwater! Waitress!

The sun was partly down past the far mountains. They were a grand shade of purple. It all looked the way Mr. Waldrip's mother used to watercolor when she got old and as loony as a bullfrog and decided that painting was her vocation and got to wearing her slippers on her hands. All of her paint would run together and it was unlikely anyone could guess what she had meant anything to be.

I rounded the airplane to get a better look at Terry. He had his eyes open. They were vacant and gleaming like the marble eyes in the trophies that Mr. Waldrip's hunting friends had all hung up on their walls to their wives' dismay. I never let Mr. Waldrip keep any of his own in the house. I have always had the opinion it was macabre to hang heads on a wall.

Terry was chewing on that broken piece of jaw. I shuddered at the sight of him. I had never before witnessed such a helping of violence. Mr. Waldrip and I did not go to the kinds of pictures that had it. I had seen people pass away, but not like that. Father had gone at peace in a goose-down bed five years before, and Mother shortly thereafter in a similar manner at the age of ninety-three. Davy got the ague and died sleeping in his bed when he was eleven years old. God rest his soul.

There was a hole over Terry's right ear. I say a hole, but what I ought to say is that a good portion of his head was missing. It had gotten scooped away somehow or another and some of it was on his shoulder like an epaulet of melon pulp. He had started singing quietly in falsetto a song called "Time After Time," which I have since learned was made popular a couple years before by a young lesbian named Cyndi Lauper. Dear Mrs. Squime later informed me that Terry had never mentioned the song nor would it have been the kind of music she would have expected him to enjoy and she could not fathom why it appeared on his lips before his death.

I sat on the ground in front of him. I suppose I did not want to be alone, even if he was not particularly good company. He sang that song over and over again until I had learned all the words. The last of the sun was gone and above us shone a bright full moon. Terry got quiet after a while. His marred face did not move anymore.

His eyes were stuck wide open yet they no longer looked about unseeingly and the blue in them had grayed. I was then sure he had finally passed. I had never seen a thing like it and I hoped then that I never would again. It haunts me yet.

I climbed back into my seat in the little airplane. It was colder now. My coat had been in my bag and that was missing with the other half of the airplane, which officials found some weeks later scattered across the north side of the peak in nearly the shape of a hexagram. In the bright red suitcase that had fallen on me during the crash I found a wool sweater with a colorful zigzag pattern such as I had seen some young people wearing on television. It is mighty fine luck that Terry was a large man, for his clothing yielded a wealth of fabric and proved very useful against the cold. I wrapped myself in the sweater and sat back again in my seat.

It was terribly quiet then, save for the memory of Terry's song yet warbling in my ears. I endeavored not to worry on my situation, or worry that Mr. Waldrip was still in that spruce. And I made an effort not to stare at the back of Terry's head. From where I sat it looked eerily the same to how it had before we had fallen out of the sky, such as if some pieces of the world had halted in time and others had gone on.

After it was plenty dark and I could not guess what time it was, I climbed ahead to the cockpit where a small yellow light blinked in what remained of the controls by Terry's legs. It was a radio. My heart leapt! I grabbed the receiver and held it to my mouth. I recall shaking wildly and warming up around my neck and behind my ears. I held down the button on the side of the receiver and said, many times, My name is Cloris Waldrip, help, my name is Cloris Waldrip, help, is anyone there? My name is Cloris.

Lewis, eyes bloodshot and lips purpled, scrubbed a dark stain from her uniform. She rinsed the olivedrab shirt and held it to the light over the kitchen sink. She sank it back into the water and took up a brass badge and washed it under the faucet. She passed a thumb over the relief of a conifer and set the badge aside and looked out the window above the sink. The small pinewood cabin overlooked a dim and narrow wooded ravine and the mountain range beyond.

She left the uniform to soak and went to the living room with a glass of merlot. She sat on the couch and turned on the transistor radio on the end table, but there was no signal. Over the fireplace was mounted the head of a runt doe her ex-husband had shot when he was a boy. She watched a wasp land on the dusty black nose. She heard voices out front. Lewis turned down the static on the radio. Boots thumped on the steps to the porch. She finished the glass of merlot and switched off the radio and went to the door. She opened it to the screen.

Ranger Claude Paulson leaned on the frame. He had a nose the color of gunmetal after a bad bout of frostbite, but Lewis figured his face was handsome otherwise. He lifted from clean dark hair a campaign hat and held it at his waist. Hey, Debs, he said, sorry to bother after nine like this on a Sunday. Saw your light on.

That's all right, Lewis said.

Claude lived next door in a small blue-washed cabin with an old golden retriever he called Charlie. He had no curtains to his bedroom window and Lewis often saw him in bed reading or asleep, mouth agape. Most mornings she had a cup of coffee and merlot and watched him iron his uniform. Once she had seen him awake past midnight naked at the foot of his bed weeping into the dog's coat.

Lewis opened the screen door and a man staggered up the steps behind Claude, struggling with a video camera as if it were a cinder block. Pigeonchested, the man propped himself against a post, jaundiced there under the porch light. He swung the video camera off his shoulder and trembled a hand over his skinny neck. He scratched at the red stubble down past his shirt collar. Evenin, ma'am.

Claude jabbed a thumb over his shoulder and introduced the man as Pete and said that he was an old friend from high school. He's goin to be stayin with me and Charlie for a little while.

My old lady left me, Pete said.

Goddamn sorry to hear that.

I'll be all right, ma'am, thank you. Claudey's agreed to put me up while I'm hurtin.

Claude told Lewis the plan was for Pete to help him finally get the ghost of Cornelia Åkersson on tape with his new video camera. He said that it would also do Pete some good to volunteer in the Friends of the Forest program and get some fresh air.

Pete glanced behind him at the dark mountain road. So it's just you and Claude the only rangers up here? Maybe I'll be some help, then, while I'm hurtin.

Pete's had some ciders.

We been out lookin for that one-eyed ghost you got up here, Pete said. He retied a meager auburn ponytail and adjusted the strap to the video camera. Claudey here wants me to get a picture of her, but I told him I ain't any good at takin pictures. He's always had more faith in me than what I got in myself. I know Claudey since we're in high school back in Big Timber. It sure is good to be with old friends while you're hurtin.

Lewis nodded and looked to Claude. The porch light showed the dog hair on his uniform. He turned in his hands the campaign hat like he were steering a car.

So what is it, Claude?

I'd say that's a hard one to say.

We got a distress call over the radio, Pete said.

Claude put up a hand. I'll give her the information, Petey. We can't say we know it was a distress call. All we can say is we heard a humanoidal voice say *cloris*. Thrice it said it. *Cloris, cloris, cloris.* Like that. It was garbled.

Cloris?

Cloris.

I tend to frighten, so it spooked me some, Pete said.

What's a goddamn cloris?

I can't say that I know, Claude said. If it's some kind of code, I can't say that I know it. And what for, to what end?

Maybe you misheard it.

Maybe. Maybe. Don't think I did.

What sounds like cloris?

Morris, Pete said.

Where were you?

Out by Darling Pass.

See your goddamn ghost?

Claude smiled. All right now, Debs. No need to have fun at my expense.

Pete raised a red eyebrow. You don't believe in the ghost, Ranger Lewis?

I've never seen it.

I guess it's hard to believe in somethin especially when you can't see it, Pete said. I tried to believe my wife loved me. But after a while she said she wanted to make a change in her life before change was too late to be made. She said I was repressed. Sometimes she likes to use words I ain't never heard of to make me feel bad about my education. But I told her she ain't goin to get another way of life like she wants, not at thirty-nine lookin like she's sixty-nine, not a clean tooth in her gourd.

Pete's had some ciders, Claude said.

Did I tell you what she said, Claudey?

Why don't you tell me later?

No, go ahead, Lewis said. What'd she say?

Said I had a weird heart in a weird chest. Said I looked like an ugly woman with derelict breasts.

I'm sorry, Petey. She shouldn't talk about you like that.

Well, I'll be all right. I know I got a weird chest, had it all my life, born with it. Pectus carinatum. But a weird heart? Been wrackin my brain tryin to know what she meant by that.

Sorry again about the hour, Debs, Claude said, turning to her. Just thought I'd brief you on this cloris word in case you thought we should act on it in some way didn't occur to me.

Lewis steadied herself on the doorjamb and looked up to the dark sky. She recalled the coat of a black Labrador she had once watched her father euthanize in his clinic. She looked back to Claude. You don't need to check on me every goddamn weekend. I'm all right.

I know that.

All right, she said. Man's voice or woman's?

Couldn't say. I'd say might've been a woman or a young boy.

Pete fanned out a hand of small fingers. To me that voice had the sound of a forlorned woman, he said importantly.

All right. I'll make a note of this tomorrow mornin. You two ought to get on home before Cornelia eats you guys' tongues and takes you to Neptune.

Come on now, Debs, don't poke fun.

What's that? Pete said.

The goddamn ghost Claude's got you lookin for, Lewis said. Gums off tongues, hair, and balls.

She closed the door on the two men, then she went back to the kitchen sink. The stains in the uniform had not come out. She dropped the shirt in the wastebasket. She had another glass of merlot and took a long bath with another bottle and listened to *Ask Dr. Howe How*. A thunderous woman phoned into the program and asked how it was that she and her husband seemed to be behaving like unrealistic and impractical people. She asked if it were common for people to behave like characters they had seen on television. In a reedy and pragmatic voice like that of a physician in surgery, Dr. Howe offered that, yes, it was common, perhaps because to do so was easier than assessing and acting on our authentic impulses and concerns.

Lewis switched off the radio and climbed from the bath. She dried herself and stood naked to her bedroom window looking out at the dark pines and the valley below. She took to the fogged pane the tip of a finger and outlined her tall reflection. Beyond, in the forest, distant flashlights worked the dark and struck the trees. Lewis figured it was the men searching yet for the ghost of Cornelia Åkersson.

She wiped the window clear and returned to the bathroom to vomit in the sink and then went to bed where she slept a restless night of dreams she was sure she had dreamt but none of them could she recount upon waking. In the morning she said to herself, God only knows what happens to me in my goddamn dreams.

Lewis stopped the Wagoneer to clear from the road a flattened goshawk. She sailed the carcass like a discus into the trees below and marked the incident in the notepad she kept in her chest pocket. The sun was not yet up, the road still dark. She drove on and came to the one-room cedar structure perched high up the mountain. She unlocked the front door under a sign wood-burned with *National Forest Service Backcountry Station* and went inside.

In the kitchenette she started a pot of coffee and took three aspirin and splashed her face at the sink and clicked on the space heater. Her desk was flush against a large westfacing window with a view of the same wooded valley she could see from her cabin. Mist sat in the evergreens and was just burning off under a rising sun. Great clots of dark birds turned in the sky. Lewis took off the campaign hat and set it to a hook on the wall. She sat and powered on the radio equipment on the desk and waited for it to warm up. She leaned over the paging microphone.

Ranger Lewis to Chief Gaskell. Ranger Lewis to Chief Gaskell. Come in, Chief Gaskell. Over.

Mornin, Ranger Lewis. Readin you loud and clear. What're you doin at the station this early? Over.

Somethin was buggin me, couldn't let it wait. John, you know anythin about a cloris? Over.

What's a cloris? Say again. Over.

Cloris. I don't know. I was hopin you would. Over.

I don't. Over.

Is it not code? Stand for somethin? Over.

Not anything I know. Over.

Ranger Paulson received a transmission over his handheld last night out by Darling Pass, worried it might've been a distress call. It just said cloris. Thrice it said it. Cloris, cloris, cloris. Could've misheard. Over.

Cloris? Say again. Over.

Cloris. I'm spellin it C-L-O-R-I-S. Cloris. Over.

Cloris. Copy. Cloris. I've never heard of that. Cloris. I'll check around. Darling Pass? Was Claude out lookin for that ghost he says rides that turtle? Over.

Goddamn Cornelia. He was. Over.

He's a strange bird. How're you holdin up up there? Over.

Lewis leaned back and looked out the window. A black beetle was climbing the inside of the pane and appeared there an immense animal using for stepping stones the peaks beyond. She hunched again for the microphone. I'm all right, John, thanks. Over.

All right, well you let me know if there's anything I can do. We're thinkin about you. Marcy says she's thinkin about you too. Divorce is hard times under any circumstance. Over.

Appreciate it. Over.

That everything, Ranger Lewis? Over.

That's everything. Out.

Lewis stood from her desk and went to the kitchenette and poured a cup of coffee and splashed a little merlot in it from a bottle hidden in a cutout behind the cabinet and turned again to the window. She went back and leaned over her desk and flicked away the beetle.

Mr. Waldrip and I had a calendar of 1986 from First Methodist pasted to the pantry door. Prior to us leaving on our trip to Montana, Mr. Waldrip had circled the 31st of August with black pen and had neatly written in the appointment we had with Terry Squime for the flight to our cabin in the Bitterroot National Forest. I have always thought it noteworthy that the 31st happened to fall on the first Sunday of Kingdomtide. If you are not a Methodist of a certain age likely you have not heard of Kingdomtide. It is meant to be a season of charity and unity in the Kingdom of God observed after Pentecost and before Advent. Not many churches observe it anymore. For me, ever since my time in the Bitterroot, it has turned out to be a season of considerable hardship and grief.

I now have the calendar here with me at River Bend Assisted Living on the wall above my desk. Mr. Waldrip could not have foreseen he was marking the day he would wind up in a tree and I would be stranded in the wilderness, but that is just the way these fateful moments go. Often we do not know the significance of a thing until it is good and well in the past. It is seldom now that I shut my eyes without I should see that calendar and the first Sunday of Kingdomtide circled in the glittery dark you can find on the inside of your eyelids. I fear it may be the last thing I ever see.

There was painful little sleep to be had that first night. I must have said my name into the radio near to a thousand times. I was hoarser than a pioneer preacher on a Monday. I was not certain whether the radio still worked, but I made an effort nevertheless. When I did endeavor to get some shut-eye, I learned how mighty afraid I was. I did not care for staying in that little airplane with Terry's disfigured body looming up in a terrible silence, but I came to reason it was a sight better than sleeping out in the open with the dark and all the unknown critters that call the dark their home.

When I woke the sun was high and my shoulder and knees ached something terrible. I was getting thirsty. Dried blood flaked off my forehead like paint off an old prairie home. A filthy latticework of scratches and scrapes covered my arms. I was not even sure they were my arms. They seemed to belong to some old and pitifully treated indigent woman. I sat up and climbed out through the gash in the little airplane.

Terry was still strapped in his seat, warped up like an old cigar-store Indian left out in the weather for a considerable long while. His fingers had buckled into an array like buzzard talons and his jaw was crooked and dried out. I cannot know what on earth compelled me but I covered my mouth and went closer to him. Tiny gnats danced on his opaque eyes and I studied the way the bigger flies throned the tongue in his gaping mouth like little green potbellied despots.

I left Terry and went to the edge of the escarpment and stood next to Mr. Waldrip's boot. My poor husband was down there yet caught in that spruce. He had not moved. I prayed then and there that this would be the most heartless sight to which I would ever bear witness. I got a handful of pebbles and chucked them at him. Some missed entirely and others bounced clear off his back. Mr. Waldrip did not move. I was reminded of when he had been hospitalized for his back surgery in 1974. When they put him on the morphine he went quiet and helpless. I had never seen him like that before. I had certainly never seen him deceased before. He was a mighty sweet man, dear Mr. Waldrip, God rest his soul. I miss him very much.

A young black woman who is a therapist here at River Bend Assisted Living has told me that there is a woman in Switzerland with one of these doubled surnames that are fashionable today, Elisabeth Kübler-Ross, who believes that there are five stages of grief: denial, anger, bargaining, depression, and acceptance. I am sure that she means well, but I do not believe she has it exactly right. The stages of grief are myriad and you could not endeavor to name them all. A stage for every recollection, for every ever-failing memory, and these stages are nameless and they are many, so that cast before you is a measureless spectrum of unparticular nostalgia and loss. Grief is the cold end of the night, I believe.

I turned back to the airplane and decided I would try the radio again. By then I had grown used to the foul way Terry smelled so that I did not even flinch when I crawled in around his legs and took hold again of the receiver. I said the same thing I had said all night prior: Help me, my name is Cloris Waldrip. Our airplane went down.

I repeated this at intervals some one hundred times or better. I was getting mighty hungry and thirsty so I looked for my purse and found it had tumped over on the floor next to my seat. I put back what I could find: my gallbladder medication (which I had nearly finished and did not especially need to take anymore, thank goodness), a packet of tissues, my little copy of the King James Bible, my house keys. I did turn up a handful of my caramels under the seat, but I could not find my copy of *Anna Karenina* nor my pocketbook. I did not imagine I would need my pocketbook, but I would have liked to have had the copy of *Anna Karenina*. I could not find any water.

I backed out of the fuselage with my purse and I unwrapped a caramel and ate it on a short boulder close by so that I could still hear the radio should anyone come through. It was a Monday and I usually had my Panhandle Ladies' Breakfast Club on Mondays out at the Goodnight House. (Colonel Charles Goodnight was a celebrated cattleman who helped settle the Panhandle, and his family have kept up his fine estate as a landmark of historical significance.) We often ate on the veranda. Had Mr. Waldrip not convinced me to go on this crazy trip, I would have been sat between Sara Mae Davis and Ruth Moore, the sun in Ruth's dyed orange hair like a Christmas light, both of them yammering about the new establishment in downtown Amarillo that was said to be an iniquitous place for women who liked women and men who liked men.

I had reached into my purse for another caramel when suddenly Terry shuddered and growled! Dear me! Flies blew out like smoke from his nose and mouth in a great retch. I let out a terrific scream and covered my face in horror. I fell to my knees and prayed.

A kind pathologist would later inform me that Terry had eructed. Unpleasant a thing as it is, during decomposition a corpse will build up internal gas that has to escape somehow. I understand the gas is sometimes called cadaverine. It does not sound right to me, but this pathologist was a medical man so I am inclined to believe him. It would be a shame if he were pulling an old woman's leg.

After I had prayed for some time I opened my eyes. Terry was much as he was before. The flies had resettled him and his mouth was black with them. I was in dread for fear he would move again. After a spell, when finally I decided that he would not and was very deceased, I looked to the sky for the time of day and could not tell what it was. If I had been in our little house I would have been able to tell by the way the light falls through the windows in the sitting room. Living that long in a place makes it something of a clock. Everything tells you the time. You could know the hour by the shadow of a chair leg on the carpet. But out there on that mountain the light fell about so strangely that I was hardly ever too certain.

I guessed it was late afternoon and I decided I would take a look around before dark. I was just then beginning to get my wits about me and think rationally on what I ought to do. Though I do not believe I had as of yet understood my situation entirely. I scouted around the escarpment, but never left sight of the little airplane. The place was not large. It was a narrow chance we had stopped there instead of farther down the mountain in the timber. I found little else besides granite cliff faces, which I could not climb. However I did spot a raccoon with a white eye hiding in a shrub that grew straight from the rock. I watched it for a spell and it watched me back best it could. It reminded me of a pet raccoon that an unusual neighborhood boy had named Duodenum and had kept in a messy dog kennel and fed scraps of cooked meat, except that Duodenum had the whole of its sight.

I went back to the airplane and shuffled some more through the debris in the cockpit and turned up a tore-up map of Montana. There was also an issue of *Time* magazine from the year prior about President Reagan's colon surgery. I sat on a rock and read it until the daylight had all but gone. Then I returned to the radio. The little light in it had gone out. I tried it but did not hear the static I had heard before. It occurred to me that I ought to have stayed after it earlier until it had died.

Night fell after what I hold to be the longest day in creation. A gentle rain began and I sat back in that little airplane and held my eyes shut and thought about Mr. Waldrip out there in that spruce. I was mighty thirsty but I was too frightened to go out for a drink of rain. Something rustled around outside. I told myself it was only the white-eyed raccoon and did not open my eyes to find out for sure.

In the morning I woke to an awful shock. Terry had slid out into the aisle and his face was within a foot of mine. His eyes and nose and lips were all but gone. I suspect that the white-eyed raccoon had made a meal of them and was sleeping soundly someplace with a red muzzle. My goodness gracious, I hollered like a steam whistle and scrambled from the airplane. I fell to my knees and shut my eyes and prayed for some time. When I opened them they were on the mountains and the rolling valley. In the valley I saw a thing which at first I took to be swifts flying. But I rubbed my eyes and saw better that it was smoke! Lead-colored smoke over the treetops.

I stood up and dusted off my stockings and tidied my hair. I went up to the edge of the escarpment. The smoke was from a campfire, I reasoned. Here I was to make a fateful decision. Best I stay near the airplane and wait for help? There was no water at hand and I had no way to know if anyone had heard me over the radio. How long would pass before they would know to look for us? Or should I venture down to the smoke with the idea that there might be a campsite? The smoke was at a considerable distance, but I judged I could reach it before nightfall. Although I was concerned I could injure myself (seventy-two-year-old women are not meant to climb anything), that little airplane had become a mausoleum of wickedness and I dreaded another night there more than anything else. Troubling a decision as it was, and fateful as it would prove to be, I made up my mind that I would leave the airplane and make a pull for the smoke. I had a good idea that it was a nice family down there cooking breakfast.

I happened to look down at my side. Mr. Waldrip's boot was still upright there at the edge of the escarpment. It was full up to the ankle with rainwater. I was then mighty pleased that I had bought him those good alligator-skin boots, being that alligators are waterproof. I knelt down and got that boot and gulped the water until it was gone. I ought to have sipped it and saved some in the toe, but you do not think that way when you are thirsty.

I went back to the airplane. It was cooler than it had been, so I had decided I was going to take the big wool coat Terry wore. If Mr. Waldrip had been there with me he would have done the same thing.

I imagine he would have been disappointed with me if I had not salvaged everything I could both from the airplane and from Terry's person.

I inched closer to him but kept my eyes on the ground. He smelled like a dead horse. I grabbed for him and felt for the seatbelt and unbuckled it. He slid out of his seat and toppled to the rocks with a heavy thud and an upwelling of many flies such as dust beaten from an old cushion. I turned him on his side and worked one arm free from his coat. His joints popped. I told myself I was only loosening up the stiff leg on the old card table we used for bridge night at First Methodist. I rolled him and did the other arm. He ended up on his back, and I was stood over him with his coat. It was a gray color and was patterned with blood and looked now a little like red damask. I had the thought that I had robbed him. I looked him full in the face or what else there remained of it. It had been gnawed away and there was no blood nor flesh to it, only such as would be left on a watermelon rind after a picnic.

I turned out his hip pockets and was careful not to disturb his dignity. The stench was powerful and I held my breath. I found his billfold and a book of matches from a gentlemen's club called the Polecat printed with a multicolored cartoon of a masculine and muscled dancing skunk. I have never known a man to frequent one of these establishments, although I have been told that many do. I wager I have met quite a few of them and did not even know it. I ought to mention here I do not include the description of the matches as a comment on Terry's character. Men and women alike lead common secret lives that necessitate common secret places. I pass no judgment on them.

I put the book of matches in the coat's breast pocket. I opened his billfold and looked through the photographs he kept. There was a photograph of an attractive blond man fishing and another of a young girl holding balloons next to a waterfall. I found the one of Mrs. Squime he had shown us on the airplane. I replaced it and laid the billfold over his heart. It is fortunate that I had worn my good walking shoes, so that I did not need to take his boots. They would not have fit me, and I believe there is an old caution about wearing a dead man's boots.

A funny thing occurred to me while searching Terry's body. When I put my hands on another man who was not Mr. Waldrip, even one deceased and bodily abused, something stirred in me and I recalled a boy named Garland Pryle. Garland grew up down the road from me on a little ole alfalfa ranch. Our mothers sat next to each other in the old Methodist church house. He was four years my junior and played war games in the pasture with my brother, looking everywhere for sticks that were shaped the most like firearms. Garland was a mighty handsome, green-eyed boy, and his chin was the finest chin I have ever seen. I will soon tell what there is to tell about Garland Pryle, for I will not cower from the truth as I recall it. But for now all I will say is that while the years can sure put a memory in its place, some memories are darn ornery and like to return at inconvenient occasions.

I put on Terry's big coat and was very small in it. I crawled back into the fuselage, and under Terry's seat I found a plastic sack containing a small black hatchet and an old blue umbrella. I was sure happy to find these. There was also a tennis ball with the word *stress* written on it in marker and a flashlight that would not turn on so I left it where it was. I rolled up the issue of *Time* magazine and the tore-up map and put these in my purse. I climbed out of the fuselage and did not once look back at the little airplane. In hindsight, I ought to have left a note telling anyone that might come along where I had gone.

At the edge of the escarpment I picked up Mr. Waldrip's boot and stuffed it toe-first into my purse as far as it would go. After scouting around I found a suitable enough slope with soft dirt and loose rocks. I dug in the heels of my shoes and carefully climbed down to the floor of the woods below. I had not been in the dirt like that since I was a little girl. After I had caught my breath I pushed on through the trees.

I had not gone far when I spotted Mr. Waldrip's glasses on the ground. I looked up. Mr. Waldrip was hung above me in the spruce. His arms were out wide as if to greet me in a way he had never done before. His head sat mauve and swollen on his shoulders at a funny angle. There were no cuts nor blood to his face. The expression on him was one I had seen when someone talked to him about a drought. That dab of jalapeño jelly was still on his chin.

I recall wanting to bawl, but I did not. I suppose some things are just too sad that tears cannot do them justice.

When Mr. Waldrip and I were a young couple, we would argue about small infractions just as young couples do. I recall one summer night in the backyard of our new home under the water tower when the cicadas were very loud and I was as mad as a wet hen and we had raised our voices at each other. About what I do not now remember. But while I was still hollering and pointing up and pointing down and going red in the face he had calmed. He smiled. He reached out and brushed away my hair and said, No matter how angry you get, Clory, I always know you still got your kind little ears.

Standing under his body then, I wished to be the woman I was when he had loved me the most. Mr. Waldrip always said I was the most whip-smart woman or man he had ever met and that I could outword a dictionary. I thought that if I could manage to be that woman for just minutes at a time, maybe I just might survive this ordeal. Perhaps I had a way out of this immense and terrible place. So I fixed my hair around my ears best I could, knelt down, and picked up Mr. Waldrip's glasses. I stowed them in the breast pocket of Terry's coat and set out through the trees in the direction of the smoke.

II

Tuesday morning Lewis sat at her desk before the wide window and watched with bagged eyes the light change on a page of the *Missoulian*. She had come into the station again before sunrise and by the time Claude and Pete arrived she had already drunk two cups of coffee and a mugful of merlot from a bottle she kept under her desk. She had read twice the front-page story on the disappearance of a ten-year-old girl, vanished from her bed in the middle of the night. She flipped back to the newsprint photograph. The girl wore a deely bobber and smiled crookedly before a painted canyon landscape.

You read this about the missin girl? Lewis said. The Hovett girl? Sarah Hovett?

Claude was hunched over the narrow desk at the west wall, touching ointment to the blue end of his nose. I did, he said. He laid a hand on the head of the old dog snoring at his feet. I'd hate to know what happened to her.

I sure do appreciate y'all havin me in your place of work, Pete said from the kitchenette. He steadied the video camera on the counter and put an eye to the viewfinder, recording the percolator drip. I appreciate the company durin these tryin times.

We know you do, Claude said. Don't use up all the tape on pictures of coffee.

Lewis folded the newspaper and dropped it in the wastebasket. I can't figure why sittin up here on a goddamn mountain with us'd make anybody feel better about anythin.

Pete shrilled like a hag and turned off the video camera. He poured two mugs of coffee. You sure are funny, Ranger Lewis. He gave Claude a mug and kept one for himself, then put a hand to the wall and faced the window and sipped. He gestured out the window. Ain't enough to mention it's just plain gorgeous.

White clouds lay banked high in the mountains and below in a valley went what Lewis figured to be a herd of elk. Sentient points of black in an otherwise senseless landscape.

Sometimes I'd like to live in a goddamn city, she said. With all kinds of goddamn people around.

Pete brought to his malformed chest the coffee mug and nodded as if troubling at a riddle. The rest of the morning he drank coffee and videotaped angles of the station and listed for Lewis the infidelities his wife had committed in their toolshed under the cover of darkness, and told how she had contracted syphilis from a nineteen-toed lounge singer who mowed the lawn next door.

She just got to where what she had weren't enough for her, Pete said, adjusting an angle on Claude's wastebasket. And look what it got her. Look what it got me. She's selfish and makes a real good play of makin you think it's healthy. Boundaries, she calls it.

Claude sighed and threw away the empty tube of ointment. The old dog raised its head and lapped its ragged mouth. Don't tell her about all that. Talk about somethin regular. My God.

What kind of work you do, Pete?

He's in finance, Claude said.

I put some money I'd saved workin at the cannin factory in my nephew's TV game. It's doin better than just makin hens meet.

Ends meet, Claude said.

Now I got some money in a cheddar-flavored soda pop I got real high hopes for.

The sun now stood high in the window above a coalblack thunderhead beyond the mountains. Lewis poured another mugful of merlot in secret. She told the two men that there was not a goddamn thing going and that they could start hunting Cornelia's ghost and leave her to finish out the day alone.

Cornelia's nocturnal, Claude said. I'd say you know that.

Pete hoisted the video camera to a shoulder and asked Claude to tell him more about Cornelia's ghost for he did not entirely understand what they were doing.

Claude leashed the old dog at his feet and stood from his desk and went on to explain how Cornelia Åkersson had been born male in Sweden in 1841, but had feminine features and chose to live as a woman. He told how she had come to Montana in 1859 with her husband, Odvar, in a caravan from the Boston seaport and how she was only eighteen years old when three men from the caravan camp raped her and found out what she was. Thereafter they pulled her teeth and left her in the Bitterroot to die, Claude said. Then they murdered Odvar and tossed his body in a crick.

Pete had leveled on Claude the video camera. You been sayin she's got one big eye.

Her eyes've grown together in the center of her forehead, Petey. Happens to greater shades over time. These mountains keep most of the souls of their dead, so we've got lots and lots of shades here. Even the spirits of prehistoric animals that died millions of years ago. I'd say that's the reason why Cornelia rides aback the phantom of a megafaunal armadillo from the Cenozoic called a glyptodont. Imagine gettin that picture.

I can't, Pete said. He took his eye from the viewfinder and turned off the video camera and let it go slack about his neck. You ever go snipe huntin when you was a kid?

Lewis told again the men to leave her to it and they went out and took the dog. She refilled the mug from the bottle under her desk. She sipped at it and filed a vandalism report on a campground boulder that Silk Foot Maggie had spray-painted gold and covered in cat hair and rubber nipples.

After a while a transmission came in over the radio. Lewis leaned over the paging microphone.

Ranger Lewis here. Over.

We got somethin developin here, Ranger Lewis. Yesterday the wife of a small aircraft pilot named... Terry Squime... contacted Missoula authorities concerned about her husband's whereabouts. She said he was due back in Missoula late Sunday. Due back after he was to fly a pair of senior citizens to Lake Como. An elderly couple named Richard and Cloris Waldrip. Over.

Cloris Waldrip? So Cloris is a goddamn name? Over.

Yeah. Turns out. Over.

You figure they went down, John? Over.

We checked at the cabin the Waldrips were supposed to be at, but they're not there. Proprietor said they never were. Squime's flight path was to be over your way. I'm dispatchin search-and-rescue. You'll act as department liaison for this thing. Go with them, chopper over, and check it out this afternoon. Expect a Steven Bloor with a team in about an hour. Bloor's a real interestin fella, you'll like him. Poor guy's a widower. He's a good guy, a good old bud from the National Guard. You two can help each other. Hopefully you guys can beat the storm. Over.

Roger that. Over.

This's some excitement. How're you holdin up up there? Over.

I'm fine, John. Over.

Good. Let me know if there's anything I can do. If you ever need to talk, we're here for you. Marcy says she's here for you too. Over.

Thank you. I'm all right. Over.

Well all right. We're all prayin for you. Marcy included. That's what the ranger community is for. Carin for the land and servin people. Over.

Thank you. That everything? Over.

That's everything, Ranger Lewis. Out.

Out the station window dark thunderclouds lay slung over the mountains like blueblack viscera jumbled and discarded as if the heavens had been hunted and gutted the way Lewis often found the carcasses of poached bears and elk ditched on service roads. The elk had gone from the valley, and wind from the stormhead combed the grasses and shook the forests and moaned through the station. In the wind Lewis figured she heard a woman orgasm. She shivered. She finished a mugful of merlot and poured another. She turned from the window to the front of the station and put a hand to a cheek and figured she had a fever. She watched the door and strained to hear again the woman.

Then the pineboard steps croaked without, and the door opened.

A tall man ducked into the station and removed a pair of sunglasses. He took a hand to a mullet of feathery blond hair, so sparse it was in front that the ruddy dome of his skull gleamed underneath. He wore civilian clothes—hiking boots, a button-up, and khakis—save for a bright orange windbreaker which bore the letters *SAR*.

The man hung the sunglasses on his shirt and showed bright white teeth like those of children in beauty pageants. He said, Koojee.

Lewis stood and drew a sleeve across her mouth. Sorry?

Do you have kids?

No.

The man shook his head. My daughter, he said. His voice was faint and high and he sucked over each word as if it were a lozenge. Her disgusting boyfriend clerks at a dollar store and has a dead tooth. Political, everything is always political, you know. I'm a progressive man, but...

Are you with search-and-rescue?

He clicked his teeth together and nodded. I hope you're the ranger I'm here to see. I misplaced the name John gave me. Wrote it down on a napkin. A waitress threw it in my beans.

Ranger Lewis.

Ranger Lewis, of course, my apologies. Please take your seat.

That's all right.

You prefer to stand?

Yes.

The man closed his eyes and sighed. He opened them again and raised an arm to the window behind her. There's a storm waiting for us, he said.

I'm ready to go.

The man came closer. No, Ranger Lewis, he said. He looked her over. If we chopper out there in this weather and go down, who'll rescue us? He put out a hand. A fine white dust covered his fingers. Steven Bloor, he said. Search-and-rescue.

Lewis took his hand. Don't you figure since it's an emergency we ought to go anyway? Weather be goddamned?

If you speak with my colleagues from Tacoma to Missoula they'll all tell you that I'm a prudent and professional and progressive man. Tonight that may save our lives. He squeezed her hand and let it go. We'll wait till tomorrow. I predict the storm will have abated.

In a goddamn emergency—

It's not much of an emergency, Ranger Lewis.

How do you mean?

If the plane did go down, those aboard are more than likely deceased. Koojee.

Bloor unzipped a breast pocket and brought out a photograph and a small cake of hand chalk like that used by gymnasts. He passed the photograph to Lewis and slapped the chalk between his palms.

Lewis studied the photograph and brushed it clear. It showed a young couple posed in foam Stetsons smiling before a low geyser in a state park.

That's Terry Squime, Bloor said. The pilot, there on the left. Mrs. Squime sent us the picture. My guess is she's the pretty woman in the blue hat. Xerox it for your personnel.

You mean Claude?

I probably do. Bloor studied her and pulled out the chair behind the smaller desk against the west wall. He sat down and pocketed the chalk. He stretched out his long legs and thumped the pineboards with the heels of his boots. You know, my wife always told me never to stand while there's an empty chair in the room.

Do we have any more information on Cloris Waldrip and her husband?

Retired, Bloor said. In their mid to late seventies. Small-town Texans flying up here for a pleasant few days in a cabin. Koojee. You live up here all year round, Ranger Lewis?

What does that mean?

What does what mean?

That goddamn word you keep sayin.

Koojee?

Yes.

It's a word my wife used to say to express most types of emotional concern. It's exclamatory. You know, it just stuck with me. So do you live up here all year round then?

I go down for groceries and gasoline.

Bloor put an end of the sunglasses in his mouth and nibbled. It's not unpleasant up here. Only I get the sense it'd be lonely for an individual with an active mind. Loneliness can be dangerous. You could go nuts. Do you have a companion?

You mean a dog?

No. An intimate companion.

No.

Do you have a dog?

Claude has a dog. I'm divorced.

How long?

Almost three goddamn months now.

Where is your family?

My dad was in Missoula. He's gone.

Your mother?

Long gone.

I hope I'm not being too forward. Sometimes I'm too forward. My wife always told me I was too forward and that it made people uncomfortable, because forwardness is only permitted in children.

It's all right.

I'm a progressive man, Ranger Lewis. It's important to me to become familiar with the people I'm to be working with. I'm a people person. Are you a people person, Ranger Lewis?

Goddamn it, I don't know.

Bloor took the sunglasses from his mouth. A little about me, he said. I was married in Washington State. Lived in Tacoma, you know. At heart I'm an art collector. I only keep working in search-and-rescue anymore to have a reciprocal relationship with society. Just recently I procured a wonderful piece by a tractor mechanic in Washburn, Arkansas. Jorge Moosely. He uses his comatose mother for his canvas. Paints her head to toe in landscapes, then photographs her. I have his *White Water Vapids* piece back at our house in Missoula. It's heartbreaking.

I'm goddamn worried we ought to try and head out there, see if we can't find—

I don't want to die out there, Ranger Lewis. Do you? Bloor clapped his legs and stood and left on his khakis two white handprints. I'll return six o'clock tomorrow morning. He looked once clear into her eyes, winked, and replaced his sunglasses. Lewis recalled a man who had worked as a janitor in her father's clinic. In the evening hours, when she would work at the clinic after school, she would find this man pacing the blue halls with a carpet steamer, or washing dung from the pens with his thumb on the end of a hose, or folding into the plastic bin next to a lightning-scarred oak the bodies of euthanized dogs and cats. The last time she saw him there he had winked at her too.

That evening Lewis drove the mountain road to her pinewood cabin, listening to *Ask Dr. Howe How* on the radio. A man with a hurried whisper like that of someone hiding under a desk during a home invasion phoned in with concerns about an inability to throw punches in his dreams. I'm gettin killed in there, Doc.

Lewis turned up the radio and pulled over to a shoulder overlooking a deep gully. She drank from the thermos of merlot and listened to Dr. Howe tell this man that he had gone to sleep with unsettled anxieties of sexual inferiority and that he would do well to remember that all men are created inferior in some way and are therefore all equals. Practice enjoying sex and fulfilling your partner in a respectful intimacy, Dr. Howe told him.

Lewis finished the thermos and climbed from the Wagoneer. She squinted out over the land and the evening mist that settled it and the thunderhead in the mountains. The last of the sun colored her face and was gone. Lightning burned beyond. She touched to her tongue her fingers and wetted them. She sent them into her government-issue trousers and closed her eyes to the dark.

Hateful swarms of mosquitoes kept that steep and rocky little wood. Most of the time there was not a thing to do but go straight through them. I just covered my mouth, pinched my nose, and held my breath. Mosquitoes have always been a special nuisance to me. When I was a little girl our house was by a seep pond and Mother would leave the window open on hot summer nights. You could count on those little winged devils to find out the holes in the flyscreen. I would swat at them until the moon was gone. I am not fond of that awful whine they like to make. Gracious, how gargantuan they sound when they get right up to your ear and sing that song which I imagine is sung in the halls of damnation.

I was slow getting down that mountain, being that I was mighty careful where I put my feet. All about were barrows of rock and motts of twisted pine and big old spruce. I held on to low branches to keep from falling over and stopped often to rest my breath. I was mighty thirsty again too. One good spill dirtied up my skirt and the zigzag sweater, but I managed not to hurt myself. Mr. Waldrip and I had been taking calcium tablets with our breakfast, so my bones were good and strong.

I am sure it was near three hours before I got to that little clearing where I had marked there had been smoke.

When a mind has had seventy-two years' worth of thoughts, it has the opportunity to start acting a little funny. It runs the way my vacuum cleaner ran after twenty-three years of Mr. Waldrip refusing to replace it. The rubber belts inside go slack and the work of it smells like warm hair and dust. Now, I had never worried much about dementia before; Grandma Blackmore's mind could skin a buffalo right up until the day she ended her earthly career at ninety-six. Still, as I set my old back to a great spruce and sank to the ground, my worry was that my cognition had fooled me good about the smoke I had seen rising up from the clearing. It occurred to me that it might have been wishful thinking, the way men lost in deserts see lakes where there is nothing but sand. There was not a thing in that clearing save rocks and grass and somewhere a terribly noisy owl. But I was sure I had seen smoke.

Clouds blew in above and the shadows under the trees grew together. Suddenly all was darker. I had a pain in my stomach. I had not yet passed the jelly and toast I had eaten at the Big Sky Motel the morning of our fateful flight. And I was mighty hungry. I sat for a spell holding my stomach as what was left of the sun crowned the mountains. The place had the look of evil and I was scared. True dark would come soon and I had no airplane to shelter in.

I decided that I would build a fire. I set about gathering twigs and sticks and pine cones and I piled them in the flattest place I could find. I drug a rotted log to the pile and sat there. I took out the matchbook from Terry's coat pocket. Once more I studied the muscled dancing skunk on the cover and then I struck a match. The flame did not want to take to the log and it burned my fingers and went out. Three more matches were left.

Mr. Waldrip and I used to visit the Panhandle Plains Museum in Canyon, Texas, where there are life-sized plaster figures of cavemen and cavewomen, hairy and mean, squatting at the limits of a campfire with paper flames. One of the cavewomen was meant to have set it. My thought was, if she had been able to set a fire back then in that hard way of living, surely I could too.

I tore up some pages from the *Time* magazine about President Reagan's colon surgery and stuffed them under the wood. Then I lit another match and dropped it in the makings. It burned some and went out. I tried again with the penultimate match and had not a thing on my mind save that cavewoman. The flame took and slowly wound its way up the tinder. I had never before given much thought to what Darwin called his *Origin of Species*, but I did then. I can see how it might have come about. The people that could not get a fire going would have perished in the cold. And I suspect it was womankind that spared Man from extinction.

The fire caught into a fine blaze and I watched it there for a little while. I was feeling mighty pleased with myself, so much so that I risked a little cheer out loud. It is true a fire is a great comfort even in the most dire of circumstances, but it does make the dark it cannot reach a great deal darker. I endeavored to keep my eyes from the dark and watch the glow in the rotted log instead. Little bugs trapped there hissed and exploded like popped corn. A poor daddylongleg was scurrying from the heat but its fine appendages singed away and the fire overtook it.

By then my stomach pained me something terrible and my bowels began to move. I hurried to the other side of my fire and looked around at the dark. I do not take any pleasure to include this here, but bless you, I will not shy from relating this story in its entirety. It is important that you believe I am relating the whole and pitiful truth of the strange events yet to come in this narrative. As a tree kept my balance, I undid my skirt and rolled down my stockings and I relieved myself right there in the firelight before all creation.

I have always considered myself a well-bred Texan woman, but I suppose even the best of us have bowel movements. My generation is mighty ashamed of them and precisely why that is I do not know. But I was sure sorry for myself and I teared up a little and swatted away the little black flies and mosquitoes that pestered me. I was a pitiful sight to behold. After I had finished, I kicked some pine needles over it and went back to where I had been sitting before and cleaned my ankles with grass. The notion crossed me that I was more unlike myself than I had ever been before.

I watched the fire take more of the log and exhausted I fell asleep.

I woke to thunder. It was dark yet and wind and rain clashed in the trees. The fire had gone out and the burnt-black wood hissed like a nest of smoking snakes. I backed up to the spruce close as I could, but rain still fell on me. It had created a sump and I was sat right in it. The rain washed out my permanent. I am sure I looked like a sopping wet mouse. I have always disliked the way I look when my hair is wet. I got out the umbrella I had found in the airplane and went to open it but it had a big tear in it and was about as useful as a ceiling fan in an igloo. I chucked it aside and set Mr. Waldrip's boot out to fill up. I wrapped up tight in Terry's coat. The rain was not as cold as it could have been, I imagine, but I shivered out of my bones nevertheless. How I did not perish right then and there I do not know.

I was glad that it was not long before the rain turned to scarcely a drizzle. For the better part of an hour the lightning crawled in the night above the trees. The sky seemed to me then like a cracked mirror turning and glinting and giving back all the awful true nature of the earth below, which was a hilly and scorched landscape of soot, a very unlucky and inhospitable place indeed.

One strike was not far away and it lit up a mighty strange presence ahead between the boles of two big pines. The light had come and gone so quickly that I was not too certain what I had seen. My first thought was that it had been the face of a young man, hidden in the dark of a hood. When the light was gone I was stone blind. I screamed out before the crack of the lightning reached me in the dark. I was considerably frightened.

It is a funny thing how I trembled at the notion that another person was out there with me, when another person was just what I had hoped to find. There is just something about strangers. And my thought was: what manner of lunatic would stand quietly in the dark and the rain to watch an old woman suffer? Or was it Terry's disembodied face regurgitated by that white-eyed raccoon, come to haunt me for what I had taken off his person? Perhaps there are spirits over which God has lost dominion, though I have never given much credence to phantoms.

I kept my eyes on the place in the dark, but when the next bout of lightning lit up the trees, whatever it was had gone. The woods flashed on and off for a spell, and I watched for the face to come back, but it did not. There was only that grand timber, which to me then were like great bars to a cell imprisoning me for convictions I feigned not to understand. I tucked my head to my chest and waited for morning.

Mr. Waldrip's boot filled up past the ankle overnight, but I only got a little sip that morning before I stumbled and spilt it and would spend the rest of the day as thirsty as a catfish in a catamaran. The morning was overcast but the trees all about were bright and grayly bejeweled with rainwater. The good thing about everything being wet and cool was that the mosquitoes had taken the morning off to do whatever it is they do when they are not out terrorizing us higher creatures.

I did not move for some time. I considered not moving ever again and letting myself perish right there. It might have been the first time that I had entertained the notion of resigning to what many would have said was an inevitability in the case of a seventy-two-year-old woman becoming lost in the wilderness. It most certainly would not be the last. I imagined myself looking something like poor Terry, rigid and squirreled up against that spruce, my jaw off its hinges and flies making a mansion of my skull. I wondered how long my hair would stay in and if I would be found in this most unlovely condition, or never again be beheld by human eyes. I could not decide which fate I most preferred.

I took out the tore-up map and worked to make sense of it, but it could not be done. It might as well have been a swatch of the Chinese wallpaper that insufferable Catherine Drewer had used in her sitting room. I decided to voyage away from the clearing and farther down the mountain, although not before I stepped right in my own mess and had to clean my shoe in the wet grass! I do not mean to offend, and this is again a detail I could have left out, but I believe it contributes to the absurdity of my plight and proves that I am not being false nor grand.

After about an hour I came to a rocky place where I could see out from the trees and down into a valley. My heart jumped! I spotted in the distance the asphalt of a highway, tracing a path back to civilization. I was likely as good as rescued if I could make it down there. With renewed energy and hope I made my way down to the valley. All the while I heard strange noises behind me. I had the notion I was being followed.

I reached the place after a couple of hours and stumbled out of the woods. The highway was not a highway at all but a creek. Gracious, I was disappointed. Although by that time I was mighty thirsty too, so it was hard work to be too disappointed in finding water. I wobbled on like a newborn calf, my stockings tore up pretty good now, and I collapsed at the bank of that creek. I cupped my hands in the water and drank. It was very cold and clear. I had drunk two handfuls when I looked up and spotted in the shallows the hairy corpse of a huge animal! I spat out the water and jumped back. I was nearly sick, but I held my hand over my mouth. The thing had antlers and scraps of hide trailing in the current such as some gowned pagan devil.

I went upstream past this dead monster and filled Mr. Waldrip's boot. I did my best not to let my imagination wander to what other nasty things might be lying afoul in the water. While I sat sipping from Mr. Waldrip's boot the light changed color on the mountains all around me. I was hungry and cold so I prayed and then set about building another fire for the night. I piled wood together much the same as I had done the night prior, only I gathered more of it and more dry tinder. I piled the makings near the creek. It was near dark when I sat down exhausted and took out Terry's matchbook.

The wind was against me and howled wildly over the valley, and the wide sky darkened with clouds. I opened the matchbook to the last match and tore it carefully. I steadied my hand and positioned my back to the wind. I got close as I could to the tinder pile, then said a prayer and struck the match. The matchhead hissed and blackened but did not bring a flame.

Dark came but not before I spotted the silhouette of an animal I took to be a mountain lion prowling a far ridge of rock. Scared and uneasy, and nearly starved, I had my last caramel for supper. It threatened to rain, but the wind chased the clouds from the sky and uncovered the stars and moon. The dark was hardly dark anymore under the bare heavens, which shone down on the grassy fields of the valley, the silvery creek, the woods nearby.

I did not know what next to do. I worried my situation had grown too dire. But I knew come morning I would be compelled to do something, anything at all. The dead monstrosity was yet nearby, its black antlers moonlit and the twinkling water underneath like a bed of lovely gems.

I heard something move in the woods. I recalled the face I was now certain I had seen the night before. I thought of the mountain lion too. My Bible was in my purse and I moved it to the breast pocket of Terry's coat right over my heart. But I was mighty tired, enough not to be too afraid of mysterious faces and mountain lions. There was not a thing to do but to offer up my prayers to God and succumb to exhaustion.

The pilot swung the helicopter low over gray slopes of scree high above the tree line. Lewis squinted against the crags of sunlit granite, upthrust from the depths of the mantle some eighty million years ago. She brought slowly to her lips a thermos of merlot.

Bloor, long legs folded childlike in the seat next to her, knees level to his chin, turned upon her his pale face. His voice squelched in her headset over the beat of the blades. Have you ever been to Macao?

Lewis shook her head.

An older man with clubbed fingers sat across from them. He watched the window. Bloor had introduced him as Cecil. Keep your eyes peeled, he said.

I left Jill with her grandmother and spent last winter in Macao, Bloor said, and he made a show of looking out the glass. Had to get away. Met a six-foot-three Pekinese woman named Chesapeake. They pick their own English names, you know. She picked Chesapeake.

Her friends referred to her by a Chinese word that means ladder. You're tall too, Ranger Lewis.

Cecil looked up. Keep your stupid eyes peeled.

Cecil's a longtime rescue paramedic, Bloor said. Works even though he has COPD. He doesn't like me very much.

These people we are lookin for, they are dead, Cecil said. He turned back to the window. Sun filled his eyes yet he did not squint.

Koojee, said Bloor.

They flew onward over intrusions of granite set in the earth like molars in a jaw, and they each of them searched the ground below, wearing now sunglasses as the day grew brighter. Wind shear drove the helicopter down and Lewis squeezed the thermos in her lap. The air smoothed and she drank. Bloor watched her behind yellow lenses and asked her if she considered herself an ethical person.

Lewis wiped her mouth and ran a tongue over wine-red teeth. She tightened the lid to the thermos. Not sure, she said.

Bloor brandished a finger white with chalk. I give a share of my time and skills for the wellbeing of others, so for the sake of universal balance I allow myself particular ethically selfish pleasures. Chesapeake was an ethically selfish pleasure.

Lewis smiled and unscrewed the lid to the thermos. She drank and rescrewed it.

What ethically selfish pleasures do you allow yourself, Ranger Lewis?

Goddamn, I'd have to think about that.

I hope you do.

Cecil put up a hand. Do you need me to peel them for you?

Thank you, Cecil, Bloor said.

The pilot circled two other mountains and passed over a bleak forest. Lewis kept her eyes to the land and blinked little. In the glass she could see Bloor turn his head to look at her. Twilight was already upon them when the pilot warned that they ought to turn back before they lost the light.

Goddamn it, Lewis said.

Cecil had not turned his head for a time. At long last he shuddered it around to them like some rickety piece of theater on a set of pulleys. It's difficult to think anyone of any age could survive down there at all, he said, and he coughed on the plump ends of his fingers.

As the pilot began to fly them back toward the station, Bloor spoke about the depression of people without ambition.

These are the eighties, you know, he said. I've seen thirty-year-olds dressing like teenagers. I've always been ambitious. Do you enjoy your work out here, Ranger Lewis?

They passed the black edge of the mountain in the oncoming dark. Yes, she said.

My daughter will be eighteen the third of November. I'll tell her about you, remind her that there are ambitious women out there.

Be quiet, Cecil said. You're makin the pilot crazy.

One more thing, Cecil. Then you can wire my jaw shut if you want. Listen, Ranger Lewis. I apologize if this is too forward. Sometimes I'm too forward. Have dinner with me this evening? I'm renting a large lonely cabin and I'd appreciate the company. We can go over the case and discuss our options.

Lewis watched unsteadily the man's face.

She drank a bottle of merlot at her kitchen sink and put on a clean uniform and then drove to a stately two-story cabin built of pine and painted clean white, stilted dark and alone in a far dead end overlooking the east valley. Down below in the foothills a little town glowed. No wind battled the trees and stars spun like rowels in the glassy firmament. Lewis parked the Wagoneer in the gravel driveway. She took up from the passenger's seat a four-dollar bottle of merlot and picked off the price tag.

The front door of the white cabin opened. Bloor ducked under the transom and peered out at her. His thin black shadow emerged like an insect from a crack in a floor. He put up a hand and rolled his long fingers. Lewis climbed from the Wagoneer.

Without a word Bloor ushered her into the cabin. He closed the door and locked the dead bolt. He waved in a circle a chalked hand and asked her what she thought of the place.

Lewis surveyed the large, open room. A circular steel fireplace burned in the center and a length of dark picture windows lined a wall beyond which lay a stilted deck and a hot tub and a barbecue. Long white couches were angled around a glass coffee table where there sat a bottle of wine. The kitchen was lit up through an open archway and from there came a smell of cooking that recalled a deep basement.

It's goddamn modern, Lewis said.

I thought so too, Bloor said. He took from her the bottle she had brought and her coat. Do you go everywhere in uniform, Ranger Lewis?

I expect I just got comfortable in it.

It's a handsome uniform.

I've been by here before, Lewis said. It's goddamn unusual to see a white cabin.

It's owned by a homosexual man named Cherry. Good guy. You know him?

I know he rents this place out, but I never met him.

Bloor thanked her for the wine and said, I'm sorry if I seem distracted. I just hung up with my daughter. She's been trouble recently.

I figure she's the age for it.

Bloor went over to the coffee table and set the bottle there beside the other and took from his chest pocket a cake of chalk and chalked his hands. I don't want to say she's slow, but it takes a long time to get her to understand the complexity of a thing. He took up the bottles and held them out for her to choose.

Lewis pointed at the merlot.

Bloor uncorked the bottle with a corkscrew from the table. She was caught today with that clerk with the dead tooth I was telling you about. In the school restroom. Suspended. What do you think of that?

Nothin.

Bloor poured two glasses of merlot. She told me one morning over eggs she wanted to do it. Can you believe that?

Do what?

Sex. I'm a progressive man, Ranger Lewis. Cultured, of this time. Beyond this time, even. But you know, part of me wants my daughter to be the eternal virgin.

I expect that's only natural, Lewis said.

Bloor smiled and sat on the couch. He patted the cushion next to him. Lewis went over to him and sat. He handed her a glass and raised his. To the Waldrips and Terry Squime, may Light and Love have mercy on them. May they rest in peace.

Lewis raised her glass. That's premature talk.

The two drank.

How did you meet your ex-husband? I apologize if I'm too curious. My wife always told me that I'm curious in a way that makes people feel probed and unsafe.

Lewis told him that she had met Roland at her dad's veterinarian clinic when she worked there after school and Roland had brought in his dog to put it down. She told how they had gotten married just after she had left high school and had begun working in the Missoula Parks and Recreation. After a few years, she said, she took the ranger's position in the Bitterroot Mountains and Roland was put in charge of purchasing in the small-game department at a hunting-goods store. At the time she had not thought anything of him running off on a business trip every other weekend.

He was seeing someone else?

He had a wife in Nebraska, one in Colorado, and one more in Montana. Lewis pointed to her badge.

The man is a Mormon then.

If he is he never told me about it. He's in prison for trigamy.

Koojee. At least you don't have kids.

Goddamn it, never needed any.

Kids. You know, when we moved from Tacoma to Missoula I hoped the change of venue would help. But I don't know. My daughter's already lost her virginity straddling a toilet. It's not that I'm made uncomfortable by sexuality. My tenure as a sergeant in the National Guard made sure of that.

Bloor drank off a glass, then reached for the bottle and poured himself another. He stroked together the chalked fingers of his free hand and studied the wine with eyes that did not seem to see.

When my wife passed away three years ago, he said, I thought I'd become a better person. To honor her memory, you understand. I haven't. Not at all. I don't know why.

Sorry about your wife.

Bloor looked at the ends of his white fingers. I love people, he said. Do you know what she used to tell me?

No.

That I could rule the world with love and compassion.

All right.

I miss her. When I tell people about her I can see it in their faces they don't understand what a visionary woman she was. They don't know what she meant to me.

I expect that's true.

I've always lost people, you know. I think it's why I first started in search-and-rescue. My mom disappeared watering pansies one morning when I was an infant. Nothing left but a pair of size-six clogs and a water hose running. My dad was already long gone, somewhere dead or alive in a country we had no idea about. Some people thought he'd come back and kidnapped my mom and drowned her in one of the Finger Lakes. They never found her. My sister raised me. Then she died of food poisoning in a hotel lobby ten years ago this Thanksgiving. Koojee.

Goddamn sorry to hear that.

Room service killed her. The hotel settled handsomely in court. Now I never have to work another day of my life if I don't want to.

I figure that's a good thing.

Losing my wife, Adelaide, was the hardest. We knew each other since we were kids. But I don't think she ever was a child, you know. She always spoke like she'd been born with a life already lived in her. Most everyone didn't know what to make of her, so they were vile to her. The boys at school tormented her. But I don't think any of them ever really had the upper hand. It was even then like she'd wanted them to be vile to her in just the way they were. As if she'd orchestrated the whole thing for a pleasure only she knew about.

Sounds like she was a goddamn special woman, Lewis said. She missed her mouth with her glass and dribbled merlot down the front of her uniform. She blotted the spill with her sleeve and held out the empty glass.

Bloor poured her another. He turned his drawn face to the windows, where a blue light outside showed fog in the trees. A fingermark of chalk was on his chin. You don't even know, he said, and he took her fingers between his chalked hands. Thank you for coming over tonight. He pinched the skin of her ring finger hard and filled his lungs like he were to submerge himself in water.

Lewis took back her hand. You're welcome.

Bloor let out his breath and smiled.

Lewis, rubbing the back of her hand, pulled the Wagoneer crookedly into the driveway. The lights were off in the pinewood cabin and the windows dark. Over the radio Dr. Howe spoke gently to a woman who had phoned in with the name Ronnie and asked how she could be expected to go on and live the life she had come to live when all she had ever wanted was to leave her husband and her three children and sing country-western music all night long in Nashville. Lewis turned off the engine but kept the radio on and listened.

The woman said: I'm three hundred pounds. That's somethin to do with it. But it ain't fat that's in me. I got all this frustration poolin in my belly and my thighs and my ass. I can't be a country-western singer. I'm morbidly obese and I ain't got a particularly good singin voice. I count myself betrayed, Dr. Howe. I just knew that's what I was goin to be when I was a little girl, but here I am now and I'm not and I'm large and I'm tonedeaf. My gran was a singer. Sometimes I go to the downtown library and look through those old microfiches they got of her and the shows she used to put on around town and I just get so frickin jealous, pardon my language. Jealous of my dead gran. That's low, ain't it? Tell me it's low. And then my husband, not long ago I caught him eyeballin my baby sister at the church fish fry. That's been on my mind. She's only just able to have a legal drink and weighs nearly a hundred pounds less than me, so I ain't no competition. Where's a person like me with all this frustration poolin in them supposed to go to get their self-worth? I've just been dismissed and dismissed, even by people that'd say they love me. And I go to doin it to myself, Dr. Howe, I go to dismissin myself and I just sit on the end of my bed while the kids're at school and my husband is at work and just watch the cat come in and out of the room.

Dr. Howe said: Ronnie, life is about adjusting our expectations. It is what it is, and will be what it will be, like it or not. And I believe that the secret to happiness is to find a way not only to accept and tolerate life as it comes, in any manner it comes, but to find a way to enjoy it in spite of yourself and the conditions it sets. You can't have everything you want or you would implode and disappear. Do you understand me, Ronnie? You would have nothing at all without all that you believe you do not have.

The day after I came to the creek, I prayed by it for a spell, batting away those terrible little mosquitoes and bottle flies. I was knelt in the wet shortgrass, upstream from the decomposing creature. I drank first from my palms and then from Mr. Waldrip's boot. The water was mighty good and tasted like water from wells dug in Texas when I was a girl.

I was by now very hungry and my stomach growled something terrible. I prayed with my eyes open for a way to feed myself and watched the clear creek for fish but saw none. I watched the grass fields of the valley and wondered if there existed an animal out there slow and dimwitted enough I might catch it. Although I had seen plenty of times the hunting of small birds and seen Father shoot coyotes from the back porch, I had not ever killed a living thing myself, save for flies and mice in our house. But those are just the little ole deaths of a household, not at all like the desperate carnage which occurs in the wild. Even hunting is just a game men play at today, no longer a mortal urgency in this age of convenience. Men hunt not out of hunger, but out of boredom. Though I suppose men do many things nature no longer requires of them.

I got up from the creek and went back to the wood I had piled the night before. I had used up all of Terry's matches, and I knew of no other way to get a fire going. I considered rubbing two sticks together as I had read about the earliest Indians doing this and had seen it depicted before in a diorama at the Panhandle Plains Museum, although I was sure I possessed neither the technique nor the stamina to ignite them. If I was to catch anything for supper, I would have to have it uncooked. The notion of eating uncooked meat worried me some. I hear that some people in bright cities are fond of eating raw fish, but it does not appeal to me.

I went out with Terry's black hatchet and stalked the rocky fields. I swung the blade through the tall grass endeavoring to scare up something I might have a chance to thump on the head. This proved mighty foolish and after an hour or so I sat breathless back by the creek. I very much dislike being foolish, so I used my shoelaces to fasten the hatchet to the end of a long stick, and I set about beating the water at every dark shape that went by. No doubt at least one poor little aquatic creature was maimed. Nevertheless I sat hungry, and my arms seized up around the shoulders like the hinges on the cabinet under my kitchen sink.

I looked to that great decomposing animal in the water and I prayed aloud: Oh, heavenly Father, I do not want to starve. If I should join your holy side this day, please let me go quick, please do not let me starve.

My dear! I was sure I would die of starvation.

About midafternoon there was a sound in the sky, a clatter ricocheting off the mountains. It was faint enough that I was not sure I had not imagined it, but before I could see where it was coming from between the sunned peaks, whatever it was had gone. All that was left to be listened to was the trickling of the creek and the cry of the mosquitoes. I have since heard many stories about strange and mysterious sounds in the mountains. The ghost stories about the Bitterroot are especially peculiar and sad.

Fish swam by in the creek until the sun was gone and I could no longer see much of anything. Yet the moon kept light on the dead animal in the water where its breaching bones were blue and swaddled in its own rotten skin.

The next day I crawled in the fields eating little gray flowers. They tasted like Cynthia Weaver's summer melon salad after it had sat a few days in the icebox. Not good. I ate what amounted to a handful of them and when my head began to wobble I rested against a stump by the wood pile. The night had been cold enough to put a frost to the blade of the hatchet and I had not slept much. In the sun now I fell asleep.

I woke to a sting under my arm. It turned out to be a tick. The little monster had already gorged itself fatter than any I had seen before behind a dog's ear. The thing looked like a chinaberry. Mr. Waldrip used to heat my tweezers on the stove and pick them off his bird dogs when they got big and yellow enough to see in their coats. I jumped up and hollered and slapped it, which anybody worth knowing knows you ought not to do. Blood ran down my side in a mullion of black. The wicked thing clung to me. Its backside was blown out like pitted fruit. I picked it off. Of course the head stayed in.

I wiped the blood on my skirt and left there something like those handprints of ancient people on the inner walls of caves. The weft of blood drying in the wrinkles of my palm made a gory relief of those little life lines and love lines our dear grandniece, Jessica Pollard, had read for me one Thanksgiving and prophesied that I would finish out a long and loved existence. Jessica now lives with her olive-skinned husband and two handsome sons in Phoenix, Arizona. I might have at one time been concerned about her practicing the reading of palms, but now I think it bears little true weight on the condition of the soul.

Suddenly then I felt heat. I turned. You may not believe it yet, but what did I see but a fire burning in the wood I had piled the night before. Fire!

I froze. For most people, surely for the skeptical youth of this most recent generation, it is mighty hard work to believe that a fire could start on its own. It was hard for me to believe it too. I spun around and looked quickly over the woods and the fields, but I did not see much of anything. I crouched down. I stood up again. My goodness, I did not know what to do.

I crept up to the fire. Flies circled a steel pot on the ground. My heart galloped. A little skinless body was floating inside. I guessed it had been a rabbit. I looked around again.

Anyone there? I hollered. Hello? Hello? My name is Cloris Waldrip!

After a minute or two I sat back down on the ground. I sat there good and frightened for a spell, watching those pale flames in the daylight. Upon reflection I considered a sermon Pastor Bill had given some months prior. He had called the congregation's attention to Mark 10:27: *And Jesus looking upon them saith, With men it is impossible, but not with God: for with God all things are possible.* It was soon made plain that my prayers had been answered in nothing less than a miraculous manifestation of the Divine. They say God works in mysterious ways. This was not all that mysterious. I had been mighty hungry and I had prayed and here now was some supper. Had there ever been a more comprehensible answer to any prayer? I certainly had never heard of any since the feeding of the multitude.

I took a breath and I set about boiling up the rabbit over the fire. I prayed aloud, thank you, God, thank you, Jesus!

However I will put it down here that even then my thoughts strayed to the hooded face I was sure I had seen in the woods up the mountain. It is true I have never been one of these silly women to spin tales of ghosts and ghouls. I have always considered those the offspring of idle and devilish minds, nothing of substance in the world of God. Yet when I was a young girl, Grandma Blackmore, who belonged to an older, smokier generation of storytellers, would tell me and Davy about our long-departed great-great-aunt Malvina, and how it was that some unnamed villain had stolen her away and buried her alive in a cow swamp and ever since her unsettled spirit itinerated the whole of Texas in search of living descendants. Some nights I would lie awake after Davy had gone to sleep and I would imagine I could see her out the window, dragging herself across the prairie in a muslin dress freighted with black mud.

But I managed to put these thoughts from my mind. Those of Great-great-aunt Malvina and the hooded face and the gruesome death of Terry Squime. None were of God. I suppered that night by firelight and drank from Mr. Waldrip's boot and watched the logs glow and next to a tiny midden of clean-picked bones I slept.

I was two days at that place by the little creek, resting and pondering the miracle. Sitting around like that there is nothing much else to do but get hungry and soon enough I had eaten up even the bones of that rabbit. I first boiled them and dried them and then I took a stone and ground them into a meal that I could put to my tongue. The same as the giant in the fairy tale about the beanstalk. I used to tell that fairy tale to my kindergarteners and come up with parts of my own. I did that with most stories. I will not do it with this one. Although I have had students visit me after they are grown and tell me they enjoyed my stories better than all the rest. A tale belongs to whoever tells it best.

The bones did not taste of much, and for that I was grateful. I boiled water from the creek and drank it and in the mornings I relieved myself near a leafless bush dead and calcified like the weird piece of coral that sat on Linnie Curfell's coffee table. In the sixties she and her husband brought it back from an island in the Caribbean and ever since scarcely knew how to converse about anything else. Anyway, every time I had to use that bush I made an effort to hide myself against it best I could. I laugh as I write this now. It was as if I had become embarrassed before God out there. After the appearance of the fire and the rabbit in the pot, God sure seemed nearer than He ever had back in Texas.

When the sun was up and it was warm enough I removed my clothes and washed them in the creek upstream from the dead beast. Then I bathed in the shallows. It is not something that I easily admit, but I believe it is important; it was romantic to be naked outdoors. I thought about my first kiss. It was with a boy named Charles Manson. Now, he was not in any manner related to that terrible man who murdered those poor people in California. He only shares what has become a terribly unfortunate name. I was twelve years old and Charles was fourteen. He grew a mustache like the mold on a crust of bread. He had taken me out back a hill of dirt and tractor parts stacked in his yard.

I have forgot the kiss, save that it tickled and that it was glorious hard work not to sneeze. But I do recall his words. Open your mouth, moonrise, he said. He was a mighty good talker, Charles, and went on to become the Clarendon school system's superintendent, which he did very well until he passed away on his forty-second birthday without warning nor knowable cause. He fell to the floor in front of the icebox. His widow, Geraldine Manson, simply said to the police and anyone else who would listen that God had wanted him home, but I do not warrant that she has any notion as to what God does or does not want.

When I got out from the creek there was a shiny black leech on my leg. It would seem everything out there had a thirst for my blood and a hunger for my body. I picked the thing off and chucked it back to the current and went to the fire, where I dried my clothes and sat warm in Terry's coat, naked as a jay bird. My permanent was all but deflated and I slicked my hair back behind my ears into something like the style Father had worn all throughout the Gay Nineties. I have a daguerreotype of him then, after he had found work as a traveling salesman, selling tonics along the Santa Fe Railroad. That was before he met Mother and settled in Texas.

After I was dry I was hungry again. At home Mr. Waldrip and I ate small portions. I seldom thought much about food except for that we needed to eat and I had to decide on what to cook for supper. But out in the Bitterroot I was sure I could eat a whole burrowed generation of rabbits and whatever it was the antlered creature in the water had once been. I prayed aloud again asking the Lord to spare me from starvation. As I prayed I heard rise that same sound I had heard two days before, a clatter over the mountains, a rattle in the blue sky. Past the northern ridge hung a tiny black spot.

Bless me, it was a helicopter!

I put my arms up and hollered loud as I could. I made not words but guttural fricatives. Oh Lord, let me be loud enough to reach them, let them see me! I threw off Terry's coat and scrambled over that field waving naked and wild and unashamed. The helicopter turned towards me! I tripped over a rock and fell, scratching up my chest on a bristly kind of sticker weed. When I brought my head up again the helicopter was gone and the sound with it.

I sat a spell and worried I had broken something, but I counted my ribs and it appeared I was fine. I had bloodied my elbows up pretty good. I did not bawl nor allow myself much disappointment. I feared it would be too much. If I stopped to despair of ever being found or worry that was my last chance of rescue, or if I kicked myself for leaving the little airplane, I might not go on at all. Instead my only thought was: Now I know they are looking for me.

That night I went to sleep by the fire thinking of Mr. Waldrip and what a lovely evening we could have been sharing in the rental cabin if the little airplane had not gone down. The sight of Mr. Waldrip at the dinner table came to mind, knifing his way through a sweating steak. Even in my imagination he still had the dab of jelly on his chin. It is a difficult thing to relate, the loss of a lifelong companion, but here I will suggest to you that it is akin to losing your name. Such as if you and no one else in the world knows what to call you. It is not something I like to dwell on.

A pungent odor woke me in the morning. You may not believe me, because I am a funny old woman and you could think my mind is a nest of dead spiders. But I mean to tell you that when I opened my eyes I saw a big ole trout laid out on a rock. A note was pinned to it by a twig through the gills. It appeared to be written on a piece torn off a brown paper bag from a grocery store. In the blue block letters of a child's penmanship were the words: *Go Downriver*.

III

Koojee.

Lewis and the two men in the station looked up.

Bloor leaned in the doorway. He rolled in his palms a fresh cake of chalk. I'm terminating the search, he said.

Lewis stood at her desk and knocked to the pineboards a mug of merlot and coffee and cursed it where it broke.

I'd say it's time, Claude said.

The old dog at his feet raised its head to look at the halved mug on the floor. Claude was untangling a telephone cord at his desk. A busy signal burred dully in the receiver.

Bloor returned the chalk to a pocket in the orange windbreaker and stepped into the station. We've flown over for three days now without any sign of them. They've been missing for close to a week. If somehow they survived impact, there's little hope they could've survived this amount of time exposed in those mountains. But we cannot let it get to us. We did our best. You know, Ranger

Lewis, people die all the time all over the world and we know nothing about it.

The old dog wheezed and got up and went to the spill and lapped at it. Everybody watched.

Pete grunted and all turned. He sat atop a stool in a corner of the kitchenette, hunched over an embroidery hoop. He wore a white coif like Lewis had seen actors wear playing medieval peasants on television. The video camera framed him from a tripod.

Claude sighed. What is it, Petey?

Pete brought up a needle and scratched the red stubble of his neck. Back in Big Timber my little nephew got his head caught on fire Fourth of July and I just happened to be standin by with a full squirt gun. You don't count on there bein a miracle like that for these people?

Bloor said that he did not and asked Pete what he was doing. Claude answered on his behalf that he was needlepointing.

Pete took the slack off a ball of magenta yarn at the foot of the stool. I'm prayin it'll keep my mind off my heart.

And the hat? Bloor said.

Pete straightened the coif. Found it in Claudey's closet. Figured it'd kind of go with my new peaceful attitude.

My mom used to work at a Renaissance fair, Claude said.

Bloor looked at the two men and turned to Lewis. I'll tell you something, Ranger Lewis. When I worked in Yellowstone a man came to us about his nine-year-old boy disappearing from their campsite. We mounted a fullscale search for the child for two weeks, you know. Vast amount of resources apportioned. Come to find the man had killed the boy back at their home in Boise weeks earlier and fed him down the garbage disposal. In the meantime an albino girl about my daughter's age had been reported lost in Pine Park, but my men and I were exhausted that night and I know we didn't look as hard as we could've. We found her body the next day under a dogwood. Dead of exposure, white as an onion.

All that goddamn story means to me is we ought to hurry up, Lewis said.

The dog had finished with the spill and now was at licking the dust from her boots.

My wife always told me that true wisdom was to know when a situation was hopeless.

Pete raised the embroidery hoop in Bloor's direction. Your wife sure must have been a fine woman, Officer Bloor.

Thank you. You have no idea.

Claude held taut before him the length of telephone cord. He hung up the receiver. The Waldrips were an older couple. I'd say maybe explodin on a mountainside's a better way to go than dyin slow in some smelly bed. He clapped once his hands and the old dog quit licking Lewis's boots and looked at him. I'd say they had their fair share of life, wouldn't you say that?

Goddamn it, Lewis said. We don't know what they had.

Claude retrieved a tube of ointment from his desk drawer. My uncle Jack is eighty-six and he doesn't even know what he is. I'd say *Hi, Uncle Jack* sounds to him like somebody clearin their throat.

Terry Squime is a young man, Lewis said. Just married.

Now that is a durn sad thing right there, said Pete. I bet it's real sad to be a widow.

Lewis took up her campaign hat from the desk and held it at her side. Outside fine clouds clung to the range like unearthly cobwebs.

Listen, Bloor said. It's just too many man hours and funds to apportion and bad for the ozone. My department is removing itself. You know, Cecil's already left early this morning.

Bloor stood now in the middle of the station, his head tilted as if he were listening to the ceiling. Lewis could not see clearly his face for the dimness of light, but figured she saw there a slow smile and closed eyes, an expression she had seen before on a televised judge adjudicating a most heinous crime and finding in it some cruel and selfish humor. The old dog watched him too from the floor.

Lewis dropped her campaign hat back to the desk. What in the hell're we doin up here, then?

You all right, Debs?

I'm fine, Claude, goddamn it. You don't need to keep askin me that.

Bloor neared her and leaned close. There's something important I'd like to discuss with you, Ranger Lewis. If you would. I need the perspective of a woman.

Lewis eyed the man.

Bloor passed two fingers over the back of her hand, leaving there an equation of chalk. This mountain's got me confused like I've slipped down a hole, he said. My wife always told me it was good for a man to get the perspective of a woman when he's confused.

Lewis looked over his shoulder at the two men and the dog watching her. What goddamned thing's got you confused?

I have something to show you, he said, and he asked her if he could pick her up there at the end of the day.

She told him all right.

He smiled and turned from her and nodded once to the ceiling before he strode from the building.

Pete stared after him and pushed the medieval coif up his forehead. That's one strange bird, he said.

After Bloor picked her up they drove in his black truck down the mountain road. Out the corner of her eye Lewis watched him steer with hands chalked to the wrists. She sipped from the thermos of merlot. The inside of the cab was marked everyplace with handprints and scuffs of chalk.

In my eleven years up here I never been department liaison, she said.

Never had anybody lost up here?

We had a couple drunk hikers go missin for a couple hours till their wives found them. Only time I found anybody was about three years ago. I found Ranger Paulson after he'd got turned around in the woods behind his cabin and ruined his goddamn nose. I just know Terry Squime and the goddamn Waldrips are alive out there. They need somebody to keep lookin for them.

A woman's intuition's a powerful thing.

I'm not talkin about a woman's goddamn intuition, Lewis said.

Have you enjoyed my company while I've been up here?

Lewis fixed on the man a pair of bloodshot eyes. His cheekbones were low and his thin blond mustache shone through like glass. I don't know, she said. I guess it's been all right to have some fresh faces up here.

They came to a shoulder of broken trees and rusted dumpsters and he pulled the truck over. The sun was nearly down and gold light lay aslant on the ground. He turned the ignition off and the lights in the cab went out and Lewis studied the shape of him in the murk. The motor cooled and it was quiet.

Bloor got out and Lewis followed him in the sundown, toting the thermos, and he led her behind one of the dumpsters.

This morning I brought my trash here and I found this, he said.

There leaned a stinking homunculus crudely composed of garbage and cat skeletons glued and woven together with electrical tape and melted dinner candles. It had for a head the yellow skull of a bobcat and for eyes a halved tennis ball. It wore a redly stained ranger's uniform and used tampons for earrings.

Goddamn Silk Foot Maggie.

Who?

State allows her to live up across from the point, Lewis said. She does this kind of thing. Don't know why.

Bloor bowed his great torso over the hodgepodged carcass and looked it over. She's an artist?

I don't know if you'd call her a goddamn artist.

I thought it was especially fascinating because of the uniform. It's yours. Ranger Lewis. Says it right there.

It's vandalism, Lewis said. You got to burn or goddamn bury somethin if you don't want her to get her goofy hands on it. It's a pain clearin these goddamn things up. This what you wanted to show me?

I need a vacation. You know, my wife always told me I was a hungry vulture eating dead hearts, but one day I'd get tangled in some power lines and they'd all start beating again in my stomach.

I don't know what the hell that means.

I need recreation, Ranger Lewis. I spoke to Cherry and extended my stay.

You want to stay way the hell up here?

I've fallen in love with it, Bloor said, and he went on to tell Lewis that he did not yet know how long he would stay, but that he was driving down the mountain Wednesday to pick his daughter up from the bus station and that she would be staying with him for a time. He said that Chief Gaskell had suggested she volunteer in the Forest Service.

Goddamn Friends of the Forest?

I'm hoping it'll pull the fog off her, Bloor said. And it'll look good on her college applications.

Flies haloed the skull of the homunculus and some muddy color dripped from its pawed appendages.

We already got goddamn Pete Trockmorton participatin in some limited capacity.

She could benefit from a conversation or two with a strange bird like Pete.

Goddamn it. I don't guess I can see any goddamn harm in it.

He thanked her and told her how rare Jill Bloor was. He said that he would never say she was slow, but that she had not developed the way some people her age might have for when she was a baby he and her mother had answered an advertisement for test subjects in a study at Seattle University. He told how the experiment had involved her mother behaving coldly with her and then comforting her and then behaving coldly again and how they had photographed hours of her crying.

I don't expect a child'd understand any of that, Lewis said.

No. And then we homeschooled her in the sunroom until the lymphoma finally got Adelaide. Koojee. I couldn't keep working and maintain my passions while continuing her education myself. So I enrolled her in a public school, you know. I'm telling you I think the confusion in her upbringing has left a mark on her.

I ought to be headin back.

Bloor took the cake of chalk from a pocket and passed it over his fingers. I like to get involved, you know. Now that I know she's sexually active there's little left unsaid between us. I keep a calendar of her cycle on the refrigerator door back in Missoula.

You got any goddamn gloves in your truck?

I might.

Don't much want to use my bare hands to get rid of this, Lewis said, glancing at the homunculus.

I'd like to have it if you don't mind. If you think this Silk Foot Maggie wouldn't mind.

Lewis looked to the creation and back to Bloor. Do what you want, she said.

Bloor smiled. I'm sure you'll be a valuable influence on her.

Who's that?

My daughter.

I don't know somebody like me has any business bein an influence on anybody.

Why do you say something like that, Ranger Lewis?

You can call me Debra.

I would prefer to call you Ranger Lewis, if it's all the same to you.

She drank from the thermos of merlot and eyed the man. I don't figure I'm a people person, she said. Sometimes I just don't give a goddamn about anyone. I have to work at it. Remind myself everybody else still exists even when I'm not lookin at them. You figure sayin somethin like that tells you somethin about me?

My wife always told me that people are the most fearsome and unruly animal ever to have walked the earth, but that it was possible to train them not to shit on the carpet.

Lewis spat in the dirt.

Bloor brought a tarpaulin from the truck and he wrapped up the homunculus and laid it carefully in the truck bed. He stopped Lewis before she climbed in the passenger's side and he pulled her close to him and held her. He gave her a pat on the back and apologized for the behavior of her ex-husband. I don't want you thinking that all men are created equal, he said.

He let her go and she looked to his white hands. Why do you do that with your goddamn hands?

I don't like them getting too moist, he said. One of those quirks you get when you've got an active mind, you know. Adelaide always told me it was the clearest indication that I was mentally ill. I stopped for a while, but I picked it up again after she died.

He drove them up the dark mountain road and let her off at her pinewood cabin. The tarpaulin flapped in the bed of his truck as he drove away. When Lewis undressed later that night she found on the back of her uniform a handprint left in chalk.

In 1972 a handsome young couple moved into the little yellow house next door to ours below the water tower. They were clean and had good postures and they looked after their lawn. They had a little legless Chihuahua dog they had found stuffed in a vase abandoned on the side of the road. On warm evenings they took that little dog out in a kind of tiny bespoke wheelchair. People got a kick out of that. This couple was well-mannered and they went to the Episcopal church off Pond Street.

But one night the young man decided he had to go beating on his wife. I heard the commotion and crept from bed. Mr. Waldrip did not wake. I went to the sitting room and from there I saw their shadows warring on their window blinds. I was not snooping. I am not one of these bug-eyed women who hardly does a thing but leans on a windowsill. Still I watched them from my sitting room for a good spell, quietly, like it were a shadow play.

Of course I had not heard what had been said between them, however the next morning that pitiful little Chihuahua dog was strung up by the wire in their porch light and the young couple had come up missing. The limbless animal swung dead there like a pendulum for a day or two before the mailman cut it down. I did not think to do it myself. That poor little Chihuahua dog! Often as not it is the helpless and the meek that pay the debts of others. Shortly thereafter the house was put up for sale and I never heard word of them again. I worried I had showed myself a big ole coward for not having acted in some way better than what I had, at the least to have spared that poor creature the indignity of swaying in the hot breeze like a windchime struck dumb. But I did nothing and told not a soul. I spoke of it only to God and it is unclear his opinion on the matter.

I thought about this young couple once out in the Bitterroot and teared up, not for them or their little Chihuahua dog, but for myself and those mighty cruel occasions on which I had been shown my awful lack of character. I fear I may be what psychologists call a narcissist. The very nice black therapist here at River Bend Assisted Living, Melinda, does not think so, but I do. Perhaps she simply does not know me well enough.

I had been in the wilderness for ten days now, and I had counted three days since I had found the mysterious note. I followed the creek down like the note had said to do until the creek became more what I would call a river. Far ahead it disappeared into a thick wood. It seemed this river could wind on into the depths of that wilderness without end.

Each night as darkness fell I would spot a flickering light ahead and soon find a fire burning and a fresh trout laid out on a log or a rock. I had gotten to where I could clean one well enough with the little black hatchet, but I sure made a mess of the first. I toted along the steel pot I had found the rabbit in, and every night I fried the trout in the bottom of it and scraped it up and ate it off the blade of the hatchet like a pirate from Robert Louis Stevenson's *Treasure Island*.

One cloudy day more helicopters zoomed over to the big mountain where our little airplane had gone down. I counted three of them. They were blue and one was wide and very loud. I waved and hollered but it was no good. They could not see me. I went on down the river slow as a graveyard.

I do not imagine I made much more than four miles a day. Naturally I was younger then than I am now, but I was still an old woman and I was unaccustomed to traversing such difficult terrain, much less while carrying all that I was in my purse and in the pockets of Terry's coat. The most Mr. Waldrip and I ever did was take a leisurely stroll after dinner, less than a mile out to the west pasture, where there was a polled steer cross-eyed and roped to a lazy old windmill. Occasionally kids would glue a corncob pipe in the poor creature's mouth for mischief.

Miss Lauper's song that Terry had sung prior to his passing rattled on stubbornly in my head. At the time, not knowing how the melody was meant to go, I only heard it in Terry's broken plainchant: *If you're lost you can look and you will find me, time after time*... You might suppose I would not want to hear that song ever again. But now that I have heard it performed by Miss Lauper I do not mind it, though it is not as musical as Ruth Etting's "Crying for the Carolines" or most anything sung by Perry Como.

On what I counted as the fourth night of my journey downriver, black clouds covered the sky. The wind picked up and the smell of rain filled the air. There blinking ahead was another fire. I made some haste to it. It was burning hot and was hissing and sputtering as the first of the rain came. Nearby on a felled spruce lay a thin creature akin to a squirrel, cleaned and with little blood. Being special tired that day and not very hungry, I decided to hide best I could from the rain and eat the inscrutable creature in the morning.

The rain did not last all night, thank goodness, and I managed to keep the fire burning. At last the sun rose over the mountains, and the trees and the grass glittered and reminded me of the awful gaudy jewelry Catherine Drewer wore every Sunday to impress upon the congregation how well her pepperhead husband was doing in the oil business. I wrung out Terry's coat and put my shoes out to dry. I got a stick and skewered the strange skinless creature I had been given and burned away its limbs and ate little of it. I kept the rest in the pot and traveled on downriver. After a while I was near in a trance. My body ached and like an old salt lick my head was not all there. I felt the way I had when Mr. Waldrip had taken me to the hospital for an endoscopy and a young nurse with old hands had given me some tablets the color of cream. I made little progress down the river that morning.

Afternoon came and the sun burned and insects chattered. Not the way they do in Texas, where it sounds like there are rattlers hanging in the mesquites. No, these insects in the mountains are more softspoken. All creation seems to whisper.

I do not hold any belief in devilment or magic, but those savage mountains had begun to work a kind of spell over me. As often as I looked to them on the horizon I could not for the life of me get familiar with them. They seemed to shift and collapse in the manner of waves on an ocean. Not long ago I watched a television program on the Public Broadcasting Service about the expedition of Lewis and Clark. I learned that a travel companion of theirs, Sergeant Patrick Gass, wrote that the mountains in the Bitterroot were the most terrible mountains he had ever beheld. I am inclined to agree with him.

I got mighty dizzy and lost my footing. I caught myself and climbed up on a rostrum of granite to get my bearings, but I went on being mighty dizzy for some time and then I was just plain ill. Unable to stand, I crawled on my hands and knees to the riverbank and splashed water on my face. I watched some little tadpoles go by and I was sick in the water.

I lay there and listened to the water play against the reeds and imagined I was listening to Mr. Waldrip run himself a bath after a day hunting with his friends Bo Castleberry and Bob Guffine. Mr. Waldrip was not one for showers. He liked to take his time in the tub and mull the day over. He would take his open palms to the water and perform a measure of percussion so distinctive I doubt I will ever hear the like of it again.

Shortly my feet were sweating and I had been sick three times. Heat filled my eyes the way it does when you have a fever, and I could have placed my hand on my Bible and sworn I saw Mr. Waldrip watching me from a nearby mott of spruce. I shut my eyes.

I got to wondering if it was not God that had led me downriver, providing my supper and building fires, but Satan himself. My gracious, I feared I had been led astray. Poisoned by the consumption of that unknown creature, some kind of wrong spider feline escaped from a demon's kennel, ailed with an ague incubated by the malarial climate of hell itself. I knew I had not correctly atoned for my sins. Perhaps all that I had done poorly in life had sought me out and found me there at the end of a purposeless parable.

Now I ought to put down here some about Garland Pryle.

The trouble with Garland began at the grocery store his family owned. It was the only grocery in Clarendon at the time. He worked there in an emerald-green apron that matched the color of his eyes. He would have been twenty years old and I twenty-four. I had not been married very long to Mr. Waldrip and we were both of us still very young. I wish it were true for me to say that Garland lured me against my better judgment to his parents' home one evening while Mr. Waldrip was in Colorado at a cattle auction. But this Cloris Waldrip will not dishonor the memory of her dear departed husband by dealing poorly with the truth. I will commit to this account that it was I who stole Garland aside one rare day of heavy rain and gripped him by the belt of his apron in an aisle of canned peas and begged him to take me home under his umbrella. I have always wondered if Mr. Waldrip knew what had happened somehow or another, and for whatever kind or pitiful reason just never said a word about it.

I sat up and put my back to a stump by the river and kept my eyes shut against the sun. The blood in my eyelids made a monstrous wall of thumping red. Beads of sweat chased each other off my forehead and down my arms and tickled me something terrible like the little black flies and mosquitoes that pestered me most hours of the day. However I did not move. I was sick again and still I did not move nor open my eyes. I was a mighty pitiful sight.

A very nice doctor would later suggest to me that I had most surely ingested giardia from drinking unclean water out of my late husband's boot. However I hold to this good hour that it was the animal I had eaten the species of which to this day I cannot name.

I thought again about how they might discover my body, terribly defiled and molested and inhabited by all manner of crazy wildlife. Likely my bones would be flung far and wide and no doubt the investigators would not be able, nor possibly see it necessary, to reassemble and identify them as having once belonged to an old Methodist from Texas named Cloris Waldrip. I wondered too if they would be able to tell how old I had been by the marks in my bones as they do with the rings in a tree.

Soon the afternoon had all but gone and the sun was hidden among opposite mountains and the colors of the valley deepened like day-old bruises. I mustered what little strength I had left and took the hatchet from my purse and scratched my given name into that stump. In my life I had not ever once considered that I would come to rest unburied at the foot of a grave marker of my own making, especially not one so evil and poor. It seemed as if my name there were a curse word meant to condemn me for all that I had done wrongly in my days. I suppose it just goes to show how awful little we can control the outcome of our decisions. Cloris. What a terrible word it was cut into that pale wood.

What I next recall was this: two eyes bodiless above me in the dark, the sky mighty black behind them, no starlight nor moon to it. Two bright emerald-green eyes such like those of Garland Pryle gazing down at me from the heavens. Here may be the face of God, I thought, bared before me. Or perhaps that of an angel lowered into the Bitterroot. A strong warm hand held the back of my neck and another cradled my head and raised me up. Then a soft voice told me to drink and I felt on my lips the cool brim of what I imagined was a silver chalice. The voice was gentle but strong like that of the masculine young woman who tended the service station back in Clarendon. Stokely, I want to believe her name was. She wore powder the way Chinese women do in costume plays. I drank. I do not recall the taste. I slept. I dreamt.

I dreamt of a humid room with no clean light where a translucent man shaped like a water tower stepped carefully around me with boots the size of cast-iron skillets. He endeavored not to wake me, but he did not know that I had been awake for centuries. I dreamt of a palace of mirrored floors where I could see up a gown I wore as I wandered its ornate halls, and in this palace was a woman with red hair. I could see up her gown too and under it was a series of inverted mountains and cosmic voids and angry children in multitude. But I dreamt most vividly of the little Cessna 340 airborne from Missoula, and in one of its bright windows I had a vision of a woman I had never seen before, a sad woman with dark hair cut short same as a man's, looking for someone in those merciless mountains, her countenance incorruptible and without fear.

My dreams ended there and I could not blink nor shut nor open my eyes anymore and I woke to find that it was still very dark yet. I sat up and I put my fingers where I had scratched my name into the stump. I endeavored to get my wits about me. Firelight played over my name. Out at the river a man sat crosslegged by a twisted fire, stirring it with a smoking stick. Behind him the river shone in the firelight like a macabre river of blood. A white shirt masked the man's face. The shirt had eyeholes cut out of a printed image of eggs and pancakes and the arms of it were tied around the back of the man's head over a wild mane of long dark hair like a neckerchief. I suspect the shirt was made to be worn by the employees of a diner.

I had a notion the man was watching me, but he did not turn his head in my direction. He was a dread frightful sight, dirty and shadowy. However I was not all that afraid. I had put it together that this must have been the man who had been building fires for me every night and giving me supper. Despite the mask and his appearance, I was hopeful. And I mean to tell you at the time, as funny as I was feeling, I was not very sure if he was of this world or not. Either way sure enough there he sat.

I waited a little while before I asked him who he was.

The masked man looked up from the fire and dropped the stick. He wiped his hands on his blue jeans. He made no reply.

Then I asked him if he was an angel.

Still he said nothing and stood up at the fire, casting out a maniacal shadow. He looked like some timber-born deity. He was lean and must have stood five foot nine in his socks but his big old boots put him taller than that. He had on his hip a magnificent scabbard like I had seen worn in Shakespearean plays at the Little Theater in Amarillo. Later I would get a closer look at it and see that it was intricately metalworked with a bas-relief of what I have determined to be the English Battle of Marston Moor in 1644.

I said, My name is Cloris Waldrip.

He took a cautious step closer and in a deep and steady voice asked me how I felt.

Better, I told him.

Anyone else survive?

I shook my head.

How many people on the plane?

Two others, I said. The pilot and my husband.

The masked man sat back at the fire and picked out another stick and stirred the coals. I'm sorry, he said.

It is mighty strange the words people say to comfort each other.

I hear them often in the halls here at River Bend Assisted Living. And I allow that there is no better recourse in the face of the grieving and sorrowful than to apologize, as if it were the fault of every man and woman who had ever begat a child that anyone should ever hold grief in their heart. I imagine that we are all culpable in every loss, every familiar window shuttered, every summer swimming pool drained, because surely we are loss itself. I am inclined to think that we alone on this earth know such a thing as grief exists, though my dear grandniece has informed me that some whales mourn their dead.

I sat against that stump and wrapped my arms around my legs and at last bawled into my knees like a crazy little girl until my face was fuzzy and fat like a dish sponge. I carried on that way for some time and when I did finally look up the man had gone but the fire still burned hot and bright.

Lewis, naked save for her boots, spun slow ovals in the living room and guzzled down a glass of merlot. She steadied herself at the mantelpiece and looked to the head of the doe mounted above. She smacked her lips and toppled over to the couch. Night blacked the windows and the radio sizzled after *Ask Dr. Howe How* ended with a frustrated caller complaining about the biennially scheduled anal sex in his marriage. Lewis grabbed a bottle of merlot from the coffee table and drank from it.

The regional office had mailed a photograph of Richard and Cloris Waldrip. Lewis took it up and studied it for maybe the dozenth time that hour. The old couple smiled together in front of dormant lovegrass and busted and blown mesquite. All but the woman's hair keeled in the wind. Far behind them a white church house bowed askew, the copper steeplecross candescent like a branding iron held to the sky.

Lewis eyed again the doe's head above the fireplace and looked back to the photograph. She looked closer at Cloris, the white hemisphere of hair, the miniature face and pinched smile. She left the photograph on the coffee table and stumbled from the couch. After she had dressed in her uniform and buckled the holster to her waist, she pulled from the wall the doe's head nail and all and took it with her out the front door. She went around back of the cabin and got a shovel. She came back around to the front and dug a shallow hole in the gravel driveway and buried the head.

After she had tamped down the grave she threw aside the shovel and got in the Wagoneer. She swerved back and forth down the mountain road to the large white cabin at the windless dead end. She went to the front door and rang the electric doorbell. The windows showed a light was on and a shadow toiled inside. She waited. She banged a fist on the door. The night was still and a far wolf bemoaned a thing she could not know, the way sentenced dogs had done from the chain-link kennels behind her father's clinic.

The door opened onto Bloor posing in an argyle bathrobe. Ranger Lewis? What's wrong?

What?

Your shirt's on inside out and you drove over the hedge.

Get on the horn and get your goddamn chopper up here first thing tomorrow mornin.

She went to turn but Bloor brought her inside by the shoulder and closed the door. He gestured to the couch.

Lewis did not sit. She leaned against a wall and lifted heavy eyes to the high white ceiling over the atrium. She sniffed the air. The homunculus of cat bones and refuse slouched in a corner of the room. God, she said. Damn.

Can I get you a glass of water?

Reconsider the search for Terry Squime and the Waldrips, she said. Merlot if you have it.

Bloor went to the kitchen and brought back a glass of water. She shook her head at it. Bloor lowered himself to the couch and set the glass on the table. He took from the robe pocket a worn cake of chalk and rolled it over his fingers. Ranger Lewis, he said. Try not to get unduly upset about the problems of strangers.

Not upset.

Have a seat.

Lewis shook her head again. No, thanks.

We're here for the common good, you know. Please sit down.

Lewis stood where she was and put a finger to her chin. You want me to give up on those goddamn people.

Do you think maybe why you're so upset might have something more to do with the unresolved conflicts in your own life than with our missing persons?

Don't talk to me like I'm some goddamn goofball.

I'm sorry. Maybe it has something to do with being up on this mountain all the time? Are you happy up here?

Bein on this mountain all the time is my goddamn job. This's my job. How about that merlot?

Bloor stood from the couch and held her by the shoulders. You've had too much to drink, Ranger Lewis. Koojee.

Please don't say that word.

You've had too much.

Usual amount.

Lewis dropped her head toward the floor and saw under the hem of the argyle robe Bloor's feet flashed over with blond hair and chalk dust. She looked back up to his face. It was equine and highbrowed like that of an aristocrat in some old movie she had seen.

All right, she said. I'm sorry to come here like this. Late. It's goddamn unprofessional and inappropriate.

Bloor stroked circles over her shoulders and left there in white what a child might draw of a sun. You know, I've been in SAR a long time now, he said. One summer I found the body of a boy who'd been lost in the Sonora Desert for three days. Looked and smelled like a roast pig. Only wanted an apple in his mouth. Later I commissioned a haunting portrait of his body from a friend in Saratoga Springs who usually does portraits of cats. I wish I'd brought it. I'd have liked you to see it. In the portrait the boy does have an apple in his mouth. Albeit he looks a bit like a cat too. You see what I'm telling you?

Not at all.

My wife always told me to make something of something else, Ranger Lewis. Especially those things that make you want to scream at a closed door, you know.

All right. I don't know what she meant at all, but all right.

Bloor let go of her shoulders and stepped backward into the living room and raised his long arms. He lifted a hand as if to swear on a Bible and then he pointed at the homunculus. Sublimation, Ranger Lewis.

You ought to throw that thing out, she said. It stinks.

It's art.

Take me out there one more time. I'll put it all to rest if we don't find anything and you never have to see me again. I can get Gaskell to okay the extension. Just get on the horn with your man about the chopper.

He won't want to fly on a Sunday.

Just one more flyover is all I'm askin for, Lewis said. I know they're out there just waitin for us under a goddamn tree. I know where to go. I can see it, goddamn it.

The pilot dipped an old helicopter between the mountains and struck out westerly over a yawning gulch in the batholith. He wore a ratty beard down to his lap and a helmet plastered with discolored bumper stickers and Christian symbols. The high winds shook the blades and he gripped the stick and sang a falsetto hymn.

Lewis pressed flat her nose to the glass and cast her bloodshot eyes over the land below. Bloor nudged closer to her seat and touched her knee. She turned from the window and vomited in her lunch box.

We've only got a few hours up here, Bloor said over the headset. Daniel has to make his evening worship at eight.

Lewis nodded and wiped her mouth with her shirttail. She clasped the box and held it in her lap. We should push farther out, she said. Claude was out near Darling Pass when he picked up the signal and he said it was weak. It could've been a goddamn fluke of reflection.

My wife would've enjoyed spending some time with you.

Lewis rolled her eyes and turned back to the window and brushed the damp from her brow. The valley and the gray mountainsides went by.

The pilot sang louder now, a hymn about fishermen, and barreled them farther out into the rough wind, past a mountain hung with clouds and over another pastured valley and braided forest. They circled a place where Lewis figured she had seen something moving, but there was nothing to be seen there and they flew on. The pilot snapped his fingers and warned them that they had forty minutes before they had to turn back.

You know, Adelaide always told me that we give up on people all the time in the course of our lives, Bloor said. At some point we all have to give up on each other and leave each other to our own demises, you know? There's no real rescue in the end. I wish them the best. I really do. Koojee.

Lewis clapped a hand over her mouth and held back the sick and did not speak but watched yet the chaparral valley.

The pilot screamed the cadence of another hymn and brought the old helicopter around a tall mountain into a downdraft and dropped altitude. He lisped a curse word to the sky and grappled with the stick. He wailed anew a birthday song for Methuselah. Then Lewis braced herself and caught sight of a glint of steel and a black ring of condors down below. She put a hand on Bloor's knee and she called out for the pilot to shut up and turn back. The pilot quit his singing and touched his headset and told her that he did not abide yelling.

He circled back. There the wreckage of a small airplane lay on the mountainside.

The pilot lowered the old helicopter onto a level elevation up the mountain. What a calamity, he said.

Lewis was out before the skids touched down. She ran for the wreckage and slowed to a stop before she had reached it. A severed arm still in its sleeve lay at her boots. The fingers were balled, gnawed to five glaucous points. Red ants coursed over them like veins yet leading blood.

Bloor peered over her shoulder.

Lewis stepped over the arm and went on to the wreckage and covered her mouth against a stench the same as that of the burn pile out back of her father's clinic, where often the fire did not find all of the animal and left anatomy behind to rot in the ash. She came around to the other side of the airplane. A naked body with one side peeled of its flesh was laid upon a slab of stone like some miscarried sacrifice, its abdominal cavity vacant and no face to be seen. A round load once a head now a muddy orb glittered, fasciae left here and there white in the morning sun like embroidered silk. Lewis stared and tightened her grip on her mouth. She heard footsteps behind her.

You see, Bloor said, there's another one. This part always puts a cloud in my stomach. Koojee.

Lewis turned where Bloor was directing a chalked finger. There in the height of the trees beyond the edge a bloated corpse was roosted black with slow flies. Lewis figured it looked like a fat man wearing a skinny man's clothes. She wiped her eyes and figured she was crying for the brightness of the sun.

She went back to the wreckage. Again she held a hand over her mouth against the smell and put her head through a hole in the fuselage. A raccoon with but one eye to turn the light watched her from under a seat, waiting. The strewn interior stank of urine and sour hair and was knobbed with dark droppings. Lewis picked up from the floor a tan-colored wallet. She withdrew her head to the daylight and opened it. Inside were club cards, a laminated Psalm about the Kingdom of God, and a Texas state identification card for Cloris Waldrip. Lewis squinted at the tiny smudge of a picture, the dome of white hair. She handed the card to Bloor, who looked at it and gave it back and told her to return it to where she had found it. Lewis put the card back in the wallet and leaned into the fuselage again and put the wallet back on the floor, then she withdrew her head and took a deep breath.

Bloor came around and looked inside the fuselage. Then he too brought out his head and took her hands in his. She recalled the dryness of her father's skin after he had worn a pair of surgical gloves. They stood sweating in the sun. Bloor searched her eyes. The high winds intoned a solemn pitch in the wreckage, and from the helicopter came the faint music of the bearded pilot, who sang:

A little kingdom I possess,
Where thoughts and feelings dwell,
And very hard I find the task
Of governing it well…

I count two bodies, Lewis said at last.

Bloor brushed a fly from her cheek. I bet the third's somewhere around here, he said. Maybe fell out a couple miles back. Probably dragged off and eaten by goats and scavengers. It's not the kind of thing we like to think about. But it's likely the truth, you know.

I count two goddamn bodies, she said. Two men. Where's Cloris?

Two days of mighty fine weather were had and I recovered on the riverside by the stump into which I had scratched my name. I count it was the 14th of September by then and I had not seen hide nor hair of the masked man since the night my fever had broken. But when I slept the fire did not burn out and still I woke to crawfish or trout in the steel pot. Even then I asked myself if I had ever seen the masked man at all.

I have put it down here before that there is some question about what an old mind will do. At seventy my Aunt Belinda was convinced that there was a pride of mountain lions behind the facility where she spent the rest of her days. The facility is in Franklin, Tennessee, where it is my understanding that there are no or very few mountain lions. What she had been watching out her window, according to Cousin Oba, was a party of derelicts and vagabonds so inebriated they could hardly be upright. So drunk they were that they slunk around on their hands and knees, crawling and growling in the alleyway. You never know what fantasies a mind will conjure.

When I had got back enough of my strength I aimed to continue on downriver. I prayed that the masked man was still out there somewhere watching over me. The night before I planned to depart I sat awake waiting for him to appear until I could not help but fall asleep.

I woke late in the morning and there were no victuals of any kind, but I boiled some water and filled up Mr. Waldrip's boot and in the late afternoon I set out downriver anyway. I looked back at my grave marker. It struck me how strange it was to be leaving it behind, like I was a ghost errant from the tomb. Dark soon overtook me and it was not long before I had to stop. I had not gone far, I do not suppose more than a couple of miles.

The masked man was no place to be seen, and I did not have a way to build another fire nor did I have a thing to eat. Thank goodness it was another warm night. I sat for a spell in the dark and a pretty blue mist rolled over the river shimmering under what little moonlight escaped the clouds. Frogs croaked and crickets chirped and animals I did not know spoke tongues I could not fathom. A bobcat prowled the brush, its eyes like silver dollars. This bobcat had been stalking me for a couple days. I had spotted it once in the daylight. It had a little yellow tag in its ear. After a little research I would later learn that it was a particular variety of lynx bobcat being studied by some students at the University of Montana at the time.

I had been fiddling all day with a piece of crawfish stuck in my teeth. It had been bothering me something terrible and I just could not keep my tongue off of it. I had sucked at it for hours like a dolt with no manners, such as I had known Mr. Waldrip's hunting friend Bo Castleberry to do after he had chewed the meat off a handful of quail and left nothing on his plate but a tidy cairn of bones and shot.

I went to a shallow place in the river and washed my hands and face. I popped out my dental bridge and washed that too. I must note here that I have a dental bridge not because I did not take care of my teeth. (I did and we all ought to.) Haunting my father's bloodline is a blight of geriatric gum disease and tooth decay. Grandma Blackmore used to tell of my Saxon great-great-grandfather, Wetley Blackmore, wearing false teeth carved from a piece of black marble stolen from the steps of the Cathedral Church of Saint Peter in Cologne, Germany.

Well, while I was fiddling with that piece of crawfish my dental bridge slipped from my fingers and plopped right in the shallows! I plunged my arms into the cold water but could not reach the riverbed, so I held my breath and put my head under. The water was terribly cold and the current very swift. The tips of my fingers could just about reach the bottom. I did this for a good long while, but I did not find my dental bridge in the cold muck and smooth stones nor in the handfuls of unknowable black mud I brought up and threw back. I lay there on my stomach on the bank of that river in the dark, cold and mighty frustrated, dragging the tips of my fingers over the stones and sediment. Still I could not find the little thing.

When I sat up again and wiped my hands on my skirt I was colder than I guess I had ever been before. I stood up, shivering and sopping wet, and faced that black wood behind me where the valley narrowed. I was then despondent. I hollered like a crazy person with no articulate language into the trees, which all bowed and swayed like gargantuan congregants of the same whispering cult. I do not doubt but that the sounds I made were of angry nonsense, like a coyote on a pulpit.

After I had hollered all I wanted to, I hugged myself in Terry's coat and prayed without words that the masked man would return and help me again. And I prayed aloud that I was not the same as Aunt Belinda and that the masked man had not just been a phantom of a very tired, frightened, and desperate old mind.

I sat up the night shivering something terrible and tonguing my gums. I was just as cold as an electric chair in Wisconsin and damp and I expected that would be the end of me. I was sure to die of exposure that night.

Around when I had just near about given up hope, there came a rustling from the trees. I had the awful notion that it was not the masked man but something else. Perhaps it was the tagged bobcat or the menacing gopher the size of a toaster oven I had escaped the day before. Or perhaps it was a larger presence, a perilous predator such as a grizzly bear with a hankering for old women. Shaking like a sickly devil with the cold, I got up and fixed my skirt. I reached for the hatchet in my purse. I raised it out in front of me, not too sure what I would do with it in battle against a grizzly bear or a mountain lion. I listened. Whatever it was had stopped moving.

Hello, I said. Hello?

Nothing answered. Then all of a sudden from the gloom of the trees came a bulky form of arms and legs and skull and soon by the light of the moon I saw that it was him, the masked man after all! I cannot say how very glad I was to see him!

He moved awkwardly and cradled a bundle of firewood in his arms. He walked past me quickly. He sure looked to be a man of real flesh and blood and not some wild senile vision like I had feared. He did not say a word. I do not believe he even looked at me. He dropped the firewood and took from the back of his belt a red baton and one of those little lighters that you flip open. Then he wedged the baton into the firewood and lit it with the lighter and the pile caught.

He came around again past me towards the trees.

Wait! I said. Please wait! Where are you going?

But he did not turn and kept on at a sure pace away from me into the dark. He was gone again before I knew it and I stood shaking wildly and holding on to the hatchet for dear life. I watched the place where I had last seen the growing firelight touch him. It was not long until he came back with more firewood. He lumbered by me again, as if he were in a trance, heaving muddy boots, the mask slipping around on his head.

He dropped the entire armful into the fire and stood in the upwelling of sparks that carried off over the water like little lightning bugs. He fixed the mask and lined up the holes with his eyes. He took a seat in front of the fire then with his face turned away and put out his legs. Neither of us spoke a word. I had forgot about the hatchet. I dropped it and sat down on the other side of the fire and warmed myself. It was mighty good to get warm again.

We did not talk. I stole glances at him through the flames. He wore big floppy leather gloves and a great puffy eiderdown coat the color blue of postmen. Around his neck was a pair of binoculars and around his wrists were bunched many-colored pieces of elastic like the bands to undergarments. He reminded me of a figure somewhere between a storybook marauder and a homeless man named Leonard who Mr. Waldrip used to employ from time to time to clean the dirt from the eaves and repaint the cattle pens. Leonard was good help, but after a while my powder and a dress or two had come up missing from my closet. Not much later Mr. Waldrip said he spotted an ugly and oddly familiar-looking woman in a similarly familiar-looking dress hitchhiking on an I-40 access road. I do not hold this transformation against Leonard, but I do not believe it is nice to steal things.

Finally I said to the masked man: Has God sent you here to help me?

He watched the fire. His eyes gleamed like metalwork in the holes of the mask.

I told him that I was very frightened.

He looked up at me. Where are your teeth? he said.

It was a moment before I had an answer. I lost them in the river, said I.

In the river?

I told him that it was a dental bridge.

Can you chew all right?

Middling, I said.

It occurs to me that in nature if an animal is old and toothless surely they are not long for this world. This must have occurred to the man too because he looked at me with some worry in his pretty emerald-green eyes. Nowadays civilization keeps a person alive much longer than ever before. I mean to tell you there is a lawyer I know from First Methodist, Dalton Mills, who is 104 years old as I write this and has divorced three wives and has had six different cancers removed from his neck and is all but blind. He has a stainless-steel machine that breathes for him while he sleeps and he smells deathly of olives and talcum powder. I have no concern of his reading this, so I will say that if he were an elephant the herd would have left him behind to die many years ago, which, I am told, is what elephants do.

The man looked back to the fire. Then he said: If you keep downriver you'll come to a forest in little under a week. If you keep moving all day. The river will go left, and you'll want to go right. Into the forest. Watch for two tall pines that make the shape of a keyhole like to an old-timey house. Go between them, straight ahead into that keyhole. You'll meet up with the old Thirsty Robber hiking trail. There'll be a sign with a wooden flower. Follow the trail and you should hit the highway.

How far is it to the highway?

Far, he said. But it's your best way out. You'll have to hurry. It's not safe out here and bad weather's coming.

I am not sure if I can make it, I said.

The man unsheathed the long strange knife from his hip. It looked to me like the kind of spey blade I had seen our cowboys use to geld the workhorses, only larger. He must have heard my breath quicken because he told me he was not going to hurt me and he set about digging mud from the treads of his boots with the point of the blade. Go to sleep, he said. You'll have to leave at daybreak. You won't see me, but I'll be with you as far as the keyhole. Go into the keyhole. Then you'll be on your own.

You are not coming with me?

No, he said. I'm sorry. But you can make it after the keyhole.

I asked him why he was wearing a shirt over his face. He did not reply, only worked at his boots. I wanted to ask him more questions, but I decided against it. At the time I did not know what to make of him. I was nearly sure he meant me no harm, but I could not guess what a man would be doing out there with his face covered up like that. I suppose at the time I took a comforting notion that he was an eccentric hermit of some kind or an earthbound angel or somehow both of those peculiar things at once. The man said nothing more and after a spell I curled up there next to the fire and drifted off watching the light of it flash the blade of his knife and dance over his white mask.

The fire had smoldered out and the masked man was nowhere to be seen. The sun had yet to rise. A fearsome and colorless light haloed the big mountains. Beyond them, I imagined, lay civilization entire. Painted homes and fenced lawns, watered gardens of little foreign flowers, cats belled and little old dogs tethered to telephone poles, and clothed men and women following those sidewalks and roads paved for their shod feet and wheels. Streetlights aglow.

I got up and brushed myself off. I had left a pitiful and fetal shape in the grass. The notion crossed my mind that as long as I had lived I had not lived long enough. I had gone from Mother's belly to that fearful swale in the Bitterroot in the blink of an eye. And all those years in between had not set me right for what I was to face out there. God makes us one way, and we make ourselves another. It is a mighty troublesome misadventure to learn this in the evening of your life.

When I was the librarian at Clarendon Elementary School I often watched a wall clock tick away the minutes of the day with not much else on my mind other than the passage of time itself. The library was located in the basement of the school building and it was cold and musty and there were no windows to speak of, only high cuts of fogged glass that put out the same light no matter the hour of day. I had the idea that my library was where time went when it was wore out and needed some shut-eye. I thought that to live forever a person would only need to sit in that library and watch that wall clock. I retired and left Clarendon Elementary School and forgot about that wall clock. Well, I can sure tell you it did not forget about me and suddenly there I was out in that wilderness an old woman. And even more suddenly here I am at my desk and an older woman yet.

The hatchet lay on the ground. I wiped the dew from the blade and returned it to my purse. On a flat rock near the softly smoking coals was a small compass and a little red canteen the masked man must have left for me in the night. I stowed them in my purse and then I struck off downriver, thinking all the while that Father Time was slinking around after me in step with that tagged bobcat.

The National Transportation Safety Board arrived on an overcast day in September to clear and catalog the crash site. They came in three blue helicopters. Men with rubber gloves photographed and removed the decomposing remains and zippered them away into thin shellwhite bags like amniotic sacs. Lewis watched the men count two bodies and bag the wallet she had found in the fuselage. They photographed the place and the wreckage they would leave behind to rust and fall apart and a straight-backed bald man glided around with a clipboard and took notes.

That evening in the helicopter back to the airfield Lewis asked this man what he figured had caused the crash. He told her that he did not know yet, but said that he was not getting paid enough to find out, for his grandfather had been a butcher and the smell of old meat turned his stomach. Whatever had caused the crash, he was close to certain that Cloris Waldrip had perished along with the others, even if they could not find her remains.

The next day Lewis drove down the mountain and tacked to the telephone poles in the town there flyers of Cloris in black-and-white. *Help the United States Forest Service find Cloris Waldrip.* Nobody save Pete volunteered, yet Lewis did receive a phone call in the night from a man who told her that Cloris looked as he believed his mother, missing since 1953, would look after thirty-three years. Lewis told him that Cloris did not have any goddamn children and had been born and raised in Texas. The man cursed in a language that was not her own and hung up.

Lewis tipped back the brim of her campaign hat and looked up at the spruce. The wind pulled at empty broken boughs stained dark and hung with flies black and fat like overripe fruit. Dark bands of old blood candycaned the trunk to the ground. She drank from the thermos of merlot.

Pete leaned against the spruce and shrugged the video camera on his shoulder. He wore an orange reflective vest which bore the word *Volunteer* and a matching baseball cap pulled down over the coif. Lewis figured he looked like an imbecile someone had taken hunting for small birds.

Come out from under there, Pete.

He looked up to the top of the spruce. He pressed a hand to his malformed sternum and gripped a plastic whistle there. He stepped back. Lord, my life's sure gone weird.

That's where we found Richard Waldrip.

It sure does give off a smell, don't it?

And they knocked him down three days ago.

Pete did not take his eyes from the rotten place, thumbing the whistle as a Catholic would a rosary. There ain't no guessin at it, he said. The man who was up there sure couldn't've guessed he'd end up in a tree in Montana. No guessin at it. No guessin at it at all.

They hiked down a ways and found Claude writing in a notebook before a mossy clearing the size of a school bus.

No sign of your old woman, he said.

Lewis brushed a mosquito from her cheek and left there a stroke of blood. Looks like somebody came through here, she said.

Claude whispered the name Cornelia and touched a tissue to the blue end of his nose. I don't expect we'll find anything. I'd say the skeeters alone could have drunk her up. We got a long hike back to the truck and I got to walk Charlie.

Lewis told the two men they would search the place for an hour more and she went off ahead, calling out to the forest, Mrs. Waldrip! Mrs. Waldrip! Cloris!

She took from her chest pocket the picture she had been given of the Waldrips. She looked again at Cloris, the small face and orb of white hair. She drank from the thermos and strode on calling for the lost woman.

She let the men off at Claude's cabin and drove alone back to the station. She drank a mug of merlot at her desk and listened to the static purr in the radio receiver. Nothing to be heard in it. Outside the window the range was turning dark.

A motor rumbled out on the road.

Not long afterward Bloor stepped into the station and held open the door behind him. Here followed a sizeless teenaged girl. Her thick amber hair was middleparted in curls down her back and she was bucktoothed.

Lewis swallowed the last of the mug and set it on the desk and stood to better look at the girl. She figured the most unusual part to her was that over her face lay a perfect web of rosy scars outward from her nose.

Bloor passed over the girl a chalky hand and introduced her as his daughter. She's almost a perfect carbon copy of her mother, he said. Jill, this is Ranger Debra Lewis.

Do you ever leave this mountain? the girl asked. She spoke with a strange Northwestern accent and a slight impediment.

Probably go down an average of two times a week, Lewis said.

Bloor brought from a pocket a cake of chalk and passed it from palm to palm. We were driving by and saw the light on, he said. You're working late, Ranger Lewis. I hoped we could convince you to let us rescue you. Give you some dinner.

Was just fixin to lock up and head home.

Gaskell phoned me today, Bloor said. He told me you took your men and hiked all the way up to the crash site to look for Mrs. Waldrip's body? That's quite a drive, quite a hike.

Weren't lookin for her goddamn body. I figure she's hikin down. She left the airplane alive.

Bloor clicked his tongue and looked past Lewis out the window behind her. Do you know what you are, Ranger Lewis?

I expect you're about to tell me.

A fascinating and indefatigable woman.

Lewis turned to the window herself. Off in the mountains mist fell in the moonlight as if spun from it. All right, she said.

Jill moved now through the dim station, blinking her eyes and chewing a little finger. She swatted as if to shoo a fly Lewis could not see, then came around to the corkboard on the north wall and pointed to a picture pinned there: a police composite sketch of a young man with a strong jaw and short dark hair. Jill asked who it was.

The Arizona Kisser, Lewis said. The FBI figure he's hidin out here somewhere.

Out here?

Maybe. He was last seen in Idaho buyin bulk foodstuffs.

Jill asked what the man had done, and Lewis told her that he was wanted for questioning about the disappearance of a ten-year-old girl.

Jill turned and rubbed her eye. Is he attractive to you?

The Kisser?

Yes.

Don't guess I ever thought about it.

We took Jill to the ophthalmologist today before driving up, Bloor said. He put away the chalk. Apparently she has myodesopsia. Floaters.

No, I'm haunted by the ghost of a gnat, Jill said, and she picked a place in the air with her finger.

It's not something you'd normally see in a young person. Koojee.

Goddamn sorry to hear that.

A scented candle burned low on the dinner table. Lewis sat across from the girl, drinking a glass of merlot and squinting often at her in the poor light. The girl held her scarred face by her palms, her thin elbows at either side of a plate untouched. Her father sat at the head of the table and showed them both in alternate a slow winecolored smile. His hands lay chalked white and forgotten on the arms of his chair.

Lewis looked beyond him to the fetid homunculus now leaned in the opposite corner like an alleyway drunk. It gazed mindlessly back at her. You guys got any special plans while you're up here? she said.

No, Jill said.

Bloor stood and emptied a bottle of merlot to the brim of a glass. He set the glass before the girl. In most countries it's legal to drink at her age, he said.

Jill took up the glass and gulped it down. You're drunk and you want us drunk to keep your ego company, she said.

Bloor laughed and shook his head and told them to go out back to the hot tub and get to know each other while he cleaned up. He curtsied to them and the homunculus and left to the kitchen.

Jill pressed a thumb to the empty glass and held it up to the candlelight. Just in case, she said, and showed Lewis the whorl of a thumbprint. So they will know I was here.

Pardon?

She held Lewis with her blue-painted eyes. In case he murders us.

Lewis excused herself and went down a hall to a clean white bathroom. She rinsed her mouth and combed through her hair a row of wet fingers and sat on the lid of the toilet. The barrel of the revolver in her holster clinked against the porcelain.

When she returned to the table Jill had gone out back to the deck and Bloor was still in the kitchen. She took a bottle of merlot from the table and joined the girl's small figure at the deck railing. The plaid cotton dress the girl wore was draped on the wind. Rain fell far away in the mountains, and the treetops bristled like the hackles of many thousands of enormous dogs.

Lewis drank from the bottle and held it out. You think you'll like it up here?

Jill took the bottle. Do you think being in these mountains for a long time can make a person nuts?

Lewis looked at the small face. Anglewise the girl recalled to Lewis a beautiful and fineboned boy in her high school class she had never had the courage to befriend. I'm not nuts, Lewis said. And I've lived up here eleven goddamn years.

I think it's nuts that people believe what other people say about themselves.

You ever listen to Dr. Howe?

No. What is that?

Lewis took back the bottle and swigged it and loosed a mouthful down her front. You lookin forward to spendin time up here with your dad?

Jill lit a cigarette. He says he has anxiety and depression like it's an excuse to be selfish. She took back the bottle and finished it. Are we going to get in?

The hot tub was in a corner of the deck, wood-paneled and etched with suns and crescent moons. The two uncovered the water and Jill stripped down to black underpants and a brassiere. The girl stood lean before Lewis, her bony shoulders drawn in against the chill.

Lewis stripped too and the cold raised the dark hair on her arms and she folded her winestained uniform on a deck chair and set the revolver on top. She wore tan briefs and a white undershirt.

They got in the hot tub and circled each other in a clockwork of pale suds until they both found a corner. They did not speak yet. Jill kept her head back and upward to the night sky. She pinched the bridge of her nose and swatted often at nothing. By the green of the lights in the water her small face and fatless body glowed like the vision of a drowned girl.

Your dad mentioned you want to volunteer for the Forest Service, said Lewis. Goddamn Friends of the Forest program.

The girl said nothing.

You're welcome to if that's what you want.

He told me you would be a good influence.

I don't figure he's right about that. I don't know what I'm doin most of the time.

I don't need a good influence, the girl said. I'll be eighteen in November. I plan to leave.

Where're you plannin to go?

Maybe out of the country. But I don't want to sit around this cabin and watch my dad try to understand himself. So I'll help you look for that old lady while I'm still here.

Good. I'm sure she's anxious to be found.

They sat in silence for a time in the tub and Bloor came from the cabin, bared to the flesh save for a pair of small shorts patterned in bald eagles. He carried yet another bottle of merlot and three glasses. He showed Lewis a garish smile purpled like her own and he slid into the water between them the length of his white body and let out a joyful groan.

My gals, he said. My tub gals. I'm a lucky man tonight. Jill, I'm intoxicated. I don't normally like to get this intoxicated. I wanted to tell you how grateful I am you're here. You know, we're going to have a meaningful experience together and when you're my age you'll look back on this time up here with your dad and think how formative it was. It is essential you learn about hard work and the value of a day spent in the service of others. We're both going to get better up here, you know.

Clouds stopped the stars, and the girl's face was dark turned away from the green lights below.

Bloor pulled the cork from the bottle and dropped it into the water. He poured three glasses. Ever since your mom died I've been turning into someone I always worried I could be but never was before, he said.

Jill turned from the sky and looked at her father.

The fringe of his mullet had gotten wet and was stuck together like the feathers of a sick bird. He trained his gaze on the cork in the water. What does it want from me?

What does what want from you? Lewis said.

Bloor nodded at the cork. That.

He's drunk, Jill said. We don't have to answer him.

Bloor drained his glass. How did your partner's nose turn blue, Ranger Lewis?

You don't have to talk to him.

Lewis drank off her glass. It's all right, she said, and told the story of how three winters ago Claude had gotten lost in a snowstorm looking for his dog. Lewis had found him at daybreak, balled up under a ventifact of sandstone with a face frostbitten nearly black, mumbling about a redheaded one-eyed shade he had seen riding a giant armadillo. His nose just hasn't gone back to normal, Lewis said. Maybe his mind hasn't either. I never hear the end of it about that goddamn ghost. I reckon that's round the time I developed a real taste for merlot. Roland never liked it.

Bloor held his hand to the sky and palmed the moon. People need to do whatever it is they want to do while they still want to do it, he said. Give in to our temptations before we can't even care enough to be tempted anymore. Someday we won't have any temptations at all, Adelaide used to say.

Jill looked at her father and climbed from the hot tub and wrapped herself in a towel. Good night, she said, and she took with her the bottle and slid open the door. Before she went inside she glanced once over her shoulder and met Lewis with an expression she could not place.

Lewis raised a steaming hand from the water and bade the girl good night.

Jill slid the door to and Lewis found Bloor's eyes walled and following his daughter through the picture window. He mouthed at the ends of his fingers like a suckling infant.

Are you feelin all right?

Are you, Ranger Lewis?

Lewis sent her eyes roving to the wild dark. The trees reeled blackly there in the wind. Mrs. Waldrip's still out there, she said. I'll bet she's goddamn terrified. Just goddamn terrified. And we're sittin drunk in a goddamn bathtub doin not a goddamn thing but talkin shit about stuff we don't understand.

Bloor brought her to him through the water. Let's not get upset about dead strangers tonight. He put his hand behind her neck and drew her head level with his. He did not kiss her yet but brought his lips to within half an inch of hers and told her that she was a powerful woman. He put out his tongue and licked her bottom lip. Lewis put her arms around his neck and kissed him.

Soon he was on top of her. The pair of bald eagle shorts roiled with the cork in the green water. He grappled with her. Together they flailed in the foam and splashed and he held her still by the shoulders. He could not penetrate her for he was not erect. He pressed himself to the inside of her thigh and rotated his hips like an exotic dancer. A light rain had begun to fall and he asked a question into her open mouth so that it rang in her head as if they had shared a voice. What can I do for you?

What?

What do you want me to do? What do you like?

I don't know, she said. Whatever.

He held up two fingers and took them underwater and he pinched at her sides. Lewis laughed and he held her there. His face was set humorless and empty like a death mask. He pinched her harder and she quit laughing, and he went on pinching her under the water many times as she watched black rain fall from the sky.

IV

For three nights fires smoked downriver in the twilight. Victuals were put out for me on a flat stone or a log. The first night it was trout and crawfish. The next I believe I ate a vole of some kind. The animal had a similar skeleton to critters I had exhumed from stacks of old newspapers and gardening periodicals in Mother's basement after she passed. On the third night it was a cleaned and halved feline. Its big ole head had been left on and it had a numbered yellow tag in one of its ears, and I am nearly certain it was the very bobcat that had been tailing me. I believe the number was 147, if I recall aright, but I cannot put my life on it. I have a powerful memory, but this has been some time ago now.

I never could get enough to eat. I was working up a mighty big appetite even on my pitifully slow pace across the floodplain. The masked man had said that I would not see any more of him, and sure enough he had not showed himself since instructing me on how to get to the highway. Every night however while I had the supper he had provided I kept my eyes on the woods. I suspected he was watching me.

One day I saw a fox chase something through the grass. I recalled a dog we had when I was a girl, a spirited little dog with a happy face. Before long the dog grew old and very ill and I overheard Father tell my brother it had outstayed its welcome. Davy cared a good deal for that little dog. Pepper, its name was. I thought about how we had all loved this dog when it was playful and well, but when it got to knocking blindly about the house, dragging its hind legs and messing behind the furniture, we were ready for it to be gone. Father took it out to the pasture and shot it. I have had occasion to think about this; about how conditional we are when it comes to love and affection.

On the fourth day I came to an inviting shallow in the river that led out to a braid bar of red sand. At that time I did not smell at all like myself. Or perhaps I smelled more like myself than I ever had in the civilized world of soap and detergents. Whichever way it was, the sun was high and hot, and I took it in my mind to cool off and have another bath. I had not had one in some days, out of modesty, being that I had the idea the masked man was out there watching me. At the riverbank I kept an eye out for him. But there were only the mountains and the eternal snow blown from their peaks, the valley, the nice grass. The valley was narrowing and yellow-flowered shrubs grew thickly in the fields. Firs and pines bordered it all. It was a mighty fine spot.

I took Terry's coat and the zigzag sweater from around my waist where I kept them cinched by the arms when it was warm enough. I unbuttoned my blouse. The masked man could be watching me right then. I went ahead and disrobed all the same and there I was in my pitiful undergarments. The holes in my stockings made funny shapes of my skin. Since I had grown old my body had gone soft and misshapen like the crab apples at the foot of my crab apple tree in our backyard. Like most women my age I wore practical undergarments. The manufacturers like to call the color *flesh color*, though I am not sure whose flesh they had in mind when they decided to call it that. Maybe there is some poor person out there who is this color they call *flesh color*, but I do not think it is likely. I have never worn dark-colored underclothes, and I have always had hard work believing, as I know many do believe, that we are primarily on this earth to attend the sexual purposes of men.

When I was a girl, not more than eleven years old, Mother and Father would take me and Davy to a swimming pool in Amarillo. There was a small changing room that smelled of surfactants and chlorine and the floors were slick and rocky such as the inside of a cave. It often happened that a bald man with a sunburnt head would watch me from a little oval window at the top of the wall. Either he was a giant or he must have had to climb up on a chair to see in. Only the crest of his pink head and his beady eyes were visible in that foggy little oval window. I did not holler and I did not say a word to anyone. I have wondered from time to time about myself and why it was that I disrobed even though I knew that man was watching me. I suppose most everyone likes to be desired, often even in the most undesirable of circumstances. Perhaps it is our greatest flaw as people.

I removed my brassiere and rolled down my stockings and folded my clothes in the grass. Feeling strangely light, I did a turn, entirely naked to the natural world. I have always had a slight figure and I have always taken care of it as best I could. But out there in the Bitterroot, for the scarcity of provisions and the great deal of walking, I had grown so thin I had nearly misplaced my shadow.

I looked down at myself. I will admit here in this account that as a girl I often had prideful and immodest thoughts. I have since learned that is considered by many psychologists to go hand in hand with what is thought to be the natural development of a woman. I never knew much about psychology until in recent years when people became interested in mine. It is curious to see how people try to understand one another with what seems to me a confused science, not much better than phrenology, which was popular in my parents' day. A mind endeavoring to understand another mind is like using a hammer to fix another hammer. Anyway, psychology might be closer to poetry, but less helpful. Particularly when it comes to discussing sex.

Nowadays women are allowed their sexual desires. Back when I was young the existence of a woman's sexuality was a dirty little secret that everyone shared. I recall wanting men to notice me when Mother would walk me and Davy down Main Street to the old First Methodist church house dressed in our Sunday clothes. That was before they tore it down and built the one on Washburn Street. I preferred the old one. I had a blue cotton dress that I thought looked just darling on me for how it complemented the color of my eyes. One Sunday when I was fourteen years old, Mother took me aside and warned me that I was not to walk in the manner I had been walking, or to look at men in the manner I had been looking. She called me a little fire ant and was sure that I would find trouble someday. In one way of looking at it, she was right, but I never did half of the things that Phyllis Stower did, and she ended up more or less the same as myself, except that God gave her four healthy children, all of whom are alive and well as I write this and have children of their own.

I stepped out onto the sandbar. The water came up to my ankles. It was mighty cold, but I was determined to have a bath. I waded out and it came up to my knees. When you get older your balance is not what it used to be, and the current was stronger than I had anticipated. It took me by surprise and toppled me, and I went under!

My body seized up in that cold like I had been stuck with a cattle prod. I kicked and clawed at the rocky riverbed. Suddenly there were no rocks to grab ahold of. I struggled to the surface and got my head above it. The trees and the riverbank had changed and now it was all rushing by. I could no longer see where I had folded my clothes.

I endeavored to holler out but I was too cold and water filled my mouth anyway. I gulped and spat and coughed like a crazy person. Locked helpless in that current, I caught my breath before plunging underwater again. It was terrifically difficult on my lungs and my arms. I was very scared. Just before I went under again a figure sprang past me along the riverbank. Dear me! That is what I said to myself.

Something crashed into the water ahead of me. I wiped my eyes best I could and made out a great big rotted log. A deep voice hollered for me to grab on. I swam in earnest and reached for it. I grabbed the end of it just in time! Suddenly the water rushed past me. I had disturbed some insect, perhaps a centipede, that lived in the log and it stung me right between the fingers. I did not let go even though it was terribly painful.

When I blinked away the water, the masked man stood at the riverbank with his heels dug in, hauling on that log. Gracious, what a sight! His huffing and puffing over the noise of the water grew louder the closer I got. It sounded the way Mr. Waldrip's ranch manager, Joe Flud, would grunt and growl whenever a cow was calving and he had to wrestle it into the chute.

Before I knew it I was close enough to make out the print of the pancakes on the white mask. The cotton over his mouth sucked in and blew out in a damp oval. He dropped his end of the log and drug me out of the water by the pits of my arms onto the bank. I was flat on my back, gasping for air. There I was cold and naked and wet as a Baptist, but I was alive.

People have asked me what I had on my mind just as that little airplane went down in the Bitterroot. It is always the young people who ask me that. And I always have to disappoint them. I cannot recall having a thought in my head. My mind was as empty as one of Mr. Waldrip's Coke bottles out on the back porch, hooting in the wind. However I will tell you that when I nearly drowned in that river I did have something on my mind. I thought of Mr. Waldrip. I wanted for him to be the last thing on my mind before nothing else would go there, so I repeated his name over and over in my head until I saw that I was going to be all right.

Above me was a blue sky and not a cloud in it. The man leaned over me. The mask, wet and clinging to his face, revealed the shape of a bearded jaw. I was sure I could see myself, a pink and naked old woman, in his emerald-green eyes. Being that he had come to my rescue, I knew then he had been watching me when I had disrobed and gone out to bathe.

Are you all right? he asked me.

I told him that I was.

The man wrapped me up in his down coat and made a fire. It was late afternoon and the wind was up. I sat on the ground, rubbing my hand where the little critter had stung me. The fire burned sideways, singeing tall riparian grasses and warning away the mosquitoes and gnats. Fire looks mighty strange and false in the daylight.

The man went back upriver for my things: my purse, the hatchet, the canteen and the steel pot, Terry's coat and my filthy clothes and Mr. Waldrip's boot. He disappeared behind a rise of stones and grass. I waited. I put my hands in his coat pockets to keep them out of the breeze and in one pocket I found a small skeleton key. It looked like an antique. In the other was what I first took to be a handkerchief but was instead a women's undergarment. It was blue cotton and did not have any special thing about it other than that it appeared to be clean. I put it back and did not think much of it at the time.

There naked in that man's coat I recalled when Father would take us swimming out at Greenbelt Lake. I would sit on the shore, small and wrapped in a towel, letting the Texas sun dry my plaited hair. Father was not a very religious man. He attended church for Mother and the neighbors. He was raised wild in Colorado by nearly blind Grandma Blackmore, an unlettered gold panner. The true breadth of her past was a wonderful mystery to him. He always told big stories that she had been at one time married to a tongueless court jester in Central Europe and had sold petrified monkey hearts in the markets of Marrakesh. I get my storytelling ability from his side of the family. Anyway, he would take me and Davy and we would all swim as naked as newborns. Mother put a stop to that when she found out. She sure could cow my father with the thousand ways she knew to say his name. By the end all he ever did was what she told him to do.

After little more than half an hour the man returned from upriver wearing Terry's coat and my purse. He set my purse and a neat pile of my clothes and Terry's coat beside me. He did not say a word and sat with the fire between us and turned away.

I thanked him for helping me again. I seem to be an awful lot of trouble, I said.

He made no reply.

I stood and let his coat fall to the ground and was naked again. The sun was setting then and the large mountain put a limitless shadow over us. All that was left of the day burned a royal color behind the peak. The firelight was not flattering to my naked body. I set about getting dressed. With my stockings in tatters, I rolled them up and stowed them in my purse. I combed back my hair with my fingers and sat back down by the fire.

I told the man that I was dressed and that he could turn back around. Still he had his masked face to the far rocky land.

There's not enough day left for you to make any headway, he said at last. You should stay here tonight.

I wrapped myself in Terry's coat and looked at the man through the whipping flames. Will you stay with me?

I can't stay here, he said.

I asked him why that was, but he would say nothing.

Did Jesus send you? I asked.

No, he said.

My name is Cloris Waldrip, I told him. What is your name?

The man straightened the mask and got up. He produced a square of chocolate in a foil and told me that it would have to do for supper. I took the chocolate and went to touch his hand, but he shied away like a dog with a past. I apologized.

Tomorrow you'll cut through the forest, he said. The keyhole I told you about is just right down there. You'll see it in the morning. The man pointed to a place of darkness where the woods began. Just right down there. Stay on the trail. You'll see the sign, remember? That goes straight east. Watch out for mountain lions. Snakes too. You can reach the highway in a little under a week if you don't stop too much.

I asked him to please come with me and said that I did not believe I could make it without him.

Ma'am, he said, I'm really sorry. And he gathered up his coat and set off into the dark of the woods.

Being that I was very tired, I slept well and the morning came quickly. The fire was out. I did not look for the man. On the ground was a small box of oats and four salted fish wrapped in newspaper pages of showtimes for a small-town picture house in Idaho. I cannot recall the name of the town. Beside that there were six fire-starter sticks and a lighter which bore the likeness of a silly cartoon pig playing a saxophone. I righted myself and stuffed the cereal box in my purse along with Mr. Waldrip's boot, which held the hatchet, and stowed the fire-starter sticks and the lighter and the little red canteen in Terry's coat pockets.

I was by that time mighty curious about the masked man. I had only ever heard of criminals wearing masks in the commission of their crimes. It is not often that you hear about a person hiding their face for an act of altruism and charity. Still, and perhaps I was being silly, it did not yet occur to me that he could be a criminal.

By then I counted that I had been out in the Bitterroot wilderness for twenty-one days. I was getting used to being outside all hours of the day and night. But gracious, I ached something terrible and was as tired as a tumbleweed. I was ready to go home. So I filled up the red canteen the masked man had given me and I stood a little taller when I looked out at those mountains and that wild land. I was a little braver when I faced that dark opening in the thick woods he had pointed out to me. The place shaped the same as a keyhole.

I later learned that back in Clarendon about this time the church held a candlelight vigil for myself and Mr. Waldrip. I was told that most of the congregation turned out. Even Mrs. Holden, who had lost the use of her legs and weighed a good 250 pounds and had to be carried in on a piece of canvas by her four grandsons like she were being pallborne alive. The vigil was held on a warm Wednesday evening on the mowed lawn of the courthouse, they said, and as Pastor Bill began the prayer of the lost, a wild truckful of bibulous hooligans drove plumb through the front window of the pharmacy across the street. By the grace of God no one was hurt, but some took it as confirmation that we were not coming back.

I turned around and looked up once more at that great mountain where the airplane had gone down. I thought about the impact and the sound that was not sound. I thought of poor Mr. Waldrip still up in that spruce, and imagined vengeful birds pecking at him as if they had learned he had hunted their kind every season since he could walk. I got one last look at that vile mountain and through the keyhole I sallied forth into the dark wood. What awaited me there I cannot easily forget.

In the blue dawn Lewis tucked the campaign hat under her arm and rang the doorbell to the white cabin. Bloor answered the door.

Thanks for coming to get her again, he said.

More than a week had gone since Jill had arrived on the mountain and every morning Lewis had collected her on heading into the station, and they would ride together without words, listening to the whir of the heater.

It's on my way, Lewis said.

He leaned over and kissed her on the cheek. She's out back, he said. Having a little trouble getting going this morning.

He gave Lewis a mug of coffee and she went out the sliding glass door and found the girl smoking at the deck railing and staring at something. Lewis went to her and followed her gaze. An emaciated squirrel, perched on the bough of a pine, was turning in its paws a wriggling knot of damp fur.

It's eating its baby, Jill said. Like Ugolino.

The young squeaked and clicked and the squirrel rolled over the minor skull its bared teeth, stripping flesh like a hand plane. Lewis sipped the coffee and grimaced and pulled from the end of her tongue a toenail clipping. She spat over the railing and flicked the clipping from her fingers, then faced the white cabin. Bloor stood in the window watching them.

Lewis turned back to the girl and lifted the campaign hat to the coloring sky and told her they ought to go for they had yet to collect Ranger Paulson and Pete and would be going a long way out today.

Jill blew a ring of smoke. She nodded at the hot tub. I heard you both.

Heard what?

You and my dad copulating in the Jacuzzi.

I don't know what you mean.

Last week, the night I got here. I heard you having sex.

No. Lewis watched yet the squirrel work the newborn like a nut. Maybe you heard some goddamn animals.

I convinced a boy to copulate with me, and after we did he told the school my vagina looked like an old army boot.

Lewis poured the coffee out off the deck. Boys can be mean.

Men who act like whatever they think men are supposed to act like should be gassed. Women who act like whatever they think women are supposed to act like should be gassed too.

Maybe we need the people we don't like. For some reason.

Maybe, Jill said, swatting at nothing. Like we need gnats for the ecosystem? Maybe if we lose all the annoying people it could be the end of society.

Lewis turned again to the window. Bloor was behind the glass in shadow still watching. He smiled and held up a chalked hand.

I'm beginnin to think your dad doesn't give you enough credit, Lewis said.

When my mom was sick she couldn't move her body. She couldn't even talk. And he would get her from her wheelchair and copulate with her on the living room rug. Up until the week she died.

Maybe that's romantic.

It's not, Jill said.

Lewis watched the girl suck her cigarette. Smoke swam from a perfect nose, light catching the pattern of scars on her face.

The girl said: I would like to be one of those people that change many times before they die. I could be married to a man in Tokyo and he cheats on me when he's volunteering for UNICEF in Africa. I could be a librarian with an Iranian-American girlfriend. She's a hot dog vendor in Central Park. I could have a shoe store that floods, gets mold, and is condemned, and I become a counselor at a homeless center. I could be in jail for fish gambling with a son in Newfoundland. As long as it's different from this and everything else.

Don't you figure you ought to finish high school first?

Jill stubbed the cigarette out on the railing and turned to Lewis. You could take me seriously.

You just might regret not finishin school.

Do you regret anything?

Probably.

If somehow that old lady is still alive out there, do you think she regrets anything?

Well, you can goddamn ask her when we find her, Lewis said.

If the crash didn't kill her, she has probably killed herself by now.

Lewis looked back to the pine. The squirrel had gone.

She checked the rearview mirror. Jill, asleep in the backseat, jostled against the window. The old dog lay balled on the floorboard under her feet. Pete, his red hair matted under the coif, sat in the seat next to the girl and worked at his needlepoint. Lewis imagined him as an ugly peasant woman living in Holland before the discovery of America. Over the three hours she had been driving he had raised the video camera now and again and taped Jill and the embroidery hoop and the dog and the nape of Claude's neck in the front passenger's seat. He had once fixed it on her and caught her drinking from the thermos of merlot.

She drove them on for near an hour more over worsening roads and darker forest, and often they stopped and dragged away a fallen branch in their path and Lewis would sneak around to the back of the Wagoneer and refill the thermos from a bottle she kept hidden there.

Jill woke when the engine quit and the others had climbed out and slammed the doors. She blinked at Lewis as if she had forgotten her and asked if they were there. Lewis told her they were and that they would walk side by side and comb the forest trail until they came to Black Elk Creek, where they would continue on for about a mile more and then turn back before dark if they had not found Cloris Waldrip. Her guess, she said, was that Cloris would be at the creek.

She gave Jill and Pete reflective orange vests and the team followed an overgrown trail marked by wooden posts rotted thin and washed pale red. They chanted in round *Cloris, Cloris, Cloris, Mrs. Waldrip*. Claude kept time with a machete on the pines and the old dog wavered at his heels. Downward to a scrub valley they went like a pilgrimage in prayer, and Pete hauled about his neck the video camera, wheezing and halting to clutch at his pigeon chest and to straighten the coif.

Don't get left behind, Petey, Claude said. We'd never find you.

They left the forest for the grass and the few windspiraled pines of the wide valley. Ahead of them was the river. They spread out and Pete and Claude went together. The dog trotted after them. Carrion hunters patterned the peaks.

What d'you think of it out here? Lewis said.

You should see Tokyo, Jill said.

Lewis tightened the straps on her pack and spat in the grass. You been there?

No.

How d'you know then?

I've seen images in a magazine.

What about bein out in goddamn nature?

Tokyo is nature, said the girl.

Lewis sucked her teeth. Maybe you're right. Maybe this isn't all that different.

They went on and the team reached the river and stopped there. Jill sat on a rock and lit a cigarette.

Don't you goddamn leave that out here, Lewis told her.

Claude and Pete milled about downriver some hundred-odd feet away. The dog snuffled around and ate grass and gagged. Pete set the video camera on a stump and fixed it on Claude, who stood before him gesturing wildly to the water and forming claws of his hands and making a speech Lewis could not hear.

Jill brushed the hair from her blue-painted eyes and swatted at nothing in the wind. Do you hate your ex-husband?

Lewis brought from her pack a thermos of merlot and unscrewed the lid. She pushed back her campaign hat and drank. Already it was late afternoon and the mountains swayed blue over the river. Why're you askin me that goddamn question?

The girl shrugged.

No, Lewis said. I don't hate him.

Do you love him?

Sometimes he'd fix cucumber sandwiches and bring them to the station. We'd have lunch together. He'd hold my goddamn hand, tell me he loved me. Maybe I loved him then.

Why?

Never said a bad word to me. I said more to him than he ever did to me. Maybe that's really why it turned out the way it did. I'm not an easy person. I gave him trouble for nothin. But sometimes I'd catch him just lookin at me like I was the only goddamn thing he'd ever seen. I expect that's the troublin part. He was a goddamn good man to me.

I used to love a cat but then I realized that was ridiculous, Jill said.

Lewis shook her head and licked the merlot off her lips. Talked to one of the other wives at the courthouse when he was bein sentenced. Told each other how goddamn sorry we were and how goddamn bad it all was what he'd done to us. But she said somethin. She said she thought what they'd had was one of a kind and it hurt her that it wasn't. I figure we all'd like to have somethin nobody else does.

That woman is sad and stupid, Jill said, and she put out the cigarette on the rock and flicked the butt to the river. There's no such thing as one of a kind.

I figure you're right about that.

Do you believe he loved you?

Lewis drank again from the thermos and burped and spat redly in the grass. Somebody lies that much you got to wonder. But I figure he was also sharin the best parts of himself with three goddamn women, and takin care of them and maybe he really was lovin them. You can't know. The judge asked him why he did it, and goddamn Roland said he couldn't see his way to a life without any one of us and maybe he was a greedy man but a life with just one person he loved wasn't enough for him. He said he had so much love to give and if it was a crime to give it then lock him up and give the key to a fish.

If people can believe they love cats, Jill said, I bet they can believe they love more than one person.

Lewis took another drink from the thermos. The girl balanced on the rock, hugging her legs, her locks of hair near too heavy for the wind, the sun turning in them and the scars of her face.

Your dad sure doesn't give you enough credit, Lewis said.

The girl said nothing.

I expect you're a little bit like him.

We are all the same boring person, said the girl.

Claude whistled to them from downriver and waved his arms. Pete waved too and went to whistle and instead yipped like a small dog and fell into a fit of coughing. He doubled over and Claude knocked him on the back until he straightened up.

Lewis and Jill walked down to join them and Jill lit another cigarette on the way. When they came close Claude did not say a word but raised an arm and unfurled a finger at the stump of a downed spruce.

Lewis neared it and knelt before a row of letters hacked crudely into the wood. She ran her fingers over them, then stood and cupped a purpled mouth and tottered in a circle. She called for the lost woman. She dropped her hands and cast her rosy eyes over the valley. I goddamn knew it, she said.

Jill knelt at the stump and smoked the cigarette.

Pete sidled up alongside the girl, a hand splayed over his pigeon chest. Reckon you'd lend me one of those? My heart's uneasy.

Jill shook a few cigarettes from the pack and offered them.

Pete pulled one and pressed it between his lips. He lit the cigarette and looked the girl over. Thank you kindly. Can I tell you, I see you growin up into a fine middleaged woman. Not like my wife.

Claude removed his campaign hat and wiped with the back of a hand his blue nose and snapped for the dog. The dog heeled and Claude came around to Lewis. He put a hand on her shoulder. I'd say there wasn't any positive reason she put her name in this stump, Debs. I'd say it suggests she's dead. She hoped we'd find this to let us know that. I'm impressed with this woman.

It ain't all that good a whittlin job, Pete said. I seen children what can woodwork better than that.

It's not her craftsmanship that I'm impressed with, Petey.

Jill flicked her cigarette to the river and watched the others quietly. The scars of her face grew pink in the sun.

Lewis kicked the dirt. The goddamn body?

I'd say consumed by some wild animal, Claude said.

It's a damn shame, Pete said. I'd bet she must've been some lady to get down here and carve in that wood, even if she didn't carve it all that well.

I don't see any indication of wild animals, Lewis said. No blood, no hair, no bones, not even a goddamn kneecap.

Jill looked around at the grass. I don't see anything either.

Claude ran a hand over his clean black hair. You're gettin real peculiar about this Cloris Waldrip, Debs.

Lewis swigged from the thermos of merlot and dribbled down her front. She wiped her face and showed a winedrenched middle finger to the man. You spend your nights in the forest lookin for a gingerheaded cyclops that rides a goddamn armadillo.

Claude said nothing, then wrinkled his forehead. There's no need to be rude, Debs. I'd say it just stands to reason she's gone.

I had made my way aimlessly for two long and terrible days through those strange woods and I was yet to come to the old trail like the masked man had said that I would. All I saw were trees and more trees. My gracious, there were trees!

The canopy splintered up the sun and made me mighty dizzy. It was the same effect that occurred whenever Mr. Waldrip would drive me in the truck down Goodnight Street in Clarendon. The street was lined with tall old elms, and they splintered up the sun that same way. Riding on that street was like having some crazy person switch a light on and off in your face. I endeavored to keep a true heading east with the little compass the man had left me, but the trees got the best of me and sent me to winding like a snake in a saloon. I tell you now that if I were never to see another tree again before I leave this world that would be all right with me.

I was uneasy that the masked man was not watching over me anymore. I felt direly alone like I had the night Terry had passed on in such awful confusion. The notion crossed my mind that I had been abandoned by God in some blighted fairyland. Unusual sights greeted me. Sickly and tonedeaf songbirds perched in the trees on their peeling feet and there were yellow-eyed rodents sluggish and balding and afflicted with sores. There were colorless insects the size of hands, like you could find at the bottom of the ocean, and black butterflies floated on the mist. The bare branches of dead trees clacked together above me while I watched a slimy frog eat another slimy frog. There was a shrub like a black person's hair around which schooled hundreds of bioluminescent flies.

Being that the air here was stale and little sound would carry on it, I heard only my breath like sand on paper. The ground was full of downed branches all busted up like it were the floor of a charnel house. There was a decrepit evil there and everything appeared to be ill. I was afraid, but it would take a night in the rain for the dread of it all to finally set in and for me to admit to myself how very alone I was.

That night came after what I counted as my third day in that strange forest. This is what happened: the rain was gentle to begin with but by and by it started coming down in buckets. Then I was lucky enough to arrive at a large wall of limestone. It reminded me of the facade of the old Texas State Bank in downtown Amarillo. I am not an authority on the subject, but I have read that all manner of native people once called the Bitterroot their home, so I am inclined to believe I had stumbled onto the ruins of an ancient edifice of some kind such as those in Petra halfway across the world. I climbed up on a ledge of the limestone, got up close under a kind of awning, and covered myself in Terry's coat. There was a rectangular cut in the floor of the stone and rainwater was sucking through it like a storm drain in a street.

It had gotten dark, but I fumbled around and turned up some dry pine needles and such for tinder there in a recess like that of a doorway. I hoped to build a fire. In some haste I put together a little pile in that spot. I had one fire-starter stick left. I took it out along with the silly cartoon lighter in Terry's coat pocket. There was a crack of lightning and I jumped. I dropped the lighter and it skidded away and disappeared right down that drain in the rock! I thought about putting my arm down after it to see if there was a kind of catch basin but it was dark and I could not bring myself to do it.

I slumped down on those ruins and watched the downpour and set to turning my wedding ring on my finger. I had gotten used to rain. I did not bawl about it, I just set out Mr. Waldrip's boot and filled the red canteen with the runoff from the rocks. After my eyes had adjusted to the dark I could see the woods, all black and gray. The rain fell very hard and a chill was in my bones. There was not a thought in my head, save that I was cold. I was mighty hungry too so I had the rest of the cereal, which I had hoped would last longer than it wound up doing. I did not much like the salted fish.

It was after I had eaten up the cereal that I spotted the mountain lion. It crept up out of the rain. Like everything else in those woods the creature looked infirm. It had overlarge shoulder blades that jutted up like panels on a dinosaur. In the dark the animal resembled a kind of winged mythological beast, one that was to guard the limestone ruins in which I sat. Most unusual of all, and believe me or not, the lion walked backwards. It led with its tail sweeping left to right like the head of a snake. Its mouth was slack and rain ran through its teeth. I was mighty scared but I picked up my hatchet and hollered at it loud as I could. Well, that lion lit out of there like a little pussycat. I have since read that mountain lions have an instinctual fear of the human voice.

I sat in that limestone, hatchet in hand, waiting for the cat to return. It is strange sometimes how the mind wanders off on its own, once danger disperses, and by and by when I was convinced the cat would not come back my way, I got to worrying again over the past, and the tally for and against me. I mean to say I thought of Garland Pryle.

Ours was no great love affair. I do not want to leave you the misunderstanding that it was. The women of Texas who belong to my generation generally do not talk about sex. You could live your entire life in Donley County and never be sure it was being had by anyone but yourself. But to be direct and to honor the veracity of this account, I will here put it down plainly that I committed adultery with Garland Pryle. I am not proud of it, but there it is.

It happened twice. The first incident occurred in the lovely little home his parents had on Bent Tree Street. We made love on the dinner table. The second incident occurred one summer afternoon not but a week later in the springhouse behind the grocery store. The springhouse cooled our hot and crazed young blood and we made love on the cucumbers and the squash. I did enjoy it very much. This troubled me for some time, for my amorous mind would fetch him in the night as I lay in bed next to dear Mr. Waldrip, that kindest of men. It bothered me that rainy night out in the Bitterroot, when little else made any good sense anymore and God sure seemed less like Himself than He ever had. I could not fathom the way He had worked in the masked man. I could not fathom the way He had worked in Garland Pryle so many years before. Most of all, I could not fathom the way He had worked in me. I am the greatest mystery to myself.

This is what frightened me and frightens me yet: I am near to certain I would make the same decision in that little aisle of canned peas if I had to do it over and over again until the end of time. I knew that was true every time I asked for forgiveness on my knees at First Methodist, when all of the congregation whispers selfish prayers to themselves, all of us sinners accounting the balance of our souls in that same slatted wood building, hearing not even the wind howl. I would do it again, Lord. I would do it again, and I am not even sure that I am sorry.

I did not sleep. I waited for morning as the rain slowed and then quit altogether and the clouds lightened up. I had survived yet another night. Exhausted and cold as I was I picked myself up, wrung out the zigzag sweater, and looked through the drain in the stone to see if I could spot the lighter. I could not see a thing but a trough of black water. In the light the ruins were not as grand as I had imagined them in the dark. I transferred the rainwater from Mr. Waldrip's boot to the little red canteen and then I studied the compass. I started out again in an easterly direction.

I had not gone but a quarter mile when I heard a long whistle come from a particularly shady place in the trees to the southeast. I stopped and put my hand to my ear. It sounded like the cattle pens on a windy day, slow and in the register of a school-aged boy. I have always had good hearing, I imagine because I had lived a quiet life up until that time. Mr. Waldrip, on the other hand, had lost much of the hearing in his right ear to his shotgun.

I followed the whistle through the trees until it got to where it sounded like the noises a woman makes when she is with a man. Not but fifteen yards ahead, nestled under two crooked pines, was a little blue tent. Heavens, I was excited!

I endeavored to holler out and make myself known to whomever it was inside making the racket, but my throat seized up with too much excitement. When I reached the tent, suddenly the noises quit. I went to announce myself again but could not. I was trembling. Instead I rapped on the side of the tent.

Not a thing happened.

At last I managed to say, Excuse me, help, pardon me, I am Cloris Waldrip, I have been in an aviation accident.

No answer came from within.

I do not know much about tents. I have never cared too much for sleeping outdoors. When I was a girl Father took me once out on the prairie and we slept under the stars in the bed of the wagon on top of the horse blankets. I imagine what he really wanted to do was get away from Mother for a night. Davy had passed away only the summer before and a woman had just been elected governor of Wyoming and Mother did not think that was a very good idea. She was not good company for quite some time.

This tent had zippers. It was dingy and its blue color was faded in a streak where the sun had gone over it that same way for a good long while. At the bottom the nylon was bulged and was darkly discolored like the apron of a fry cook. I was starting to get uneasy. I nudged it with my foot and announced myself again. Not a thing happened. Then I worked up the courage and reached down and unzipped the opening. Out came a smell like that of the icebox after the power had been out.

There was no one inside the tent! There was a big paper bag of groceries that had molded, and a swoll-up blackened plastic jug labeled as orange juice sitting upright next to an unopened package of paper plates and plastic cutlery. I could not for the life of me figure out what had made the noises I had heard. Perhaps it was the wind. To this date I do not know.

I hollered out. I hollered and hollered so loud I believed I would bust my throat. I had just had enough of it out there. The horror of that empty tent bothers me yet. How had it come to be there, and to what purpose or by what treacherous event had it been abandoned? I worried I had stumbled into some special kind of puzzled hell.

After I had hollered for a spell I sat my back against a pine and took a rest. My throat was sore and I was dizzy. I watched that tent and waited to see if the noises would start up again.

Something moved behind me.

Ma'am, said a hushed voice. Ma'am.

I turned and spotted him. The masked man was crouched in the trees! Dear me, I was surprised! I had thought for sure it was that mountain lion that walked backwards come for me. I was sure relieved to see the man again but when I opened my mouth to say so, he shot up a gloved finger to quiet me.

He looked about and crept out jangling for all the stuff he carried. He came up beside me and whispered, Are you all right?

I nodded and asked why he was whispering.

Why're you screaming? he said.

I told him my mind was playing tricks on me.

He crept to the tent and knelt at it and zipped it back up, then stood up and lined up his eyes with the holes in the mask. From an overpacked duffel on his back hung a little tackle box, a pan, and three rusty old traps for small animals. A fishing rod poked up behind him as if he were meant to be hooked on a wire like a streetcar.

What happened here? I said, pointing at the tent and trembling.

A gale filled the woods just then and flapped the stained nylon. Just as quick as it had come the wind was gone and all was still again. It was mighty spooky.

I don't know, he said, and looked to the sky. We need to leave.

I took one last look at that terribly vacant tent. Then the man sallied forth into the trees and I followed after him.

I thought you could not accompany me, I said.

It's too early in the season for snow, he said, but I think it's coming anyway. You'd have gotten caught in it. Come on, we have to hurry.

As it happens, the autumn of 1986 had awfully strange weather. People wore sweaters in Florida and seep ponds froze in Texas. One day people could be out on the beach scarcely clothed and the next they could be in by the fire drinking hot cider. It is my understanding that the climate is confounded for what mankind has done to the earth. It does not surprise me that we would bring about our own destruction and the destruction of our unfortunate neighbors. It would appear that we hate ourselves and the civilization we have made. Cities are bigger and technology is stranger and young people are growing younger and consuming information for which I cannot see purpose nor end.

I have put here before that our darling grandniece Jessica lives in Phoenix, Arizona. She puts in hours of time air-conditioned at her computer gazing into that Internet. I know she sees meaning in it that I cannot. When I look into that white box I am blinded by the all-colored light and the insurmountable absurdity of it all. I do not know much about the science of it, but I am afraid that when Jessica is my age she will see a stifling hot world wracked with wars fought by the poor and waged by celebrities, and from what I understand, Phoenix is going to catch fire, burn up, and blow away.

I thanked the masked man for coming for me. You are a decent man, I told him.

He said not a word and pulled on ahead.

Bloor, carrying a bottle under his arm and two glasses between his fingers, led Lewis upstairs to a candled master bedroom. On a wall hung three oil paintings of leprous zealots cradling headless lizards, and on a bedside table was a framed photograph of Jill adolescent and frowning at a lobster claw.

Bloor poured a glass of merlot and handed it to Lewis. I had some personal items shipped up from Missoula, he said. He nodded at the photograph. She used to be my little pal.

She still up or has she gone to bed?

He shook his head. Grief looks different to a teenager, he said. And anything and everything looks very different to Jill Bloor.

Lewis drank off the glass in one gulp. Picture windows kept the night and the black mountains. Across the room was a sliding glass door to a dark terrace.

Bloor asked if she had heard from Gaskell.

He's sayin it's too spendy to give any more goddamn time to it. Said he wasn't even sure the carvin spelled out her name. I figure he's just gettin pretty goddamn tired of hearin about it.

Bloor raised a finger to the paintings on the wall. I got these in today. A Norwegian artist. She's in jail awaiting trial for molestation charges. It's interesting what turns a person on, don't you think?

I don't know if it's all that interestin.

What turns you on, Ranger Lewis?

Lewis hooked a thumb in her belt and looked at the paintings again. Usual things, I expect.

What are those?

I don't know, kissin, goddamn slow dancin, nothin interestin.

Bloor neared her and set his chin on top of her head and wrapped around her his long arms. He swayed and danced her in a small circle. You know, he said in a high reedy voice, my wife always told me she could remember the night she was born. She said she was born premature in a night car on a train somewhere between Yakima and Spokane. Her mom never could remember the name of the small town it was they were passing through at the time, but Adelaide swore it had a G in it and the streetlights were the color of dried menstruation.

Your goddamn wife.

He waltzed her gently across the room and pushed her to the bed. He stood over her. The light on the landing through the open door set him in shadow. He clapped together his hands and sent up a cloud of chalk. Lewis sat up on her elbows to better look at him.

He unbuttoned his shirt and kissed the air for each button undone. He laid his body next to hers and dragged his nose up her arm to her shoulder and left there a glassy circuit like the track of a snail. Remove your uniform, he said.

Jill still up? Shouldn't we shut the goddamn door?

Let's leave it open. What do you think?

Why in the hell would we do that?

It's sexy.

All right.

Lewis undid her uniform and rolled out of it and dropped it to the floor. The holstered revolver thudded to the carpet.

Now the undertop.

She undid the brassiere and threw it aside. Now she only wore underpants.

Bloor made a noise in the back of his throat like that of a rock dropped in a pond. He held aloft his forefinger and thumb and rubbed them together and studied them in the low light. He brought them down and took her left nipple between them. How long were you married, Ranger Lewis?

Twelve years, she said.

Bloor rolled her nipple. What really drove you two apart? Being up here all the time? The drinking? The other wives?

Lewis lay still and kept her eyes on the ceiling. She winced as Bloor tightened his grip on her. He pinched her once hard and she batted away his hand. Goddamn it, she said. What kind of search-and-rescue man are you?

The light from the landing carved out the dark in his face, the pools for his eyes, and the broad scythe of his brow. He grinned and his cheeks dug deep channels that left his expression wooden and mystic like a church house grotesque.

Bloor climbed on top of her. He unbuttoned his trousers and thrust himself meekly against her abdomen and she watched the doorway over his shoulder. He took chalked fingers and pinched her side. She wriggled yet he held her to him and pinched her still.

Do you want to hear something painfully honest? he said.

All right. Goddamn it.

I know I shouldn't, but sometimes I get angry that I have a... I don't want to say slow daughter, but a daughter that has a hard time understanding the finer points of human interaction and higher concepts.

Your daughter's not slow.

Bloor told Lewis how Adelaide had bought a dreamcatcher on the day Jill was born and that he had hung it in her bassinet and one day in the summer, when Adelaide was not feeling well, she left the baby under the living room window and fell asleep on the couch. He told how it did not take long for the sun to burn all but the shade of that dreamcatcher right onto the baby's face, fair as she was, and how when she woke she screamed and screamed. Her cheeks were blistered, he said. We had to take her to the hospital. She doesn't know, you know.

You never told her?

Adelaide felt so much shame she made me promise never to tell her. Of course I've kept my promise. Who'd want their daughter to know that their mom did something like that?

Bloor pinched her again. She clenched her teeth and kept her eyes on the light in the doorway. Then Bloor leaned back and gripped again her nipples and gave them two hard turns, kissing the air above him. She yelped once and bit her tongue. He dropped his body down and rocked back and forth against her thigh. She watched yet the doorway over his shoulder.

The floor creaked. Jill crossed the landing and stopped outside the open door. She and Lewis locked eyes and after a moment the girl went down the stairs to the kitchen and Lewis heard the refrigerator door open and a plate scrape the countertop.

Bloor finished himself in a chalked hand and streaked the mess on a window above the headboard and fell back beside Lewis on the bed and laughed. That was wonderful, he said.

Lewis held her damp palms over her breasts. She listened to Jill climb the stairs and saw her cross again the landing.

Bloor called his daughter's name.

She stopped in the doorway. She did not look in.

Good night, Bloor said.

Good night, said the girl, and she went on into her bedroom and shut the door.

Some transient presence tripped a motion sensor outside and a weak light came on and lit up the terrace. Lewis figured it was likely a squirrel but she thought she had seen something else there through the sliding glass door. A thin woman in shadow. It was only late September, yet snow fell without on the terrace in the cold light. Lewis figured it looked like shredded plastic in an old movie, and the spotlit heights of the motionless trees beyond the railing like set dressing to a windless stage.

Well, that settles that, Bloor said, looking out to the snow. If Cloris Waldrip did survive the crash, she won't survive the night.

Snow hung low the boughs and cauled the granite forms roadside and stilled the tall grass. Lewis drove Jill in the Wagoneer, yawing edgewise an alpine forest, static humming low on the radio, tire chains biting into the last of a paved road that had earlier been plowed. Lewis put to purpled lips the thermos of merlot. She sipped and turned the Wagoneer up a dirt road mottled with ice and mud.

Jill watched her from the passenger's seat. Are we going to get stuck out here?

No, I won't get us goddamn stuck. Lewis drank again from the thermos and replaced the lid. She gave the Wagoneer some gas.

Are you drinking wine out of a thermos?

No.

They drove on for some miles over the dirt road, guttering heavy places of snow and spitting past boarded-up hunting lodges. Leeward a hut with no windows hung a poorly butchered carcass, bottom up, frozen to a muddy icicle. Lewis did not stop to write a ticket. She drove on without speaking until she told Jill how she had received word that morning that the NTSB had faulted human error for bringing down the Waldrips' airplane.

Terry Squime must've lost control, Lewis said. Like he just decided he didn't know how to fly anymore. The goddamn body was too far gone for them to figure if he'd had a seizure or an aneurism or anything like that, but they didn't rule any of that out.

Jill said nothing and worked the handle and brought the pane down and got a cigarette. She struck a match in a book and lit it.

They said there could've been some turbulence and he panicked, Lewis said. Stress-related. Didn't rule out it could've been depression and he took the Waldrips with him. He'd just gotten married and it hadn't been going well. Apparently he'd been meetin men in motels. His mailman too.

Jill pulled on the cigarette and put her lips close to the window. Depression and mailmen, she said.

Lewis followed a road of black mud rutted in parabolas. A lake flashed beyond a belt of dying trees. She turned at a totem pole nailed over with snakeskins and filthy socks and a clothesline hung with the parts to a bear costume frozen at crazy angles. She slowed to a stop before a hut of plank wood leaning off the side of the road. A rusted pipe in the roof smoked green. An ironing board used for a door slid away from the entrance and a head poked out. A dark-skinned man appeared there in swimming trunks and a diving mask pushed back over curls of long icy hair. He saw what they were and came caped in a beach towel sprinting for the passenger's window, eyes wide, high-stomping through the snow in tieless combat boots.

Lewis told Jill to roll down the window all the way. Jill sighed and cranked down the pane and leaned back so that Lewis could talk to the man now resting an arm on the side mirror.

Hiya, Eric, what in the hell you doin in your swim attire?

Dogpaddlin, the man said. Dogpaddlin in cold water is all you need to stay regular. His teeth chattered. Who's this pretty baby?

She's a volunteer.

All right, all right, he said. He was nodding and shivering like faulty clockwork. What're you doin out here on a day like today, Ranger Lewis? Your outfit's liable to get stuck.

Somebody called in a complaint about you scarin some goddamn campers.

I weren't scarin no campers. Some kids was gettin drunk and drugged and pregnant on my property, so I dressed up like a bear and ran them off with a croquet mallet.

Yeah, that's what they said you did.

They was on my property.

With your property line so close to the campgrounds you ought to think about puttin up a goddamn sign or two so this kind of thing won't keep happenin. If someone gets on your land, just radio the station and me or Ranger Paulson will take care of it. Keep you from ever gettin involved. You still got your radio?

Yes, ma'am.

All right then.

You goin to write me a ticket?

Hell. I don't guess I will this time.

Appreciate it.

Let me ask you a question, Eric.

Yes, ma'am.

Seen anythin noteworthy out here in the past few weeks?

The man lowered his brow. Suddenly he was still and no longer shivered. How'd you mean?

Did you see anythin out of the goddamn ordinary? Anythin at all.

This about them bucks, ain't it?

What?

The man darted his eyes. I saw two bucks mountin each other behind my hobby shed. I'd heard somewhere they do that sometimes but I ain't never seen it in all my life. Thought it unnatural at first, but I don't know.

Anything else? said Lewis.

Well I tell you what, I did see some smoke last night while I was out in the lake.

Smoke?

Maybe t'were the night before. Like a campfire out yonder, twirlin up like this volunteer's hair here. He nodded at Jill.

Goddamn.

Was the faintest little thing too. Looked like it was comin deep from the Old Pass. It caused me to remark to myself cause I was under the guidance we weren't allowed up there anymore. I assumed it was originatin from one of those shelters.

Appreciate you, Eric, that's goddamn helpful.

Is it? Eric darted again his eyes to the girl. Jill stared ahead out the windshield. This about that sicko goofball from Phoenix?

No, Lewis said. A plane went down some weeks back and we're lookin for one of the survivors. A seventy-two-year-old woman, name of Cloris Waldrip.

The man whistled and started back shivering and shook slowly his unhinged and chattering head. Seventy-two? Tell her kin to bury an empty box and get on with they lives.

Lewis brought Jill back to the station that afternoon and poured in secret a mugful of merlot from a bottle behind her desk and set to writing a report on the smoke over the Old Pass. Pete was in the kitchenette, Claude at his desk. Jill smoked cigarettes at the window overlooking the snow and the wilderness. She pressed a thumb to the pane.

Claude looked up from a pamphlet on cryptology. You're markin up the glass.

Jill sat in an extra chair and stubbed the cigarette out on the brim of the mug she held between her legs.

She can mark up the goddamn glass if she likes, Claude, said Lewis, and she drank off another mug of merlot and showed Claude a middle finger.

Claude mumbled something about the station getting overcrowded and that Cornelia was attracted to fingerprints like a shark is to blood, and though he wanted to find her, he warned them all that he was afraid of what she might do if her appetite were whetted. The old dog under his desk sucked the ends of his bootlaces and he went back to the pamphlet and stroked the blue tip of his nose.

The girl's prints shone on the pane. In the reflection given back Lewis could see Pete in the kitchenette raising up his head now and again from the embroidery hoop in his lap. After a time he set the hoop aside and dragged a stool next to Jill and told her how his wife had dumped out all the houseplants on their bed and had left a note explaining that she had gone to make love with a docent at the Museum of Automobiles.

I didn't know what a docent was, Pete said, so I spent an hour and a half just lookin round the house for a dictionary. Couldn't find one so had to drive out to the library. Time I got there it'd closed. Took me a day and a half to figure it out. It means tour guide. Most women are just usin a man to make themselves feel all right about growin old.

Some people are deprived of oxygen when they are young, Jill said.

Lewis went back to the report in front of her and radioed into headquarters and got Chief Gaskell on the other end. She told him that she had spoken with Eric Coolidge that morning, who the night before had witnessed smoke rising near the Old Pass. Lewis suspected that Cloris Waldrip could have found her way to one of the shelters there and she told Gaskell that she needed to helicopter a team in and search the place.

Listen, Debra, I thought we'd settled this. Over.

John, she's out there and we're runnin out of goddamn time. There's new information in this case. Eric saw smoke. Over.

Eric Toothlicker Coolidge also gets in the buff and hangs himself upside down from the trees because he's under the delusion it's good for his brain. Just the other day I got a call from a very unhappy camper who had the misfortune to happen across him like that. Over.

Reckon it is good for his brain? Pete said.

Lewis turned and put a finger to her lips. Claude had gone out front with the old dog and the door had not latched. A sidelong breeze shuffled the flyers and bulletins on the corkboard to Lewis's right. She caught sight of the black-and-white composite sketch that showed the smooth, dark-eyed face of the wanted young man from Arizona.

Ranger Lewis? Ranger Lewis, come in. Over.

She turned back to the radio. It could be the Arizona Kisser. Over.

Do you have any credible reason to believe that? Over.

The FBI think he's hidin out in the area. Well, Eric Coolidge sees smoke comin from a shelter. Maybe he's hidin in one of those goddamn shelters. There're only three shelters in that quadrant. It's worth checkin out, John. Over.

There's a miner's road that runs up the Old Pass by the McMillians' dugout. Truthfully I don't have a chopper for you. But you're welcome to drive up there with Claude in a couple days after the snow's thawn a bit and check it out. I don't care much either way. Very unlikely. But I don't know. Drive up there close as you can and hike on in through that notch on the old trappers' trail. That's the best I can do for the time being. But you be careful. Over.

All right. Let me know if anything changes about that goddamn chopper. Over.

You hang in there, Ranger Lewis. Let me know if there's anything we can do for you down here. Marcy says hello. She says she's had you in her prayers. We all have. Over.

V

We traveled the day under low dark clouds. The masked man looked back every several yards or so to see I had not fallen behind. In the cold his breath steamed off his round head like a baked potato. I kept up with him sure enough, but he must have been going slower than what he was accustomed to. Often he ran his finger under the mask to get an itch. No doubt it was mighty uncomfortable to go so long with a shirt wrapped around his head like that, with naught but two little eyeholes to see his way. He did not quit, however. Bad weather was coming and a great urgency to get us to safety spurred him on.

We passed a cold night around a fire in a rocky glade. He had built the fire in the dried-out rib cage of a bighorn sheep we had found there. For supper we had some wafers from his duffel. Afterward he slept with the mask on turned away against a pine, silent as a log. The alien shadows of the sheep bones threaded over the rocks and his back, and I drank hot water from a horn he had given me. I slept fast the whole night.

The next morning we set out again. We went on the same as we had the day before and said very little. We pulled on and on and did not rest again until nightfall. My legs ached and my back was very sore. We passed another cold night in the dirt around a scant fire. The next morning we picked ourselves up again and carried on all day.

The snow arrived that next evening just before dark. An early clear moon broke the clouds and lit up the snowfall through the pines. It started soft and gentle like cottonwood seeds blown about the banks of the Red Creek back in Texas. It was very doom-ridden and beautiful.

I hugged Terry's coat around me and kept the pace. It sure was a good thing we had struck out that morning when we had, being that the snow picked up in a swell. Just when it was so heavy that I could hardly see my hands in front of me, a small log cabin appeared ahead in the last of the light. The cabin was not in much of a clearing. I suspected the foundation had been laid where the pines that had been felled to build it had once grown. Their yet living brethren grew very close against it and thick blue moss checkered the northernmost side. Two small, dark windows of dirty glass on either side of the door chattered in the rising wind. The roof was pitched, and up from it there was a blackened and crooked smokestack. It was an eerie place.

The man shoved open the door with his shoulder. I followed him inside. The first thing he did was to set his duffel down and light one of those fire-starter sticks and toss it in an iron stove similar to one Grandma Blackmore used to have in her sitting room. He then lit an oil lamp on a table in the middle of the room. He pulled out a wooden chair and shook a snowy glove at it.

The oil lamp flickered over the dingy interior. I will tell here some about the cabin. A dresser missing a leg was leaned in a dark corner and a clothesline was strung across the room. A pair of trousers and several shirts that hung there bounced shadows over two bunk beds attached to an adjacent wall. The yellow foam cots to them were without any covers and their corners had been gnawed by some desperate birth of vermin. Yellow rope like Mr. Waldrip used to use around the ranch was coiled in another corner of the cabin. On the table were some empty cans with the lids peeled back that were labeled to have once contained pear halves and kidney beans. On an unopened can of beet slices sat a lone dead fly, dusty and upright. I knew the thing was dead because it tumped over when I sat down at the table.

The masked man cleared the table and dumped the empty cans outside in the snow, as if he were embarrassed the place was untidy.

What is this place? I asked him.

The government built these in the fifties in case someone got lost, he said.

The man pulled out the other chair and sat down. He straightened the mask again so that his eyes lined up with the holes in it and the print of the pancakes was over his mouth. He took off his gloves and unlaced his boots and pulled them off, sending mud and snowmelt to the puncheon floor, then he set them by the stove to dry and pulled off some funny striped socks and hung them inside out on the clothesline. They smoked in the heat like rashers of bacon. He looked up at me in what little light there was and he cocked his head as if I had confused him, same as how Mr. Waldrip's Labrador Sally used to do when Mr. Waldrip asked her a question. The man shook his head and went about rubbing his feet at the stove.

After a minute he got up and went to the dresser. He rifled through it and brought back a light pink shirt with pictures on it of a blue castle and a white horse. He also provided me a pair of yellow socks and glittery dark purple stockings. Newspapers would later describe them as spandex leggings. Here, he said, and he put them on the table. He faced a corner to give me some privacy.

I thanked him and removed Terry's coat and hesitated in my ragged and damp clothes, the threadbare zigzag sweater and blouse and the torn skirt.

I won't look, he said.

I removed my filthy clothes and arranged them on the table. He had already seen me as naked as a nickel, but I mean to tell you it was still something mighty unique disrobing in a room with a man who was not Mr. Waldrip. I took the dry clothes from the table and dressed. They were small even for a small woman such as myself. When I put on the shirt I imagined I could smell the little girl who must have left it there. Such of apples and a mowed lawn. I did not think on it much at the time.

When I was a little girl I dreamt of having many children. When Mr. Waldrip and I were married we made an effort right away. That is what you did in those days. Mary Martha Hart, an acquaintance of mine from the Women's Historical Society, was pregnant within weeks of her wedding. She was seventeen. She had a baby boy who grew up to become a well-liked singer in Las Vegas. He had hair like a cockatoo and sang songs about lonesomeness. Another woman in my congregation, Joycie Farwell, had twins, a boy and a girl. The boy grew up to be a pink-eyed lunatic. He held some people hostage in a Red Lobster restaurant someplace in North Dakota, until one of the hostages realized he was holding not a pistol but a carrot stained black with shoe polish. I suppose what I am wanting to suggest here is that children are not a good thing to a certainty, so perhaps not having them is not necessarily a bad thing.

Finished, I said.

The masked man turned from the corner and looked me over. It was a funny outfit. I never will cease to be amazed that young people dress the way they do. I suppose often the clothes people wear only make sense to the people wearing them. He did not say a thing about my getup.

Then he sat a spell with his back to the stove, reading a book that looked like it had been in water. I asked him what it was and he told me that I would not like it. I told him that I had been a librarian for a good many years and I was interested in literature. The shape of his mouth changed under his mask and he held the book cover towards me so that I could read the title. The lettering on the cover was a faded purple. It read: *The Joy of Lesbian Sex: A Tender and Liberated Guide to the Pleasures and Problems of a Lesbian Lifestyle* by Dr. Emily L. Sisley and Bertha Harris.

I found it in the dresser, he said, and he held the book in front of his mask again and read on.

I sat there and listened to the wind toss snow against the smokestack and whistle in the unceiled walls. The lantern light played over the man and for the first time since the little airplane had gone down I wondered how it would be to return to Texas. The first thing I would have to do is to unlock the front door with the key Mr. Waldrip kept hid under the stone shaped like a steer. My ferns and zebra plant would be dried up like old goats. Our poor cat, Trixie, would have eaten all the food we had left her and she would be hunting mice to survive, something I did not believe she could do. I imagined her laid out skin and bones at the base of the front door, poor thing.

I thought about the life I would have without Mr. Waldrip. It did not make a lick of sense to me. Night after night waking to turn to him in bed just to find him gone and then remembering the whole awful story. Riding to doctor's appointments in that paddywagon of old fools the city provides these days. Taking walks by myself, down to the bluestem pasture where the idiot bull is tethered with that corncob pipe in its mouth.

No, home did not make a lick of sense without Mr. Waldrip, and I was afraid I myself would not make a lick of sense back in Texas after all I had seen out in the Bitterroot.

Snow was on the ground for two days. The masked man and I stayed warm as dogs around the stove, consuming rations of beans and canned beets. We scarcely spoke. When it came time to sleep, we bade each other good night, our teeth as red as roses. I slept on the bottom bunk and he on the top. He seldom rolled over in his sleep and it would have been easy to believe that he was not up there at all, but for the sag in the grate underside the bed. I had not slept so near a man who was not Mr. Waldrip for many years. Still I slept well. It was nice to have a soft place to lay my head.

The second night I heard a sound and went to the window. By the light of the moon I spotted that same mountain lion prowling backwards around the cabin. I alerted the man and he said he had seen the mountain lion before too. He believed the creature had an ear infection that gave it a bad case of vertigo. He said that it was merely lonely and confused and a poor excuse for a mountain lion.

During the day the masked man sat by the stove whittling inscrutable figures with the spey blade and tossing them into the fire. I read the book he had found about homosexual relations between women. It is an interesting book with explicit subject matter. I did not entirely understand all of it, but I am glad that I read it anyway. For the longest time I did not know such a thing as lesbianism even existed. It was not something anyone ever talked about, not like it is today. There was a girl who grew up with us in Clarendon, Edith Pearson, and she played baseball with the boys and was not at all interested in wearing dresses. I have learned this does not make a lesbian, but Edith and another woman, Beth Stout, did live together in a double-wide trailer in Perryton, Texas. The ladies at First Methodist could be mighty cruel about Edith, but I do not now see the point.

On a cloudy afternoon when the light outside the cabin was bluish-gray on the snow, I recalled an evening Mr. Waldrip and I had attended a performance at Clarendon Elementary School. I was a young teacher there at the time. We sat in the half-dark and watched the children put on a darling play about the first cattlemen in Texas. Not but five minutes in, Mrs. Craddock, the librarian whom I would come to replace, slid from her seat and passed away right there on the auditorium floor. She was about the age I was then sitting in that log cabin. A frail old man I knew to be Mr. Craddock crouched over her and whispered in her ear. He did not shed a tear. Others stood around and folded their hands. Dr. Gainer endeavored to revive her, holding a palm to her forehead and shaking her gently by the shoulders. This did not work. All the children stopped and watched from the stage, stricken in their ten-gallon hats and painted mustaches, save for the slow red-haired boy, Merritt Sterling, costumed like a stalk of Indian grass, who yet performed his part and swayed as if blown by the wind, unaware anything at all had changed.

Something about Mrs. Craddock's passing put a special kind of fear in my young heart at the time. Suddenly I was afraid of growing old and dying, afraid of muddling through life putting stock in all the wrong things. I was afraid nothing was as I believed it to be. I did not chew over this discomforting notion for long, however, because the next day at First Methodist Mrs. Taylor, a little woman with a vibrating sickness, stood buzzing like electric hair clippers and led the congregation in prayer for Mrs. Craddock and her family, and I was put at ease that all was safe in God and community. But then and there in that log cabin, when nothing was as it had ever been before, watching where the shirt over that mysterious man's face was damp with the shape of his mouth, that special kind of fear returned and I worried that I had made a mighty big mistake believing in comfortable things.

On our third day in that dingy old cabin, the masked man went off to retrieve more water from a nearby spring and to set some of his traps, and I took a chair out front and sat in the early-afternoon sun and watched the snowmelt drip from the trees. I breathed that cool, clean air and I was not frightened anymore. It is peculiar how the human spirit endures. A person can get used to a situation, even if that situation may have once seemed intolerable.

After I had sat a spell, the masked man came charging back through the woods. He was straightening the mask over his face. I hallooed him and he put a finger over the haunting place where his mouth was and shushed me.

He squatted close by and pointed to the place in the trees from whence he had come. He was out of breath. He said, Walk straight in that direction and call out your name.

I got up from my chair and I asked him if he had seen someone.

Don't tell them you saw me, he said. Tell them you were alone.

I have to tell them about you, I said. You have saved my life.

He said, Please, and he looked back over his shoulder.

Come with me, I said.

He pleaded with me again. Pieces of long brown hair stuck out from the eyeholes in the mask like whiskers on a cat. I told him that I would do as he wished. He thanked me.

Do you suppose they will believe it? I said. It is not an easy thing to believe that a woman my age could survive out here on her own.

You've just got to convince them, he said. He touched my arm with a gloved hand. He rushed past me into the cabin and came out a minute later with his duffel and set out in the opposite direction.

I watched after him until I could no longer see him in the timber.

I walked quickly through the woods hollering out my name. It was not but ten minutes before I found a clearing that opened up to a bluff and I quit hollering. Out in a rocky ravine, granite slopes fell to country patchy with snow and motts of spruce and pine. At a considerable distance, a troop of people in orange moved across the floodplain. They had a dog. I heard their voices echo over the range. They were hollering my name.

I do not imagine many of you can truly understand how it was for me to hear my name in the mountains and see those benevolent souls arriving to put an end to my ordeal. Few people have had the experience of being rescued. I had been out in the Bitterroot for near a month by then. I am certain a good many of you will not understand what occurred in my heart nor the decision I was to make. No doubt many of you will holler at the page, turn back, turn back, you old fool! Bless me, I suppose I do not entirely understand it myself. But a person has to make sense of their own behavior best they can and get on with it.

I stood perfectly still. I did nothing. I did not raise my arms nor wave them about. I did not holler out for help.

It was a dire sadness that came over me and at that moment, despite all the desperation I had endured out there in the Bitterroot, I could not see any good reason to go back home. It was impossible to imagine that Clarendon would be where I had left it back in the plains of the Texas Panhandle. Perhaps I did not even believe our house was still under the afternoon shade of the water tower, nor that First Methodist was holding services, nor that the congregation had bowed their heads in prayer for myself and Mr. Waldrip. At the time I was not sure how anything could exist after the great colorful ramparts of that wilderness. I worried that if I went back I would find nothing at all.

I feared a life not terribly unlike the one I live today. I live in an assisted-living facility and have been here for eleven years, since I turned eighty-one. I have a small air-conditioned single-room apartment. Most hours of the day and night I am alone. Visitors seldom come now, and when they do I am less certain what I mean to them or they to me. In truth I do not enjoy their company very much. Often I worry that compassion is perfunctory in this place, though perhaps it is that way in most of the world and nobody has caught on. But bless you, yes, there are new and dear people in my life whom I now know because of my ordeal, and in the most melancholy of ways I am grateful for that, and you dears know who you are. But at the time I could not see any potential for goodness in my return to the peopled world. Psychologists have told me that I was grief-stricken and dissociative and traumatized, but they were not there. To them those are just terms from a book. I assure you I was something else entirely.

I watched until the search party crossed out of sight into the woods. Then I turned back for the log cabin. I tossed my filthy old tore-up clothes into the stove and burned them.

The old dog limped in back of the four searchers, all of them clad in vests of orange, carrying packs and bedrolls. They came in a slow single file: Lewis, Claude, Jill, and Pete behind. Lewis led them under boughs and overhangs of rock, massaging on a forearm bruises like hourglasses, an eye hooked far on a helix of smoke. She drank from the thermos of merlot, then from a canteen of water.

Claude snapped his fingers at the old dog and it came along, nosing the tracks of his boots and stringing under the daylight silver tendons of slobber in the dirt. I'd say this isn't goin to turn out the way you picture it, Debs, Claude said.

Jill chewed the butt of a dying cigarette as she followed them.

Pete wheezed behind and tugged at the strap for the video camera. He beat a fist on his pigeon chest. How far?

Another two miles, give or take, said Lewis.

Pete shook his head and coughed into his palm and looked wide-eyed at the phlegm he had brought up.

Claude tipped back a campaign hat and searched the sky. I'd say we'd better turn back, Debs. Looks like we can't make it to the shelter and back to the vehicles before dark. It's too far out there on foot.

We're not turnin back, Lewis said.

Claude stopped and the rest stopped behind him. I'd understood the sleepin bags to be a precautionary measure.

Lewis balanced against a pine. When we find Mrs. Waldrip we'll radio for a chopper, she said.

What if we don't find her?

Think of it as a goddamn company retreat.

Jill ended the cigarette on a pine. Maybe our murders will be reenacted on television by actors that kind of look like us.

Pete dabbed his face with the coif. What if we got a real owly man up there? That Kisser fella. I just said I'd take a look around with you guys. I didn't sign on for nothin like this. Not with my heart misbeatin like it is.

It's Cloris up there, Lewis said.

Claude came around and took Lewis aside behind a tree away from the others and whispered, You all right, Debs?

I'm fine. You don't need to ask me that.

Are you drinkin wine right now?

No.

I got to say if you expected we'd be stayin overnight it's inappropriate to bring that girl out here. Let alone Pete.

I don't figure we'll be stayin the night.

Claude looked her over. Lewis figured he was looking at the washed stains and missed buttons on her uniform. She tucked in her shirt.

Debs, I'm worried, he said.

Goddamn it. Don't be goofy.

I'd say we're not the people we were when we started. Have you noticed?

I expect we're not.

Lewis went on and the rest followed.

Pete came astride Jill and hoisted the video camera to a shoulder and framed her. You doin this for your college applications?

No, said the girl.

College sure is a good thing. I didn't go to it. And look at me.

Look at you for what?

Pete lowered the lens. I'm forty years old volunteerin for a search on a mountain, just to keep from killin myself on account of my broken heart. My best pal from high school's losin his mind about the ghost of a one-eyed shemale and his colleague here's losin hers about a lost old lady. I can't find no comfort in anybody left in my life. I'd be losin my cool if I hadn't let Jesus take the wheel years ago.

Seems like he has fallen asleep at it, the girl said in her strange accent.

Pete scratched his neck and rotated his eyes high towards his brow like he were looking for an answer inscribed there on the inside of his skull. You sure do got a good head on your shoulders, he said.

The party struck onward for a time without words, kept only by the measure of their breath and the dog snuffling and jangling its tag and the clap of the snowmelt in the trees and now and again Lewis belting out ahead the name of the lost woman. Dark started to come on and the sky deepened to the color of the smoke they had followed there.

Lewis brought out a flashlight from her pack and stopped and shone the beam over her followers. They squinted back at her, resembling nothing so much as the terminally ill dogs and cats held dimly in the death kennels behind her father's clinic. She would say the same strange words to them that her father used to say to those doomed pets: *Alea iacta est*.

They neared a pair of dim windows parallactic and deep in the forest. Lewis smelled pine burning. The sky was dark and big and the air cold and the party put over the trees and granite forms tines of pale light. Lewis stopped and leaned against a boulder. The rest of them stopped behind her. None spoke. The old dog panted at their feet.

In the shadows ahead crossed a bluish body, stooped and slow. Lewis moved towards it and the toe of her boot struck something. A bronze of a perched eagle lay in puddling snow. When Lewis looked up the body was gone. She focused her eyes on the shelter. She drank from the thermos and jogged ahead, calling out Cloris, Cloris, Cloris, Mrs. Waldrip!

Behind her Claude called for her to be quiet and slow down.

Lewis reached the door and put an ear to it. Mrs. Waldrip, this is the United States Forest Service, are you in there?

Claude came up beside her. Jill followed, lighting another cigarette. Pete stood back.

Lewis drew the revolver and held it upright in one hand and the flashlight against it in the other. She leaned into the door and it gave way.

Careful, Debs.

Don't goddamn worry about me.

She went slowly into the shelter and aimed the revolver and the flashlight at the floor. She asked the dark for the lost woman. A small coal fire burned in an iron stove. Cloris? she said. She brought up the flashlight. The light slipped over the log walls and the minor furniture and the dust and smoke in the air yet did not illuminate any human form. Lewis holstered the revolver and removed her campaign hat and wiped sweat from her forehead. A clothesline crossed the room, hung with a pair of dirty green striped socks. Lewis took the end of a glove in her teeth and pulled it from her hand, then pinched a sock and felt that it was damp. She knelt at the stove and looked into the fire. A grouping of brass buttons glowed in the embers.

Claude had ducked into the room and the dog dragged its nose along the floor behind him. I'd say we just missed someone, he said.

Jill was close to the door and looking around at the room.

Lewis stood and replaced the campaign hat and pocketed the gloves. Goddamn it. Why do you figure she'd leave?

I'd say those don't look like the kind of socks worn by an old lady, Debs.

I don't like this all that much, Pete said from the doorway.

Lewis picked up from the table in the room a warped hardcover book. *The Joy of Lesbian Sex: A Tender and Liberated Guide to the Pleasures and Problems of a Lesbian Lifestyle* by Dr. Emily L. Sisley and Bertha Harris. She set it down. She asked Jill for a lighter and lit the lantern on the table and then went to a window and cupped her hands and looked out the unclean glass. Trees gnashed in the dark.

Lewis turned back to the team. They were leaned about, orange vests glowing in the murk. The dog had curled up already near the stove.

Lewis pulled a chair out from the table and sat down. She took an index finger and drew on the table a spiral in the dust. We'll stay here tonight.

No, Jill said. I don't want to.

Lewis took the thermos from her pack and drank. She wiped her mouth. Don't worry, she said. We're not in any goddamn danger.

What if they come back? Jill said.

Pete took one step through the doorway. Who? What if who comes back?

This is it, Debs, said Claude. I'm not helpin you look for her anymore. Don't care even if we get John to get us a chopper. I won't be party to it. It's not healthy.

It's a good thing to help somebody if you can, Ranger Lewis, Pete said, but it ain't if you can't. Learnt that from the hard way, at the end of a hard road of domestic torture.

They agreed to set out again for the trailhead at first light. Pete and Claude huddled upright at the stove with the dog like a covey of quail. Lewis and Jill took the bunk beds, and from the bottom bunk Lewis watched Claude fall asleep. Pete, the stovelight awash in his eyes, stared at the door. Claude whined through his blue nose, dreamspeaking low and gospel. Jill lay on the top bunk. She was quiet and still. Lewis could not know if the girl slept or not.

Lewis did not sleep and was awake suckling the last of the merlot from the thermos and listening to the loud fire of pine they had built in the stove quiet and die out. The revolver lay on her chest. Some hours into the night after she had closed her eyes, she opened them again and looked out from the bunk. Jill stood in the room.

What's wrong?

The girl came closer and moonlight in the small window touched her dark curls and the scars on her face. Can I sleep with you?

Lewis sat up on her elbows and sucked merlot from her teeth and looked at the girl. She recalled a waterspotted painting of Artemis that had hung near the basin in the restroom of her father's clinic. What?

Can I sleep with you?

In here?

I don't want to be up there by myself.

Why not?

I'm cold and I'm scared.

Aren't you too old for that kind of thing?

I'm not too old to be cold and I'm not too old to be scared.

Lewis studied the girl and said: All right.

She moved to one side and Jill brought a sleeping bag down from the top bunk and laid it on the cot. She climbed into the bunk and pushed her back against Lewis and her hair fell about and smelled the way of bloody cats shampooed after surgery.

Can you hear that?

Hear what?

It sounds like someone copulating.

Lewis raised an ear to the air. It's probably just some goddamn animal.

It's hard for me to sleep without music playing, Jill said.

How come?

I think about every little sound. Music covers them up.

There's no music here and I'm not singin.

When I was a kid I had a cassette of Jimmy Durante singing. When a side would end I'd wake up and turn it over.

You're still a goddamn kid.

Some minutes passed in silence and Lewis figured Jill had fallen asleep for she breathed slowly and twitched. Lewis touched the girl's hair and smelled her neck. The floor creaked and she looked out to the dark. Pete stood at the stove, the video camera shouldered. The black eye of the lens gazed back at her. The tape ran in the dark. Lewis did not move.

Pete squinted past the viewfinder and lowered the video camera to the floor and knelt in the corner of the room where they had stacked firewood.

The others were sleeping yet and Lewis, hunched over in her coat and hat against the chill, crept from the shelter into the dawn. She trudged out past the trees, sucking old merlot from her teeth, and she pressed her back to a wide trunk and took down her trousers. Steam rose and she breathed it in.

A scream broke the quiet and the dog barked.

She pulled up her trousers and ran back towards the shelter, buckling them as she went, and found Jill coming from the woods. The girl slumped in the doorway and the dog jangled up and licked dark blood from her hands.

Lewis told the dog to get and kicked it away and it yipped and went off. Tell me what happened, she said.

Jill raised a bloody hand to the forest. I saw someone. There.

Claude appeared in the doorway wearing backwards his campaign hat. He held out a can of bear spray. Who?

Pete rubbed his eyes and peered over Claude's shoulder. Are we bein assaulted?

Lewis knelt down and took the girl's bloody hands in hers and turned them looking for the wound. Where're you hurt?

The girl held out her left hand. I went out there to pee and I saw somebody. I ran and tripped over a metal eagle. I landed on it with my hand.

Claude held back the bloodthirsty old dog by the collar. A metal eagle?

A statue, Jill said. On the ground.

Pete shook his head. That's not the kind of thing you'd normally see out here, is it, Ranger Lewis?

Lewis found a perfect hole in the palm of the girl's hand. You're bleedin pretty good, she said. You feel all right?

Yes.

Does it hurt?

No, said the girl. Someone is out there.

Cornelia Åkersson.

Goddamn it, Claude. Quit bein a goofball and help me.

Claude gave Lewis a white plastic container from his pack. Lewis broke it open and pulled out a bottle of iodine. This'll sting. She popped the cap with her teeth and emptied the bottle over the wound. Jill winced. Lewis put some gauze to it. There were no bandages. Here. Give me that goddamn thing. Lewis snatched the coif from Pete's head and made a bandage of it. What d'you mean you saw someone?

I heard a sound and then I saw something move. There. Jill picked a place in the trees with a bloody finger.

Pete brought up the video camera and aimed it at Jill's hands. What if it's that Kisser fella?

Lewis scanned the trees. The sun had not yet risen above the range and the light was little. Wait here.

I ought to come with you, Claude said.

Stay with her, goddamn it, Lewis said. See if you can't stop it bleedin like that. Goddamn it.

Blood-splattered and stained in merlot, her campaign hat askew, she went onward with crooked footing like a war-weary soldier, sucking her teeth. She drew the revolver and held it in both blood-slicked hands and walked in a ways until she came to an escarpment. She looked out from the trees at the vast woodlands and scrub. She was alone and could not see the others.

Mrs. Waldrip? Mrs. Waldrip? Cloris?

A gust blew through the woods and Lewis heard crinkling above. She looked up. A mylar balloon was tangled high in a bleached dead pine at the edge of the escarpment. In pink block letters it bore the phrase *Get Well Soon.* Lewis blinked at it and sank to the ground and did not take her eyes from it. She knelt there for a time and watched reverently the balloon brighten in the rising sun until it burned like the bead of a welder's torch.

When she touched her face it was wet and she figured she had been crying. Behind her voices called out her name and she wiped the wet from her cheeks, blazing them in the girl's blood, then she stood and holstered the revolver.

She returned to the others at the shelter, where most things were bloodied. The two men stood outside, their hands red. Claude was buttoning his uniform. Jill sat in the doorway, her back to the jamb. Her left hand was bandaged in Claude's undershirt and Pete wore again the coif, now pied crimson. Jill smoked a matching cigarette. The dog lapped dots of blood from the floor.

Jill was cleaning her good hand in her curls. What did you see?

Just a goddamn balloon stuck in a tree.

No doubt many of you will believe that I am a crazy old bullfrog to have walked away from the search party sent after me. Perhaps I am. It is mighty difficult to know your own mind. I could liken it to when poorsighted Mr. Waldrip misplaced his glasses. Poor darling, he would bump around the house and touch the furniture like a mad faith healer, cussing up a storm under his breath. I was always the one to find the silly things, having the blessing of good eyesight as I do. I imagine that is the way it is with a mind too. You need one to find one. So if you have lost yours, you had better have another to help you find it.

I sat in that little old log cabin and watched my filthy old clothes burn up in the stove. It must have come late afternoon when I looked out one of those dirty windows for the masked man to appear. My hope was that he would return after he was sure that the search party had taken me and gone. I was ready to surprise him and tell him that I had decided that I wanted to stay with him there.

Naturally near as soon as this thought had danced into my head I was struck by what plain nonsense it was. Most people do not want one thing all of the time; in other words, I changed my mind right away. Gracious, what on earth was I doing? I needed to get out of that place and go back to Texas! My heart got to skipping like a bean on a skillet and I jumped up from the stove. I got my purse and wrapped myself in Terry's coat and I hurried out of that log cabin quick as I could, hollering my name.

Not far into the woods my toe struck something hard and I tumbled face-first to the ground and broke open my lip. I did not hurt anything else. What I had tripped over was a figure of an eagle done in some kind of tarnished metal. Of all the unusual things. To this day I do not know how a thing like it had come to be there. I looked very briefly at it as I recovered and could learn nothing about it. The mystery of it still bothers me. Perhaps one of my readers will know the answer.

I picked myself up and hurried on. I imagine I looked as silly as Catherine Drewer when she used to prance and snort past all our windows doing what she called her little aerobic walk. I told my dear asthmatic friend, Nancy Bowers, that I thought Catherine looked like a village idiot with rectal disease, and Nancy laughed so hard that she got to coughing and had to go home. She was in bed for the rest of the day. Dear Nancy passed away from complications with her asthma some years ago.

A terrible panic got ahold of me as I feared I had forfeited my last opportunity to get back to Clarendon and mourn my husband at First Methodist with some familiar faces and dear friends like Nancy Bowers and Louise Altore and Pastor Bill. Suddenly I was mighty homesick again. I might have even been glad to see stupid old Catherine Drewer again, but I am not certain about that.

I had expected to come to the lookout from which I had glimpsed the search party in the ravine, but I did not. By and by I was in some unfamiliar place. All over the ground lay strange shapes of icy snow kept by the shade of the greatest trees. Not knowing where to go, I plopped down in the crook of an exposed root to catch my breath and suck on my busted lip. The wind picked up and the trees clawed and leaned over each other like the inebriated revelers Mr. Waldrip and I used to see in front of the Empty Cupboard roadhouse on our way home from a Saturday-night picture in Amarillo. I shut my eyes for a spell and imagined I was there with Mr. Waldrip, sitting in the truck and not saying a word to each other, just driving home, listening to the road. When I opened my eyes again and looked around at the trees I was mighty confused about the way I had come and uncertain I could find my way back to the log cabin.

I would come to learn later that I had gone in the opposite direction from where the search party was approaching the log cabin. If I had gone out the door and to the left instead of the right I would have run smack into them. They would arrive at the log cabin later that evening.

Sometimes it is awful hard not to see the humor in something aggravating like that. It is hard not to see it in the sad things too. A real important rodeo man from Borger got himself killed riding a mechanical bull in a bar in Dallas. Hit his head on a light fixture. It is not funny, but it always tickled me something terrible when Mr. Waldrip would tell it. I laugh as I write this now. I wonder if this rodeo man's mother ever laughed about it. I have a hard time thinking she ever did.

I was turned around and lost. So I just settled down in those roots as a chorus of wind and darkness tuned up in the mountains. I did not laugh about anything at all right then. I could not yet see the humor in it. Instead I went back to hollering and hollering, Help me, I am Cloris Waldrip.

I sat balled up in Terry's coat shivering and hollering all night long like a crazy person until I lost my voice and could scarcely whisper. My lip was swollen up pretty good too and I was slobbering like a mule. When the sky started to lighten and the sun was just below the mountains, it was not a minute too soon. I was nearly froze to death.

Suddenly I heard something stalking through the woods. Whatever it was stopped just yards shy of where I was, but I could not see it for all the trees. There was a patter like something piddling on the ground. My thought was if it was not a mean old bear or that backwards mountain lion it might be one of the search party. I managed to pick myself up and peek around the pines, but I could not see what the thing was. I endeavored to say out my name but all that I could muster was a ghastly groan. The pattering stopped. I limped over.

Whatever it was gave a shriek and lit out of there with some haste. I chased after it, but it was awful quick and I lost track of it in the dark. I kept on in the general direction.

I did not see the drop.

My legs went out from under me and I was thrown down a slope of cold mud and stone! I tore off a whole fingernail clawing at the rock to slow my descent but I slid out over the lip of an overhang anyway. I caught the edge by my gory fingers. I could not turn my head to know how far the drop was. My legs swung free in open air and I stretched them out as far as I could to find ground if there was any. My purse had slipped off my shoulder and it lay in front of me on the overhang. I could not let go to grab it. I am sure I was a pitiful sight, dangling there in those glittery purple stockings and that pink shirt doused in black mud. My fingers burned and blood spurted from them. I was not fooling myself that I could hang there for eternity.

So I let go. There is something to be said for the graceful acceptance of the inevitable.

The fall was not far, thank goodness, but when I hit the ground my legs gave out and I twisted my ankle and knocked my head on a rock. Gracious, it hurt a great deal and I went loopy for a spell. I was sure I heard a woman above on the overhang saying my name as the sun came up. I lay on my back with my legs splayed out at the bottom of this steep escarpment, in a damp place of rocks and coarse brown shrubbery, and did not move. Above me a barkless and dying tree grew from the overhang. Snagged on a bare high branch was the kind of silvery balloon you could find with the misted flowers in the supermarket or deserted in a corner of some hospital room's ceiling. It was printed with pink words that I could not make out.

When first it caught my eye I took it for a helicopter. My heart dropped when I realized it was only a balloon. My sister-in-law, Rhonda Lee Waldrip, had brought me a balloon like that when I had my gallbladder removed in September of 1978. I accidentally let go of it on the walk from the hospital back to Mr. Waldrip's truck. It was a windy day, as they often are in Texas, and that balloon vanished into the sky mighty quick. I had the funny notion that this could be that very same balloon. It is amazing the distances they can travel.

I lay still and felt my body for injuries, but as I have put down here before my bones were strong. I had taken a spill in the grocery store a year before and had given a very nice young couple there in the produce aisle a big scare, but I was not injured.

After a time I sat up to put some weight on my ankle, but it gave me a terrible pain and I toppled over. I lay on my back like an upset turtle and considered the many mistakes I had made out there in the wilderness. It was a miracle I had survived for this long. I watched the treetops upside down and imagined Mr. Waldrip up there instead of that balloon, like deadwood that had not yet made it to the ground. But there was only that silvery balloon flapping before a big sky filling with clouds and daylight.

I set myself upright and slid under the overhang. My back was against a wall of mud and roots where it had been washed out, and I stretched out my legs and looked at my bloody fingers. I was mighty hungry and desperately thirsty. I commenced to telling myself that all I had to do was to wait and the search party would find me. They were looking for me. I had seen them.

* * *

In 1983 a man bought a spit of land down the road from our ranch. It was not more than an acre or two of caliche. He built on it a peculiar little structure, a kind of Indian sweat lodge. All hides and painted leather flagging loudly in the wind. He was not any kind of Indian that I know about. He was as white a man as I had ever seen. He wore white slacks and no shirt and a colorful little hat like a Bundt cake.

Every Thursday afternoon Mr. Waldrip would drive out to the ranch so that he could meet with our ranch manager, Joe Flud, by the cattle tanks in the east pasture. I tagged along whenever we got lunch at the El Sombrero and he did not have the time to take me home afterward. Mr. Waldrip and Joe would stand out in the grass and I would wait in the truck.

From where Mr. Waldrip parked I could see on down the road to that unusual dwelling, and a young and pretty girl, could be the prettiest girl I have ever seen, would show up on a bicycle from the north road in a swell of dust. She wore a fine cotton dress only ever a shade of blue and her flaxen hair was always combed nicely down her back. She came at 1:30, without fail, all of the Thursdays I was there to bear witness to it. She would disappear into that strange place behind a flap of buffalo hide and not come out until at least an hour had gone by. I could not then fathom why this beautiful girl, so young and vital, would be paying a visit to this unattractive and oddly costumed older man.

My awful suspicion had always been that she was going in there to give herself to the man for money. However turning it over out there in the Bitterroot, I was struck that perhaps the girl was there not because he would pay her, but because she wanted to be there. I supposed it was not impossible that she desired this unusual little man. She had ridden there of her own free will, if any of us have any free will at all. Though I often wonder if we are not all set upon roads we cannot see, enslaved to masters unknown. I have come to believe that who or what we desire cannot be helped. We are doomed from the moment we are able to know what it is that we want. And I do not blame people for knowing what they want. I only blame them for doing anything and everything to get it without a thought to the consequences.

To set this account straight, I have since done some research and met with some of the right people and discovered that the man's name was Tom Calyer, and that the girl's name was Lucy Calyer. She was his daughter and she lived with her mother not far down the road. I have even met with Lucy. She was kind enough to pay me a visit here in Vermont, where I have lived nigh on two decades now, since briefly returning to Clarendon after the Bitterroot to settle my affairs. As I had anticipated, Texas without Mr. Waldrip proved inhospitable and full of melancholy. Despite my newfound distaste for trees, I came to Vermont, a place that had appealed to me since I was a little girl and had seen watercolors of its seasons in a picture book about our United States. I had an apartment in Burlington, until my hip started acting up and I moved to River Bend Assisted Living in Brattleboro, some dozen years ago now. Anyhow, this Lucy Calyer happened to have moved to Connecticut and she assured me it was not far and that she would be pleased to pay me a visit for I have become something of a celebrity since my ordeal. We had a lovely visit. She is just as beautiful as she ever was, married and with two children of dark skin and the most darling noses you will ever see. She promised me that her father was a gentle and peaceable man, a man interested in living off the land the way that more ancient folk had done.

I include this anecdote here to suggest that there is no way to speculate nor pass judgment on the nature of a thing safely from a window, and the awful truth of the matter is that often as not all anyone can understand about a person is what they understand least about themselves.

Lewis swerved the Wagoneer down the mountain and Jill held pressure on the hole in her hand and they arrived at Marcus Daly Hospital in the foothills at about nine o'clock that night. The building was two stories and gray and outside three drunk and bloodbathed men studded with car-window glass smoked cigarettes and glittered under a streetlight like figures of crystal. Lewis refilled the thermos from a bottle of merlot in the back. Then she opened the passenger door for Jill and together they went under a flickering neon sign which read *Em gency*.

They sat side by side in a row of seats, the blood on their clothes browned in unfathomable glyphs, and they waited for an hour in a small waiting room with a tank of paling fish before a young woman beckoned them wordlessly through a door. A man in a stained cotton smock, there in a long room partitioned with sheeting, introduced himself as the doctor and washed his hands at a sink. He was wearing sunglasses and a devil's beard. Jill sat on a papered bed and Lewis swayed and leaned against a partition and watched the doctor straddle the girl's knees from a stool and unwrap the bandage from her hand. He turned it over like he were buying a cut of meat from a butcher and told her that the puncture would not need but a single stitch. He told them he would be right back and he left.

I'm sorry about your hand, Lewis said.

Do you think you'll ever see your ex-husband again?

Hope not. Why?

Jill shook her head. Will I make friends and then someday never want to see them again?

I expect so. It's only natural.

I will not want to see them anymore? Or they will not want to see me? Or we do not care enough to see each other?

Well, things change, Lewis said. Your mom not ever tell your goddamn dad that one?

Is it not true that there are people you used to know and don't keep in touch with now so it would make no practical difference to you if they were dead?

I don't want anyone to die, Jill, Lewis said. I'd like to figure they're out there doin all right even if I don't hear from them.

Even your ex-husband?

I don't want the goddamn man dead.

But you don't want to see him ever again?

No, I don't want to see him again.

Do you think you would find out if he had died or if he was doing well?

Goddamn it, I don't know.

Jill swatted at nothing and slung blood across the linoleum. Maybe you wouldn't find out, she said. He might as well be dead now. It would make no difference to you.

Goddamn, well if I don't know about it I figure it doesn't.

Everyone I've met over thirty is a low-grade psychopath, said the girl.

Down at the other end of the room a young girl with a leg in a cast screamed. Her eyes were fixed in terror on the bed next to hers, where a skinny bearded man flopped around naked on his back, pissing in his own face and singing a song about rutted roads. Bored nurses restrained him and strapped him down and spoke kindly to him as if they knew him well. They repositioned the sheeting and hid him from the ward.

The doctor returned and put the stitch in and Jill did not flinch and he called her a sweet girl and rolled back and forth on the wheeled stool. He pressed his crotch to her knees. There you go, sweet girl, he said. All better for baby.

That's enough of that, goddamn it, Lewis said, and she took Jill by the arm and they left.

In the Wagoneer they wound back up the mountain. Every quarter mile on the paved road their headlights brightened a shot-up sign warning of falling rocks. Jill sat with her knees to her chest, tethered to a line of smoke sucking out through the cracked window.

Lewis drank from the thermos. I forgot to call your goddamn dad from the hospital. I expect he's worried we're not back yet.

Jill tapped the end of the cigarette in a soda can between her thighs. She did not speak.

Lewis drove on and passed the Crystal Penguin convenience store. Townyouths from the foothills glowed a faux-sunset color under the store's sodium light. Greasy haired, frail and feminine, the three teenage boys grinned from their perch in the bed of a parked blue pickup truck missing a tailgate. They lifted thick amber bottles and whooped slow in the cadence of a siren. A fatless mohawked boy in wireframe glasses waved and flicked a bejeweled tongue.

Jill waved at the boys with her bandaged hand and said, I wonder how long we'll know each other, Ranger Lewis.

From a ways down the road Lewis spotted Bloor waiting for them under the deck light. He sat unmoving in a rocking chair, his arms folded and his boots up on the railing. Lewis brought the Wagoneer to a stop in front of the white cabin just after midnight. He stood from the chair.

Lewis turned to Jill. Thanks for helpin out. I'm sorry you got hurt.

I'm sorry we didn't find what you were looking for, said the girl.

Together they walked up to the white cabin and Bloor raised at them a chalked finger.

We had to overnight in the shelter, Lewis said.

What happened to your hand?

She poked it pretty bad. Had to take her to the goddamn hospital.

Bloor met his daughter at the bottom of the steps to the front deck and took her hand and inspected the bandage. Koojee. Are you all right?

Yes.

Bloor looked at them both and brought them into the cabin. Lewis and Jill sat on the white couch and Bloor prepared salmon and asparagus in the kitchen, reciting phrases of lyrical poetry he had written about how worried he had been that he had lost them both. The three ate at the dinner table and drank together two bottles of merlot, and Bloor asked them what had happened the night before at the shelter and they told him little save that Cloris Waldrip was not there.

After they had finished Bloor took their plates and Lewis and Jill went out to the back deck with another bottle of merlot. They sat in the outdoor furniture and drank under the clear night.

Jill put a bloodbrown cigarette in her mouth and lit it. Why do they call him the Arizona Kisser?

Kissed some young girls in Arizona I was told, Lewis said. I don't know much else about it. I don't want to.

Bloor came from the sliding glass door and carried with him another bottle of wine. He kissed the air twice and went to the hot tub and pulled the cover from it and set the bottle on its edge. A mass of black hair tumbled and rolled in the water. Ah, koojee!

Lewis peered drunkenly at it from her seat. What now, goddamn it?

Looks like a skunk got in here.

Bloor chalked his hands and drew by its tail the thing from the water. He held it aloft before them. Limp and matted, it steamed in the cold and ran dark water to the deck boards. The animal did not smell, all Lewis could smell was chlorine. Death, like a crazed taxidermist, had fixed open the skunk's eyes and mouth in a maniacal snarl. The flesh slid from the tail and the body thudded to the deck and Bloor was left holding a length of fur like a necktie.

Whoops, he said, and he knelt and picked up the rest of it and laughed once and slung the body over the railing and into a tree, where it landed draped over a high bough.

What good is that? Lewis said. Now it's goin to stink of dead skunk out here.

I'll get it down tomorrow.

Jill stood and set her empty glass on a little wood table by the chairs. She went to the sliding glass door and before she went inside the cabin she held on Lewis her blue-painted eyes and smiled a smile Lewis could not figure.

Bloor clapped and pointed to the hot tub. Do a little tubbing with me, Ranger Lewis.

There was a goddamn skunk dead in there not a minute ago.

You know, the water is chlorinated. My wife always told me that chlorine could kill anything.

Why'd she always tell you somethin like that?

Bloor stripped his clothes and sank his naked body inch by inch into the green waters until nothing save the wispy crown of his blond mullet remained above the surface. Lewis watched the man a moment, drank off another glass of merlot, stripped naked, and climbed in after him.

They bobbed in the water and Lewis spoke low about how she yet believed Cloris Waldrip had been in the old wilderness shelter. It was her, she said.

Bloor did not respond, he only hummed to himself. The wind

moved the pine where the skunk lay snagged, its eyes wide and tungsten in the light from the kitchen window, and Lewis recalled the way she had found Mr. Waldrip, caught aloft in the grave heights of the mountain spruce.

Bloor went silent and took her by the shoulders and pulled her to him.

Stop, she said.

He let her go. What is it?

She took up the bottle of merlot and drank deeply and set it back on the edge of the tub. All right, she said.

Bloor took her again by the shoulders and kissed her. He stroked the bruised places on her arms and pinched her. My leopard, he said. He turned her over and was almost inside her, humping shortly at her backside. She watched a rind of black skunk hairs ride the surface of the wild green water. After less than a minute he climbed from the tub and finished off the side of the deck. She got dressed and replaced the campaign hat to her damp head.

Are you not going to stay, Ranger Lewis?

I need to go home, she said.

You know, I wish you'd stay.

I got to change my uniform. See if I can't get the blood out of this one. I'll be by to get your goddamn daughter in the mornin.

The sodium lights were dark at the Crystal Penguin when Lewis drove by again. She passed the place slowly and leaned out the open window in the warm night. She drove the Wagoneer high up the mountain to Egyptian Point, listening to late-night reruns of *Ask Dr. Howe How*. The radio signal came and went. A caller she had heard before spoke from a heavy voice about the relativity of pain and suffering and why some people cry when a dog dies. Have they not known true tragedy and loss? said the voice. Lewis drank from the thermos of merlot she had filled at Bloor's cabin before leaving. She had also stolen a full bottle from his pantry and had wedged it in the passenger's seat and it clunked and thunked next to her up the unpaved road.

When she pulled up to the trailhead the blue pickup truck with the missing tailgate was parked there. She flipped down the visor and in the mirror rubbed a thumb over her teeth, then licked the thumb and drew it to the edges of her mouth and across her eyebrows. She removed the campaign hat and ran a hand through her hair. The holster she unbuckled from the belt of her trousers and closed the revolver in the glove compartment. The dial clock in the dashboard showed 2:40 a.m. before she took the key from the ignition.

She carried the bottle of merlot up the trail in the dark. She listened for voices in the trees and watched for the light of a bonfire. As she neared the place she saw the glow against the rocks. Ahead a group of boys cackled crazily like a coven of witches. She stopped at the edge of the clearing and stood there and listened. She clutched to her chest the bottle of merlot.

The boys chittered high and breathlessly. One of them boasted about a new used car, and another spoke about how telephones would be able to read minds in twenty years' time and how marriage would be obsolete and how psychotherapy would be done by coin-operated machines in bars and gas stations.

Then a voice like an icepick split through the rest of them. She'll be here any minute.

No she won't. She ain't comin, faggot. It's all fancy lies for sissy girls who drink diet pop and kiss boys with gay haircuts.

We stay up here long enough, she'll come.

My peepaw said he saw her up here once. Said she came up from the rocks ridin a big armadillo and moanin. She had one eye and no teeth and red hair and she had her tits and dick out and everything. He said she was hot as hell even though she was what she was.

Why moanin?

Because she died orgasmin against her will. It'll echo off the mountains for eternity, my peepaw says.

That can't happen, can it? Orgasmin if you don't want to?

I heard it can.

Lewis held tight the bottle of merlot. She took a breath and stepped forward almost into the light so that she would be seen, yet just as she was there she turned on her heel and set off back down to the Wagoneer.

VI

IV

A nice young reporter from a Boston newspaper once asked me in the most darling accent if I had ever considered taking my own life during my ordeal out in the Bitterroot. My answer at the time was no. However if this is going to be any kind of an honest document, I ought to come clean and apologize to her and put it down here that not only had I considered taking my own life, but I had endeavored to do it. And it was not the first time.

I had a mighty sad spell back in the summer of 1941 after Dr. Josiah Dove had made it known to me that I could not become pregnant. I was twenty-seven years old and embarrassed and blind envious of the women I knew who had managed it. I had the terrible notion that I was not a complete woman. Women do not worry as much about that these days, but back then in Texas motherhood was one of the awful few respectable stations in society we had.

So in the middle of a summer night I drove Mr. Waldrip's truck out to our ranch headquarters and found where the cowboys kept the bovine medicine in a dirty old drawer. After drinking all the vials I could stomach, I wandered sick as a dog out into the pasture and collapsed on a fence post like a scarecrow. Come morning I woke up there very well rested and was surprised, and relieved, to be alive. I hopped back in the truck and stopped by the grocery store for some eggs so that I would have a story for Mr. Waldrip. Bless his dear heart, he never did know much about what my crazy head was up to most of the time. If he did, he never cared to let on.

Out there in the Bitterroot I sat up the night with my back to the washout, letting little critters crawl all over me. I hollered out my name until the sun rose behind the clouds. I could not put any weight on my right leg without it giving me a good deal of trouble. If I was going anywhere it was going to have to be on my belly like a snake. But I did not know which direction to go and my purse was up there out of reach on top of the overhang. The most useful items in it were the hatchet, the red canteen, and the compass. I was sad to have lost Mr. Waldrip's boot too. I had the idea then it would have been easier to perish over a month prior in that little airplane with Mr. Waldrip and Terry.

This is when I decided to take my life out in that wilderness. I had visions of Mr. Waldrip spotted miserable with flies, an empty bed, and the obituaries that would run in the *Amarillo Globe News* and the *Clarendon Tribune*. Bless you, I saw our tragic names banal and blurry in cheap newsprint. I envisioned the article about our demise lining the kennel of a new family's first puppy dog, our likenesses specked and distorted with mess. I am aware many of the ladies at First Methodist are sure to judge me here on account of suicide being a sin. But there is not much that I can do about that.

I decided I would make a noose of the glittery stockings. I pulled them off and twisted and knotted them and looked around. Mist was on the ground and dew in the trees. I scooted over to a low branch and looped the stockings over it and slipped my head through the noose. I did not want to be discovered that way, hanged half-naked by the silly clothes of a child. What an awful sight! But when you want nothing more to do with this world you do not get a say about what goes on in it without you.

I propped myself up against the tree. All I had to do was let my legs go out from under me and let the noose do its job. I fixed my eyes on that silvery balloon high up in that pine, shining against the grayest of heavens. I let my weight go. My face got very hot and went numb. My sight turned dark.

I came to with my back flat on the ground and a lather in my mouth. I sat myself up and rubbed my neck. It was mighty sore. The stockings were still on the branch.

I then decided I would crawl for as long as I could and that is how I would meet my end and that would be that. I undid the stockings from the branch and put them back on and got on my belly. With my fingers in the dirt I drug my bad leg behind me and crawled in no particular direction, only the way that seemed to be the least troublesome and was downhill. For over an hour I went on like that, expecting to expire. On occasion I was mighty thirsty and stopped to suck on some funny shapes of ice left in places of shade.

By and by I came to a series of stony outcrops. Beneath one of them yawned a dark cave that you could just about pull a wagon through. At the mouth was a little plateau of rock and a polished dark place of creosote where I supposed there had once burned many fires. I imagined the centuries of Indians who had been there. There was also a smooth bowl such as an ancient mortar wore into the rock. I have learned that these are sometimes called gossip stones. In it was pooled some murky water where frogs had been breeding.

I crawled across the plateau to the cave and lay in front of the mouth. The sun had come out and the day was getting warm. A cool breeze blew from the entrance as from an air-conditioned department store. I hollered into it but my voice was small from the hanging. I do not know who it was I had expected to answer me. It gave back in a long echoing volley, as if the cave spiraled into that mountain all the way to the Far East where the Oriental people live and they were hollering back. I was too afraid to go too far inside. It was very dark and the air within smelled like damp carpet. I passed the day outside the cave and then the night. A mossy log was my pillow and I was hungry and mighty cold. I worried a bear or perhaps that lonely backwards mountain lion would return to the cave and have me for supper.

The next day I endeavored to build a fire so that someone might see the smoke and so I could boil up some of that foul water. The problem was this: I did not have matches nor a lighter.

I thought about what I did have. I felt the breast pocket of Terry's coat. I still had my Bible and Mr. Waldrip's glasses. I recalled Mr. Waldrip sitting out back on a hot day, reading something or another. The sunlight would catch his glasses and his book would start to smoke if he lingered on it for too long.

To make a tedious sort of story short: with much trouble I managed over the course of the day to set a fire with Mr. Waldrip's glasses and a few pages of Genesis for kindling. I know that some people will shake their heads at this bit of blasphemy, but I would only say to them that the rules history makes for us do not always hold up in practice. I mean to tell you I sure was pleased with myself that afternoon. I lay back before my fire and considered myself a worthy descendant to that cavewoman in the diorama at the Panhandle Plains Museum.

That afternoon it looked like rain. I crawled around on my belly and gathered any dry firewood that turned up and piled it at the mouth of the cave. This took some time. Then I had some words with myself and got so brave I could have played chess with a rattlesnake. I used a stick from my fire for a torch and scooted my way inside the cave.

The cave was dry and it was empty as far as I could tell, up to where my torch warded off the dark. The walls of it were smooth and the floor grew white crystals the size of rolling pins. I moved the pile of dry wood inside the cave just in time. The rain started coming down.

When I lit the wood pile with my torch, the fire warmed the cave considerably and the smoke drew out into the storm. It rained the rest of that day.

When the rain quit and night fell, every star there was came out. All was as still as death. I had not eaten anything since I had left the shelter the day before and I was very hungry. Then an awfully strange squeaking commenced in the cave. I must have known what it was all along. Bats. We do not get many bats in Clarendon and I had probably not seen but two in my life. I was mighty unnerved. But more than anything else I was hungry.

I carried my torch deeper into the cave, banishing that immense dark. I looked up to a ceiling of sleeping bats. The research I have done tells me they are uninterestingly called big brown bats. They are not the eerie variety that drink blood and serve as the subjects of scary stories. But heavens, there must have been hundreds of them! It is a testament to my hunger that the sight of that horde inspired only one idea: thumping one on the head and taking it to the fire to cook for supper.

Maybe you will not believe me, but I tell you now that is just what I did. I picked out a nice juicy plump one and pushed myself up onto one leg and balanced on the wall. I thumped that bat with a loose rock and dispatched it where it hung. It fell dead at my feet and suddenly the rest were screeching and swarming around me. I was knocked on my bottom as they flew from the cave.

I skewered the one I had got on a sprig of pine and put it on the fire to scour. The leathery wings crisped and the body bloated and burst open. To my shame the poor creature turned out to be a pregnant female. It turns out that all of them were. I had stumbled on what I now know chiropterologists call a maternity colony.

I ate all of the mama bat and her unborn offspring anyway, save the bones. I did feel sorry for it, but not too sorry to go without supper. I had a hard time of chewing it, being that I could only use my molars, having lost my dental bridge to the river. Bat does not taste terrible, I will allow. It tastes something like quail.

I would spend near twelve days in that cave in total. To my mind it began to seem I had been there for months. Before too long I was able to hobble about upright. I had turned up a gnarled and hooked branch that I used for a walking stick. I clacked about the rock with it like a pitiful shepherd of bats and vermin, the pink shirt and glittery stockings all dark with filth. My hair was tangled and crazy. I imagine I must have looked like a lunatic cave witch belonging to some period of time unkept by history.

After dusk the bats would return to the cave and I would sneak up to one in its sleep and thump it with the end of my walking stick. Eventually the rest of them did not even wake during my culling and depredations. I became better at cooking them too. I used a flat piece of limestone that I could place over the fire, rather than scorching them on a stick. For a drink I boiled the water in the pool outside the cave by heating up stones and dropping them in. I have since been told this is a technique going back to the first days of man. I ended up accidentally boiling many a tadpole that way and I ate them too.

I do not recall thinking much about anything at all during my time in the cave. It was as if I had become an involuntary function, much like how I understand a lung to work, or the heart. I had made up my mind to survive, but I do not recall arriving at the decision. I went on about my desperate business like I had been consuming bats and boiling spoiled water with stones all of my life. Being mighty weak, I spent a good many hours of the day with my back to the cave wall, watching the sun slide across the rocks.

One night, about a week into my stay at the cave, I woke to a pained cry such as that of a child or a deranged bird. I stood with my walking stick and looked out from the cave to the dark woods. The night was still and the fog glowed. After a spell, the cry came again, louder. I am familiar with the high-pitched bellering of weaning calves. I recall the cry a little Gelbvieh calf made when it could not move for a nasty protuberance on the side of its head, and Joe Flud had to mercifully euthanize it with the .22 caliber wheel gun he carried in his boot. There was a like fear and sadness in the cry growing out in the woods.

I tightened my grip on my walking stick. Out of the dark there came this little kid mountain goat, the color of caliche, not much bigger than a tomcat. Its little knees buckled and it settled to the rock and whistled at me. A creditable zoologist has recently informed me that mountain goats are the only extant species of their genus and are not authentically goats. They are more closely related to antelopes and make bird calls when they are young. I was hesitant but I took a step closer to it. It was a pitiful and sweet little thing, I dare even the hardest heart to say otherwise. My dear, was it precious! It lay still and did not move when I was upon it.

Hello there, I said to it. What is all this crying about?

It was transfixed by the fire. Its tiny body worked like a pair of bellows with each little breath it took. I sat close and reached over slowly and touched its fur. It did not shy away, nor did it appear injured in any way that I could tell. It could not have been more than a couple days old. My guess was that it had lost its mother before it had learned how to get along without her. The same thing had happened to one of Mr. Waldrip's cowboys and this left him a bad-mannered and ill-tempered young man with an awful malice for all brown-haired women. He later found his way to a penitentiary in Illinois for punching to death a bank teller who would not marry him.

I got up and beckoned the little kid goat to come along and went to the fire. After some time it inched closer and lay by me. I was up the night watering it from the palm of my hand and stroking its fur. I spoke to it and named it Erasmus, because I supposed it was a male and that is a good name. The goat seemed to get better and calmer the more the night went on and the more I talked to him. I told him about the airplane going down and Mr. Waldrip and Terry and how I had managed to survive for so long with the help of the masked man.

I fell asleep for a spell before daybreak, and when I awoke, Erasmus was up on his tiny hooves cropping the little grass that grew from the cracks in the rock. I bade him good morning and he seemed to know what I had said and he came to me and lay down again. I had occasion for the first time in some days to recall that my name was Cloris Waldrip and that I had been married for many years to a mighty good husband and that I had had a life elsewhere very different to the one I had then.

This portion of my account that I am about to commit will have a number of folk taking the stump in noisy judgment over my soul, but that does not matter a mite to me now. In truth we will all be fiction soon enough and people yet to come can decide what little truth and goodness there was in any of it. So, I was acquainted with a woman named Carol Sanders for some years. I met her at a bake sale for Clarendon Elementary. I liked Carol and she would come over and we would visit on the back porch and watch from afar as our husbands hunted quail, their orange hats bobbing through the grass. But after a while I understood that there was something terribly wrong with the way Carol talked about other people. She could sure talk about herself until there was not a gust of wind left in Texas, but when she spoke on someone else, even her children, she did not care to go into much detail.

Some people do the bare minimum to show up like they care for those they say they care about. But when it comes right down to it all they want is to get what they want out of people. A mighty fine psychologist I have met with, Dr. Ungerstaut, has told me that it is called sociopathy. I do not know if that word works for what Carol was, and I worry we are all some of it some of the time. It eventually came out that she was burning her children with lightbulbs. Thinking about her in that cave next to little ole helpless Erasmus, I had an awful notion that God was like Carol Sanders, only Carol definitely exists because I have seen her name in the phone book. I have always been a faithful Methodist, but today I do not know what to say with any certainty about the nature of God. However I sure can say a lot about the nature of Carol Sanders.

I looked down at poor little Erasmus. He did not look at me, but I did not expect him to. I took a flat piece of flint that I had worked into a cutting implement for the bats and I held him by the horns and cut his throat. It was a warm day and the blood dried quickly on the stone plateau and I rolled Erasmus aside in the shade to have for supper that night.

I decided that I would use the daylight to put up a signal fire with black smoke and to tie ribbons torn from the bottom of my shirt throughout the woods. By the time I had finished making the ribbons, the shirt was like the kind our grandniece used to wear, showing the little blue ball she kept in her navel. I tied the ribbons in a perimeter around the cave and burned some damp logs that made a great deal of smoke. By now I had survived my ordeal in the Bitterroot for some nearly six weeks.

Two days or so went by and I had eaten all of Erasmus and burned his bones. I wore his fur around my neck as a kind of stole. It did keep me a good deal warmer. I have since had it made into a pillow and it decorates my bed here at River Bend Assisted Living.

I had gotten to where I could stand without the walking stick for longer and I hobbled around and burned heavy signal fires all day and all night. Then on a warm afternoon I heard footsteps in the woods. I hollered out my name and that I was lost. The footsteps drew closer. No answer came, but I had a good hope about who it was.

Unclothed, Lewis sank up to her chin in the hot tub. The crown of her head steamed and she steadied bloodshot eyes beyond the deck on mountains like tsunamis petrified, towering blue in the dark. A full moon wheeled over them. A ways off two flashlights swung through the trees and she could hear voices. She figured it was Claude and Pete searching for the ghost of Cornelia Åkersson.

Goddamn goofballs, she said, and she shook her head. The dead skunk was yet stuck in the tall pine and she sniffed the air for it but could smell nothing save chlorine. She turned back to the white cabin.

Jill had come out and sat on the edge of the hot tub, her back to the water. She lit a cigarette and shivered and pulled an arm inside her sweatshirt and held the cigarette in her bandaged hand. Wind raised her curls and stole the smoke from her mouth.

It's cold, Lewis said into a near empty glass. You ought to get in.

I'm not going to get naked.

I didn't say get naked.

Why are you naked?

I don't know, Jill. Maybe had too much merlot. I apologize. It's inappropriate.

Jill finished the cigarette and flicked the butt over the deck railing. She stripped to her brassiere and underwear and slid in. She held above the water her bandaged hand.

Lewis sucked at the last drop of merlot in the bottom of her glass, then set it aside. The flashlights moved in the trees and she brought up a hand to the air and watched her fingers steam. I don't figure I've ever had an orgasm.

The girl said nothing for a moment and then said, How do you know?

I expect I don't.

Me neither.

My guess is that means we never had one, Lewis said, and she took up the empty glass and tried to drink from it.

Bloor, in the kitchen washing dishes, watched them from the window.

Some women have them, Lewis said. I know that. You see it in the goddamn movies. A girl I knew in high school swore she had them with a trombonist named Hamin. Goddamn embouchure. But I can't do it. No matter how hard I try.

Maybe no woman has. Maybe it's a conspiracy to keep us having sex.

Your dad really doesn't give you enough credit, Lewis said. I figure it's just cause I don't get caught up in the moment. I can't even watch a goddamn movie without I keep an eye out for the camera in mirrors. I can't just enjoy somethin for what it's wantin to be.

Me neither.

I figure everyone else can get caught up just fine. Must be what you need to do to get along with all the goddamn people. Maybe it's even what you need to love them.

There's more to it than that, I think.

On the rare occasion I do get caught up I get carried away, Lewis said. I do somethin out of hand. I let it all get out of hand.

Is that why you're naked?

Probably. It's hard to know why we do what we do.

I get carried away too.

I expect I've had too much merlot.

It's fine, the girl said.

Maybe it's a good thing we came across each other.

Do you care about me?

I expect I do.

Do you think you'll ever learn how to get caught up when you want to get caught up?

Lewis shook her head. Too goddamn old already for that. But you still got a chance. Then she leaned over and vomited on the deck.

Lewis was on the upstairs terrace. She stood at the railing in the shadows and watched Jill in the hot tub below. The girl sat yet in the water, small and pale behind the steam, and stared off beyond the deck and the dead skunk, sparking cigarette after cigarette. The flashlights had shone for hours in the trees behind the cabin and now they scanned in the direction of the road.

Bloor came through the sliding glass door and joined Lewis on the terrace. He held out before him his chalked hands. He turned them front to back and studied them under the moon. The motion light was off. Are you going back out there to that shelter tomorrow?

Lewis nodded. The FBI are sendin a chopper.

It's funny how when you look for one thing you find another, Bloor said.

We didn't find anythin. All they told Gaskell was they wanted me to show them the shelter. I'll clean off your deck tomorrow. Sorry about that.

I was talking about us.

What about us?

You know, you're a fascinating woman, Ranger Lewis. I came up here to find a downed plane and I found you. Don't you want to come in? It's cold.

Not yet.

Bloor rubbed his hands together and breathed on them. Tomorrow, he said, tell them to look under the floor. Koojee. You could've been sleeping right on top of that missing girl.

It wasn't the girl.

Bloor shook his head. You know, my wife always told me everyone's a wasp in a curtain, panicking to get out of something they can't hope to ever understand because it's too far beyond their realm of comprehension.

Lewis watched Jill and the smoke she made.

A wasp doesn't know what a curtain is, Bloor said.

All right, goddamn it.

And she always told me to get what I could get while the getting was good.

Lots of goddamn people say that one.

Bloor smiled. Not the way she said it. He took Lewis by the shoulders and kissed her. What would you like me to do for you? he said.

Sorry?

What do you want to do?

Whatever.

Bloor leaned on the railing and looked down. Lewis figured he watched his daughter below. He had a small erection between the slats of the railing. He turned to Lewis and brought his eyes to hers and exhaled. I love you, Ranger Lewis, he said.

Lewis waited before dawn at the airfield down the mountain. She drank a cup of coffee in the Wagoneer and filled the thermos from a bottle of merlot. She watched the highway.

It was 5:16 a.m. by the dashboard clock when a black sedan pulled up with three men in windbreakers. Lewis licked a flattened palm and smoothed her hair. She put on the campaign hat and got out of the Wagoneer into the cold. A mustached man shorter than the other two cradled an arm in a sling and introduced himself as Special Agent Polite. He introduced the others as his colleagues, Jameson and Yip. They did not speak except to nod and mutter, their faces like those of sullen children, turned away to the mountains.

The group boarded a helicopter and flew out to a clearing near the Old Pass and followed Lewis into the forest. They found the shelter as the sun came up. Jameson and Yip drew their sidearms and Yip pushed open the door and went in slow. Polite followed, his hand under his windbreaker on the butt of a pistol.

Lewis drew the revolver from her hip and went in after the men. The shelter was as she recalled leaving it. The striped socks yet hung from the clothesline. The spiral she had drawn in dust was still on the table.

These the socks in your report? Polite said.

Yes.

One of the men raised a camera from around his neck and photographed the socks. The flash wheezed and he went to the table and photographed the spiral.

Is this how you found it?

Yes. But I made that.

Why?

I don't know. You ever do somethin you don't know why you're doin it?

Polite looked at her. Anything different since you left it?

I don't think so.

Take a good look.

It's the same.

Polite walked around the place and stood near the pair of socks. He looked down at the book on the table and read aloud: *The Joy of Lesbian Sex: A Tender and Liberated Guide to the Pleasures and Problems of a Lesbian Lifestyle* by Dr. Emily L. Sisley and Bertha Harris. I think this is a dead end. Unlikely he would be this far out. This appears to be the work of alternatively inspired people.

It's Cloris.

What is Cloris?

Cloris Waldrip survived a plane crash not far from here about five weeks ago, Lewis said. She holstered the revolver.

What kind of name is Cloris? Dutch? Irish?

I'm not sure.

Sounds Irish.

I just don't know.

How do you know she survived, Ranger Lewis? Where is she?

She's lost. She carved her name into a goddamn stump twelve miles west of here.

A stump?

Yes.

Cloris?

Yes.

Well, maybe she did stay here, Polite said. He was surveying the room. He passed his good hand over his mustache. She's not here now. I can't see much here that interests my investigation as of yet. Jameson, make another picture of these socks.

Yessir. Should we bag them?

I don't see why we would. Did your Cloris Waldrip wear socks like that, Ranger Lewis?

I don't know. I don't figure her for wearin socks like that, no.

Did she read literature on alternative lifestyles?

I don't know. I don't expect she would.

Well then, I guess this is a dead end for the both of us.

There's blood on the floor, sir, Yip said, and he took a photograph of the floor.

That's from a member of my team, Lewis said. She injured her goddamn hand when we were here last Tuesday.

That's a lot of blood, Polite said. Did she lose the hand?

No. She poked it. She's all right.

Did you or any member of your team do anything else or leave anything else behind while you were here last Tuesday that we should know about?

Like I said, I drew that goddamn thing on the table.

Anything else?

There's a thing, a sculpture of a goddamn eagle out there layin in the dirt. That's what she poked her hand on.

You brought a sculpture up here?

No. It was here.

Well, you see, I just don't know where to place that in the situation at hand, Polite said.

Lewis went to the bunk beds on the far wall. She put a palm to the bottom cot and plucked up a strand of hair and held it up between two fingers to the morning light at the small window. Then she let it fall to the floor and went outside. She took from her pack the thermos of merlot and drank in the mist and the trees.

Polite came outside and stood alongside her. He stroked his elbow through the sling. Are you all right, Ranger Lewis?

Yes. Why?

It would appear you are drinking red wine from a vacuum container.

Lewis screwed the cap back on the thermos and held it down at her side.

Anything I can do, Ranger Lewis?

I don't expect there is.

Why don't you try me?

Lewis glanced at the man. He had a tired face. She unscrewed the thermos cap and they stood there listening to the flashbulbs snap within the shelter. You ever notice you can't get intimate to yourself, Lewis said, let alone another person?

I know that I have noticed that before, yes. Can I tell you something? I went on a Caribbean cruise last summer to meet new people, and I only stayed in my cabin by myself and read fifty-seven issues of *Life* magazine. Hated myself even more than before we pulled out of the harbor.

I expect I'm what you'd call a wino.

Too much drink can be a problem. On the cruise I had too much drink. Too much. Nobody saw. Had the chain on the door.

Lewis drank from the thermos. I figure I'm wantin to get closer to someone, but I don't know if I ought to do that with this person. Might be inappropriate for me to pursue. I can't tell what kind of closeness it is.

Why not?

Goddamn. I'm sorry. This is goddamn unprofessional.

I asked. Here. Can I tell you something else? On the last day of my cruise I was intimate with a woman who was bound to be the most unattractive woman on the ship. Maybe on any ship. She had a portrait of her stillborn son tattooed on her lumbar region. Right here, you see. It was one of the most miserable things I ever saw. Colton, she named him. Bad name too. That's nothing you want to look at when you're, well, you know.

I expect not.

Agent Polite sighed and smiled. It's good to talk to someone. Can I tell you something else about myself I haven't told anyone? I dislocated my shoulder in an automobile accident resultant of too much drink. Left the bar, drove head-on into a statue of an honored astronaut. Bad thing. All anyone else thinks is that I did it to keep from hitting a dog.

Thanks for sharin that story. I figure we ought to get back in there.

That's right. Right. I don't envy you being interested in someone you cannot or will not pursue. But you only got to decide how much you want to be governed by either impulse or regret. You do something and it may or may not be the right or the wrong thing. Maybe it turns out it is the right thing. But how do you ever know if it was? You see, maybe it turns out we'll never know right from wrong because we can't see all consequences to all possible actions and that's why some middleaged people go on cruises.

I'm just goddamn dissatisfied.

Agent Polite nodded and retrieved from a pocket in his windbreaker a cocktail sword and chewed it. He looked at his polished shoes and then at the sky. I don't have much to say about that part of it, Ranger Lewis. Except that I'm dissatisfied too.

The helicopter took off from the clearing as the sun fell and Lewis, lips purpled and tight, sat in silence beside Agent Polite while the night draped over the mountains a senseless fog, and the wilderness entire dimmed beneath. She drank from the thermos and wiped on a sleeve a clowncolored mouth. She could see in the window glass the whites of Polite's eyes flash over her.

When they reached the airfield she stumbled from the helicopter and vomited into a garbage can. She figured that Polite would not let her drive home. Yet he did, and she did, up the mountain in the dark, sweeping before her white headlights across the dewed black road and the roadkill there opalescent like broken glass. She drove with one hand on the radio tuning the static for a signal, eyeing now and again the passenger's seat and the weatherworn book there: *The Joy of Lesbian Sex.*

I thought you'd gone home, said the masked man. He was thinner than when I had left him a fortnight ago and his clothes were more ragged. He had on a different mask cut from a button shirt pictured with colorful Easter eggs. I am sure I was just an awful sight to behold, wild and filthy in dried blood and dirt like I was, outfitted in those silly stockings and that pink short top like a horrific and aberrant youth. Worse yet I had been relieving myself by the mouth of the cave where I could lean and the mess had piled up into an awful black cone about the size of a plump toddler. Vermin had tunneled through it and slept inside. It is a funny thing that I was not more embarrassed by the state I was in. I simply stood there boldly relying on my walking stick and shook my head.

He asked me what had happened and I told him that I had gotten lost and injured my ankle and had been eating bats.

How bad is it? he said.

They do not taste terribly different to quail.

I meant how bad is your ankle.

It is mending now, thank you, I said.

Those people didn't come this way?

I shook my head again and asked how he had found me.

I wasn't looking for you, he said. I was coming back because I'd left something at the shelter. Then I saw the smoke. I was afraid it'd be you.

What did you leave at the shelter?

Nothing.

Did you get it?

He told me that he had and then he said that he was afraid he would have to leave me there. He wanted to help me, he said, but nothing had changed and he still could not take me any further. He said he could leave me some jerky to see me through and told me that if I continued on east I would come to the trail that would take me to the road.

How far is the road?

You could probably make it in a few days, he said. Where's your bag?

I told him that I had lost it. Where will you go? I asked.

Where will I go?

I nodded.

Better you not know that.

Will you go back to the shelter?

No, ma'am, he said. Can't.

May I accompany you? Heavens, I asked him this before I had thought much about what it meant!

He said nothing for a moment and then: Don't you want to go home?

I told him I did not want to be alone.

He thought about this some and knocked sickled figures of mud from the heel of his boot. I'm sorry, he said.

Please, I said. I do not know what I would do anymore, even if I were to make it home.

He went silent again for a spell looking at me. Wind flapped in his mask. They won't find you, he said at last. If you come with me they'll never find you.

That is just fine, said I.

He cocked his head and righted it again. He said nothing else about it and set about building up the fire and boiling hardtack in a small iron skillet which hung from the duffel he bore on his back. We suppered as the sun went down and it was not long before I fell asleep sitting up against the cave wall, watching the flames put the masked man's rambling shadow to the stone like I were witness to the origins of mankind. I knew then that he did not want to be alone any more than I did.

The next morning he was up dousing the fire I had kept going for more than a week. If you're really coming, he said, come on.

I followed him with my walking stick into the woods. We walked for a day and come dark made camp in a dry sandy draw beneath a spruce chewed up with terrible little red snickering beetles. For supper we boiled up some more hardtack and furry jerky and slivers of a slow gray squirrel that he had stamped to death on the way. We slept. We set out again in the morning, exchanging not word one.

We pulled on that way over the course of the day and then we reached a shallow gulch upon nightfall. A skinny cold creek ran through it, silver under the moon. White pine grew bare and twisted here and there but most common was mountain grass and flows of scree.

The masked man was stopped before the gulch. He indicated a place with his glove. A particularly large and devilish pine had grown into five bone-white digits like an enormous skeletal hand. A lean-to hut as long as a school bus, partly hidden from view, was nestled against the palm of it. The hut was made up of branches held together by yellow rope and strips of many-colored fabrics and it looked sturdy enough. For a door cover it had what I took for a child's bed linen, being that it was printed with the repeat likenesses of a muscled character I had seen before on cereal boxes in the grocery store.

The masked man led me down a little path to the hut. He pulled back the sheet. Inside it was as dark as the inside of a cow and he set about lighting a fire in a little stove that had once been a bulk can of pitted olives. He also lit a kind of lantern he had made with a pine knot set in the broken skull of some toothy critter. Then I could see the place. At one end was a pallet of twigs and cloth where I assumed he had been sleeping. All kinds of clothes were piled in a corner near the pallet and a funny Swedish kind of hat hung from a sprig off the pine. Letters which spelled out the word *Russia* were carved into one of the load-bearing rafters. The hut looked like it had been lived in for a spell.

He moved the clothes to the opposite corner of the hut and in the space left he rolled out a blanket printed with illustrations of a maniacal dolphin. You can take my bed for tonight, he said. I'll make you one tomorrow.

I told him I was perfectly comfortable on the ground, which was not just me being polite. By that time I was mighty used to it. Still he insisted. I thanked him.

We ate more jerky he produced from a folded sweater. He was always a dear to remember that I did not have all my teeth, and he generally boiled everything until it was soft. It was very delicious. After all, I had been eating bat for weeks. He also cooked up wild tubers and berries for better nutrition. I was very tired and I fell asleep as soon as I had eaten. I do not even recall shutting my eyes.

He was gone when I woke in the morning, but a fire was burning in the stove and a pot of meat was simmering for breakfast. *I B BAK* was spelled out on the ground in small rocks. I spent the day patrolling the creek with my walking stick and peering into the shallows for a slow fish I could thump. Fish were easy for me to eat, but I never did catch one.

That evening I was relieving myself against a rock face some good ways down the creek when the man showed up around the bend with his tackle box and fishing rod and a line of three trout. He was not wearing his mask. My goodness, we startled each other! He dropped the trout in the dirt and hid his face before I could clearly see it. I endeavored to cover myself up without making a mess.

I'm sorry, he said, his back to me, tying the shirt around his head.

I put my clothing, such as it was, back together and stood up. You cannot come and go as you please like that, I snapped. I never know where you are!

He apologized again.

I accepted his apology and told him that I was sorry I had snapped at him.

I cooked the trout on the stove with some wild onions he had found growing in the woods above the gulch. At the time it was the best thing I had ever smelled. The man sat in the corner of the hut and watched me from behind his mask. I was wrapped in a blanket he had given me. The weather had turned cold once the sun had gone and outside the wind sang unknowable songs in that big old strange-fingered pine.

We ate our supper in silence. The inside of the hut was poorly lit, but the stove and the pine-knot lantern put out enough light to feed our shadows. Once we had finished and I had set aside the piece of shale I had been using for a plate the man looked at me again. His lively green eyes were balanced in the holes of his mask and his mouth twitched under it. He got up and went to the far corner of the hut and retrieved a big green glass bottle from behind the stack of firewood there. He held it up and gently shook it at me.

What is it? I asked.

Dutch courage, he said. I went back for it at the shelter. Not many pleasures out here. The ones we have start to get pretty valuable.

I told him that I seldom imbibed. Clarendon is in a dry county and Mr. Waldrip had been a teetotaler. As I recall I had only ever had a real drink of alcohol on Christmas Eve in 1969. Mr. Waldrip and I had driven out to spend Christmas with my niece, Mary, and her husband, Jacob, in Albuquerque, New Mexico, and I drank a glass of champagne, said something inappropriate about their cat, and went to bed.

The man unscrewed the cap and folded up the bottom of his mask just under his nose, to where the short bushy beard on his chin showed, and he took a swallow from the bottle. I could not tell you if he liked it or not, but he took a measured rest like a man playing a trumpet in a concert band and had another gulp.

I had the notion that I might as well drink, considering my situation. I put my hand out for the bottle. He got up and brought it to me. I took it and drank. The alcohol burned my throat and I coughed. Drinking gin out of the bottle is a thing I imagine you must practice a good deal before there is any grace to be found in it.

He brought me some water in the goat horn. I drank it and then I swallowed from the bottle again and coughed again. It was not long before I was good and well in my cups. I dabbed my face with Erasmus's fur. The man sat crosslegged by me near the stove and we shared the bottle between us and listened to the wind like a regular couple of cowpokes on the drive.

Struggling to keep the giddiness from my voice, I told him that I did not know how to thank him for everything he had done for me.

That's all right, he said, and he swallowed some more.

I took the bottle back from him and had another gulp and coughed and my ears got hot. Then I asked him why he lived out there in that desperate way.

Long story, he said.

I have the time, said I.

He said nothing to that.

What about your parents? I asked.

What about them?

Do you visit them?

No.

They must miss you.

They don't.

Sure, they must.

You don't know what you're talking about.

I do. You are a big-hearted angel. I surely would have been long gone had you not been kind enough to look after me.

He got the bottle back from me and drank. He looked at the fire in the stove and breathed through his nose, drinking all the while. He yanked the bottle off his lips with a great smack. I watched your plane go down, he said. I was setting traps in the valley and I saw it come over the mountain. Saw it hit before I heard it. Didn't think anybody could've survived. I stayed out there for two nights to see if a rescue effort would come. When nobody did I thought I'd get up there fast and salvage some supplies from the wreck before anybody'd show up. Thought maybe I could get a radio. I kept my distance and watched the mountain with my binoculars. I hiked up in the morning a few days after it crashed and I nearly made it there before nightfall but I saw your fire on the way. Then that storm came and I saw you.

I saw you too, I said. In the trees.

He said he knew that I had, and he said that he had waited out the storm and followed me down to the creek the next morning and had heard me praying. He said that it was then he had realized why I had left the little airplane. The fire I had seen in the valley was his.

So it's kind of my fault you're still out here, he said. I'd tried not to have a fire in the wide open like that at all in case a rescue effort was coming. But it'd rained and I was too cold in the morning. I thought I was going to get sick if I didn't warm up.

I asked: Why do you not want anyone to know you are out here?

Nobody's supposed to be out here, he said.

You could have left me and continued on up to the airplane, I said.

I felt responsible.

Your parents reared you right. You are a decent man.

Decency, he said. Yeah, that'll be it.

I watched him drink by the light of the stove for a minute or two and then I asked him again the question that yet played on my mind: Why do you not want anyone to know you are out here?

I'd rather not talk anymore about it, he said.

Just fine, I said. But if you do not want to be found, what use could you have for a radio?

The man had another big swallow. It gets really lonely out here. Sometimes I think it's not worth it. At least maybe if I had a radio I could maybe hear another voice sometime if I found a signal.

You never got your radio.

No. Got you, though.

I smiled and from what I could see uncovered of his face he smiled too. Emboldened by the drink I sat up and reached with both hands for his mask.

He pulled away and grabbed ahold of my wrists. What're you doing?

I would like to see your face, I said.

That's not a good idea.

Are you an outlaw?

The man only looked at me.

I am not going anywhere, I said, and you cannot wear that silly thing all of the time. That would be mighty uncomfortable and very likely unhealthy.

Still he held my wrists. You might not need any more of that booze, he said.

He sure might have been right about that. I was dizzy and warm. I said: Show me your face, young man.

He smiled again. I imagine he was amused by what a sotted old loon I was. He had a good smile and I will not easily forget it. He got up from the fire and gave me the bottle. He looked down at me for a moment. Then he reached up and pulled the mask off his head and dropped it to the ground.

At long last I was gazing upon the bare face of this young man. It was a very handsome countenance, not much more than twenty-eight years on this earth, as I would learn, but one of those faces that would seem young no matter what age it truly was. By the light of the pine knot burning in the critter's skull it was apparent that it was a face used to terrible worry and concern.

He sat again and rubbed his eyes.

Now does that feel better? I said.

He admitted that it did.

You remind me of a handsome young man I knew when I was a young woman, I told him.

What was he like?

His name was Garland. He was handsome and he was decent like you and he thought fondly of me.

The man drank and gave me the bottle. It's good I look like somebody else.

To my eye you do look a good deal like him. I swallowed from the bottle and this time I did not cough. Please tell me why you are out here, I said.

The man shook his head. I'm somebody nobody wants to be around.

That is nonsense.

He did not take his eyes from the fire in the stove. The wind billowed in the tarpaulin pinned to the thatched roof. You've seen how people are, he said. Nobody's ever welcome. Nobody'd know what to do if they were.

He got up and took the bottle from me and went to his pallet. He had put together a pallet for me of pine needles and grass and bedsheets. I sat on the end of it and looked at him across the hut. We were not ten feet apart. He lay there for some time. His eyes were glistening.

I asked him for his name.

I can't give it, he said.

What should I call you?

After some hesitation he said, Just go ahead and call me Garland if you want.

I suppose that will have to do, I said.

He turned on his side and put his palms together under his head. Then he rolled over the other way so his back was to me and told me to snuff out the lantern when I was ready to sleep.

I had hard work falling asleep. It had begun to rain and I lay on my pallet listening to it on the tarpaulin. The man was asleep on his back, wrapped up in those funny blankets. The stovelight flickered over his handsome face. He had such kind features. For me it was a face cobbled together from memories of handsome young men I had known, all of them long gone now, for men usually live shorter lives than women. In Hedley, not fifteen miles down the road from Clarendon, there is a Baptist church attended entirely by old widows.

I sat up on my pallet and wrapped myself in my blanket. As far as I can recall, this is the way it went: I climbed from my pallet as quietly as I could manage and knelt down by him. I leaned over him and put my face real close to his and sure enough I kissed that young man where he lay in his slumber. Lightly there on his bottom lip. I cannot put to reasonable language what it was that came over me, but I suspect it was of the drink and of my growing affection for him. I would imagine that many of the women from First Methodist will denounce me in each other's company for much of what I have put down in this account. But when they are alone with their thoughts I hope they will know what I have become and see it on some horizon within themselves as well before it is too late.

The young man stirred but did not wake and I crawled back to my pallet and went straight to sleep. I did not dream that night out in the Bitterroot, but last night a hailstorm filled the streets with ice here in Brattleboro, Vermont, and I dreamt warm in my bed at River Bend Assisted Living. I dreamt that eons after civilization as we know it had come to a disappointing end there appeared a new race of people. I dreamt that they discovered our ruins and were confounded. I dreamt that they genetically reanimated us from fossilized prophylactics excavated from the gutters of our grandest metropolises, and put us in houses and cabins and huts and studied us to find out what it was that we were all endeavoring to do to one another. I dreamt that I had always been one of these test subjects and had only helped to confound them all the more.

VII

They sat in a booth at a diner down the mountain. Jill had a soda and Lewis drank coffee and merlot and they ate hamburgers and watched from a window rain darken a leathery mendicant who waved roadside a sign of cardboard they could not read for the wording had bled. After they had eaten, Lewis had the gaptoothed waitress bring out a piece of apple pie with a candle afire in it and the waitress and a chinless cook sang. Lewis mumbled the song with them and refilled her mug from a thermos of merlot under the table. Jill blew out the candle.

The cook clapped and the waitress flattened an ink-stained hand to the girl's back and leaned over her. Lewis figured she studied the girl's scars. What birthday is it, baby doll?

Eighteen, Jill said.

What's that, sweetie?

She's eighteen, Lewis said.

Just a young and beautiful woman, the cook said, whistling. Ye gawd, ye just got yer whole life ahead of ye.

The waitress turned to Lewis. You must be one proud mama.

Lewis fixed on the woman a red eye. I'm not her mama.

She's new, Ranger Lewis, said the cook.

All right, goddamn it.

The waitress blinked and the cook pulled her away behind a swinging door.

Lewis hoisted onto the table a box wrapped in white paper. Happy birthday, she said.

Should I open it?

What else would you do with it?

Jill tore away the paper and Lewis cut the string with a pocketknife.

I went down the mountain a couple days ago, Lewis said. Came across this in that antique shop by the gas station. Couldn't believe my goddamn eyes. Had to get it. Easy there. It's goddamn heavy.

Jill opened the box. She pulled balled-up newspaper from around the bronze of an eagle taking flight off a tree limb.

I know pokin up your hand wasn't the best thing to happen to you up here, Lewis said. But I figured you could remember the other times by it too.

The girl showed her palm and the white dash there. It's healed, she said. Maybe this is the same bird and time is different.

I had it engraved there at the bottom.

Jill read aloud from the bronze: *United States Forest Service Volunteer Forest Ranger Jill Bloor 1986.*

Two goddamn months in the program. That's somethin to be proud of.

We didn't find your old lady.

Lewis took the Lord's name in vain and shook her head. Nine o'clock that morning Chief Gaskell had radioed into the station and told Lewis that the state had declared Cloris Waldrip dead in absentia. Almost everythin doesn't work out, Lewis said. We can just do our best, that's all.

Do you think she's dead?

If she's not she's probably goddamn unrecognizable.

Will you keep looking for her?

I'll keep an eye out.

The rain quit and Lewis drove the girl to an outlet store in a dismal corner of the town. Lewis strolled the aisles through racks of collared shirts and Jill tried on polyester dresses in the changing room. Lewis stood guard and kept an eye on the curtain. She scowled at a spidery boy loitering there with his hands in his pockets. Lewis told the boy to get and he did. When Jill was finished, Lewis bought her a pair of trousers and a blue cotton dress and she bought for herself a khaki shirt and then drove to a wine-and-spirits store and picked up ten bottles of discounted merlot. She loaded the Wagoneer and drove back up the mountain and the red evening sun pulled long shadows from the road signs and made bloody roods of the last telephone poles.

She caught a bottle of merlot rolling in the floorboard and had Jill uncork it with a corkscrew from the glove compartment. She parked the Wagoneer at the trailhead for Egyptian Point and they sat in their seats as the last of the sundown mist rolled off the mountains into the black wards of the valleys below. Silk Foot Maggie paced the yard behind the mobile home where she had built rust-colored castles out of used tampons and beer cans.

It was Monday and it was quiet and no vehicle save theirs was parked there. Lewis turned the engine off and let the quiet stand. She drank from the bottle. Didn't want to take you back just yet. That all right?

Jill nodded and cranked down the window and lit a cigarette. They drank together from the bottle and Jill smoked cigarettes out the window. A cloud covered the moon, leaving only the red glow of the lightbulb in Silk Foot Maggie's back porch. The girl's hair shone. Lewis reached over and touched it.

What are you doing?

Thought your hair was wet. It's real pretty. You still plannin on leavin? Now you're eighteen?

Jill said that she planned to leave the next day.

What's your dad say about that?

He wants to stay here.

You can stay too if you want, Lewis said. She took back her hand. You don't have to stay with him. You can stay with me. There's a goddamn spare room that's just boxes. It was my ex-husband's study. You're welcome to it.

I lied to you, Jill said. My dad never had sex with my mom after she was paralyzed.

All right. Why'd you lie about that?

Do you know the reasons for everything you do?

No, goddamn it, I don't expect that I do.

One day you'll not like me so much, Jill said.

I don't care that you lied about that. We all have our goofy reasons for doin what we do, Jill. Even if we don't know them all the time.

I can't stay with you.

Lewis watched the girl a moment longer and turned back to the wheel and started the engine.

Lewis, a lip wedged in the neck of a bottle, sulled drunk on the white couch. Moths knocked against the window without like a heavy rain. In the circular fireplace the false logs lay in the fire like the limbs of cats and dogs cremated in the dirt yard behind her father's clinic. Beyond the fire the homunculus leaned dry and foul in a corner, gawping at her through the flames with its eyes of halved tennis balls. A cricket sang from a hole in its skull.

Behind her a door opened and a forked shadow reached over the living room. She pried from the bottle her lip and turned to find Bloor in a lacy yellow nightgown.

Are you all right, Ranger Lewis?

What're you wearin?

It was Adelaide's.

All right. Lewis nodded at the homunculus across the room. You'd better throw that goddamn thing out before it falls apart and makes a real mess.

Thanks for taking her today.

Eighteen's a big one. Figured she'd want a day off this goddamn mountain.

Bloor let the gown slip from his shoulders and fall to the floor. He cocked a hip before her in the firelight. His long naked body was shorn of hair and his penis tight and small. His golden mullet was like a kind of Japanese headdress. He held a cake of chalk and passed it between his palms and set it on the end table, then lowered himself next to her on the couch. The synthetic leather croaked against his skin and he took from her the bottle and finished what was left. He pinched lightly her sides. When Lewis did not make a sound, he pinched harder. She put a hand over her mouth. He pinched her again harder yet and he whinnied and she took the Lord's name in vain between her fingers.

What do you want to do? he said.

I'd like to try somethin, Lewis said.

What's that?

Get on the floor and open your mouth.

Do you want to take off your clothes first?

No, she said. That's not necessary for this.

Bloor looked at her, then slid to the floor and lay there naked on his back as he was told.

Now open your mouth, Lewis said from the couch.

Bloor did so and Lewis got up and stood over him. He lay there staring up at her. She figured he looked like an enlarged and deformed girl. She settled down on top of him and put her face close to his.

Put out your tongue, she said, and he did. Lewis pursed her lips and let drool run from them. Bloor turned his head. She told him no and he turned it back. She aimed and spat into his mouth. Keep it open, she said, and drooled again. I'll tell you when to swallow. She drooled until his mouth was full and his eyes were watering, then she sat up and told him to swallow. He did and gagged and got up on his elbows and Lewis climbed off him and sat back on the couch.

He was awed a moment and clucked in the pit of his throat and jittered the sweat off his head like a water bird coming up for air, then he stood widelegged before the fire with an erection. He finished there and splattered the artificial logs and the mess sizzled and burned off in a watery smoke. He told her it was the best sexual experience he had ever had and that he loved her and he took up a glass of water from the coffee table and drank there naked.

Lewis watched him for a time and then said, I'm not all right.

Bloor set the glass down. Are you going to be sick?

No. I want to end our relationship, professional and otherwise.

You've had a couple of bottles of merlot, you know.

I've had four goddamn bottles but I know what I'm sayin. Will now, will always.

I don't think you do.

Don't tell me what I don't know. You can do this goddamn goofy thing without me. There're plenty of me out there. I'm just another kind of the same person over and over again. Same as you.

No you're not. I love you.

Your goddamn love's not special neither, she said. She cleared her throat and spat all the way into the fire from where she sat. Don't you mistake that it is. It's the same brand everybody else's got.

Bloor shuddered naked and took a step forward. Koojee. Let's discuss this tomorrow when you're sober.

Lewis straightened up on the couch and aligned the holstered revolver on her belt. Let's just leave it where it stands and move on.

You owe me some discussion.

Can you put some goddamn clothes on?

What changed your feelings for me?

I don't expect they did change.

Bloor sat down next to her on the couch. I don't understand.

Put some goddamn clothes on.

He took up from the floor the nightgown and pulled it on. My wife always told me that God has tiny feet and tiptoes through time but makes a hell of a racket in space.

Goddamn it, Lewis said. Half the time I don't know what the hell your goddamn wife was always tryin to tell you. And the other half it sounds like what every other goddamn person's already said before and it never helped anybody when it was said the first time. I can't figure why we all keep sayin the same goddamn things to each other and expect anybody to be anythin new and good. I'm not attracted to you and I don't like the sex, if that's what we're callin it.

I'm sorry, Bloor said. I was under the impression you liked it.

You misunderstood.

I hoped we could explore some of our fantasies with each other in a comfortable and safe space. I thought you had a healthy sense of yourself and were a strong, progressive woman.

Some of you people sayin you're progressive are the ones goin backward.

I had the impression you were the kind of woman that was sexually accepting and adventurous.

I'm not, goddamn it.

Bloor took up the cake of chalk from the table and turned it in his hands. You should've said something before now.

I expect so, Lewis said. But there's the goddamn joy of this, the goddamn joy of that. I just don't figure I've ever found any goddamn joy in anything. It isn't often I get what I want, but I figured I had to try.

I'll go to therapy. I'll use less chalk and we can talk more about what you like. We can do what we did tonight as often as you want.

I'm goin, Steven. You ought to go too. You ought to go back to Missoula or goddamn Tacoma or wherever the hell you come from. I don't care.

Bloor slid from the couch to his knees. He laid his head in her lap and sobbed. The nightgown cinched up around his hips. A ridge of spine disappeared into the hairless crack of his pale backside. I wish you'd stop being so mean, he said. Koojee. I have anxiety.

Whatever word you want to call it is fine, Lewis said. You're still just a person I don't much want to be around. I'm sorry you're this way. But I just don't care enough to help you.

What about Jill?

Lewis said nothing.

You know, she's come to think of you as family, Bloor said. I don't want to give you the impression that she's slow, but—

Lewis put up a hand, then she touched the man's head and stroked a length of golden hair.

Bloor wiped his face and rubbed together his chalked hands. I was in a bad way before I came up here, he said. Did you know I was on hiatus with the department?

Get up off the goddamn floor.

John called me up and said he had a job for me up in the mountains. I took it so that I could get away from my anxiety and come up here to find some healing. Then I met you and I didn't want to leave. I don't want to leave now, Ranger Lewis.

Lewis rolled her eyes and sucked the merlot from her teeth and burped up some sick in her mouth. She swallowed it and stood up and said looking down at the man: Goddamn Mrs. Waldrip would've been better off crashin into any other mountain range in the country. When you get up off the goddamn floor tell Jill goodbye for me.

Lewis walked out the door and drove the Wagoneer back to her pinewood cabin. She parked in the driveway and sat there in her seat. It was late but the lights were on in the blue-washed cabin next door and Claude let out the old dog into the woods. He did not see Lewis in the dark while he waited. After a while he let the old dog back inside and went in after it. Lewis leaned the seat back and fell asleep.

* * *

She woke to tapping on the driver's side window and opened her eyes. The sun backlit a thin figure outside. She brought up her seat and cranked down the glass and shaded her brow and peered out. Jill slouched there with luggage and the bronze of the eagle belted to a suitcase.

Jill?

It's me. My dad left. He's going back to Missoula and then Tacoma.

Lewis smacked dryly her purpled mouth and pulled herself up by the wheel. Goddamn.

I decided to stay.

You got any water on you?

No.

What'd he say?

He said you didn't want to see us anymore and we had to go home.

Lewis looked at the girl.

He said we had wasted too much time on this haunted mountain already and it wasn't good for me anymore.

What'd you say?

That I'm an adult and I would decide myself what was good for me and where I would waste my time. I'm eighteen now. Now everyone has to respect that I mean what I say.

The girl told Lewis that she would like to stay with her until she had decided where she wanted to go. Lewis shook the empty thermos over her tongue and tossed it in the backseat. She blinked a few times at the girl and told her that the offer of the spare room still stood.

He doesn't want to see you again, Jill said. He said you're a dangerous and distorted woman.

I can understand why he'd say somethin like that.

Why are you sleeping in your car?

Lewis rubbed her face and opened the door and stood from the Wagoneer. She leaned against it and vomited in the shade of it on the gravel. I got carried away last night.

He was angry, the girl said. He didn't think you would take me when he dropped me off, so he gave me money for a bus ticket home. Then he threw that gross thing out the truck window.

Lewis righted herself and wiped her mouth and looked to where the girl pointed. Cat bones and garbage gleamed on the road. A halved tennis ball lay next to the busted skull of a bobcat, and a foul uniform fluttered in a heap. Lewis squinted at the sun burning in the trees and on the granite. She pulled her campaign hat from the Wagoneer and put it atop her head.

All right. We're late for the station.

I was to call that little hut home for just shy a month. The man and I suppered together there every evening and there we slept just a couple yards apart every night. I put in a good deal of my spare time telling him stories by the skulled light of that pine-knot lantern. I called him Garland. We became quite the companions.

We had our share of little adventures too. One evening we had a tussle with a black bear cub that had climbed down a finger of the dead white pine and fallen through the roof. As the expression goes, it was more afraid of us than we were of it. Still it did give us a mighty powerful start and I chucked my supper at it. The man gave it some good whacks with a rolled-up issue of *National Geographic* he had said he had read cover to cover well over a million times and chased it out. We sat up for a spell that night waiting for the mama bear to come for her vengeance, but thank goodness she never did.

Another night after we had finished up supper, some strange doleful racket occurred in the dark outside. The noises were passionate and I was sure they belonged to a woman. I had heard them before, when I had come across that vacant blue tent in the woods. We sat and listened to them for a good long while, hoping it was only the wind in the trees. Before long the man gathered his courage and went out with the axe and his spey blade unsheathed to see what was going on. He was gone for about half an hour and when he returned he was the color of sea water and shivering. The noises did not quit until just before dawn. He did not tell me what he had seen.

Most nights we sat by the stove and I told him stories about Clarendon and Mr. Waldrip. I told him about growing up in the country in the old days, about how I had lived through two world wars, the first of which I can scarcely recall, being that I was not but three years old when Father went off to France and fought the Germans under General Pershing and came home with a wrinkly right hand that could not make a fist. I told him about the rations and the rubber drives during the Second World War, and about how Mr. Waldrip had been 4-F on account of his poor eyesight, and how he had lost in the invasion of Normandy a distasteful cousin who beat up on his wife but was memorialized as a fallen hero all the same. I told him about how I had taught at Clarendon Elementary and then was the school's librarian for over forty years, and about how I had dearly hoped to have children of my own but none had come to me, and about First Methodist and the pastors we had had over the years, including Pastor Jacob, who had renounced the church and wedded his Mexican housekeeper in an agnostic ceremony in El Paso.

My companion was not a loquacious man and he told me very little about himself. I am a notorious chatterbox and he would steer the conversations away from himself and let me go on and on until I found a natural end. I did however learn that he was born someplace in the east of the continent and that he had traveled around the world with his mother since he was eight years old and had lived for a brief time in Germany. Despite that, he came from very little money and never knew the name nor origin of his father.

His mother was apparently one of these restless women who saw no need for a husband and was, as he put it, always searching for affection from strangers. He said she would keep the local bars until they shut and she never spent a night at home if she could help it. To hear him tell it she was a pretty good narcissist. When she showed him any motherly care at all, he said, it was on account of she was seeing him as an extension of herself at the time. But being that they had often lived out in the country, he had passed much of his leisure time outdoors and had liked to go off on his own and hunt or fish. He turned out a very able outdoorsman.

He also told me a pitiful story that no doubt many of my readers will find relevant. I do not include it here to suggest anything about his character in particular, save that he told it to me and I felt sorry for him. Along sometime in his boyhood years he lived across the street from a pretty young girl who had immigrated from Bulgaria. She was in the class ahead of him and he would see her in the halls of their schoolhouse. Well, one day after school this girl approached him and invited him to a county fair. They went together and he bought her some ice cream. It was there that she took him aside and held her mouth an inch from his and taunted him something terrible about how she knew he wanted to kiss her. She called him a little pussy boy and said to him that she would never kiss him, not in a million years. He said that all he was able to do was to smell the sugar on her breath and be satisfied best he could with that.

I suppose people tell stories partly because we can tell them over and over again. You can get mighty familiar with a story and know it inside and out, front to back. But while a story has something of the true world to it, mostly it does not. You can get a handle on a story. I hold that much of what confounds young people today is that they can seldom discern the difference between a narrative and the actual events of the natural world. However if you pay close enough attention before long in your years you come to learn that there is no retelling a life and it is by your own secret hand that you are the author of your own demise. In life, no choice is made without it comes to an irrevocable end.

I believe the date of the fire was November 5th. The weather was mighty fine and the sun was out and I spent the day by the creek. A fall chill was in the air but there was plenty of sun to keep it off. I sat on my favorite rock and plaited reeds for no particular purpose while the man checked his traps and deadfalls he had set on the other side of the creek. He was sidewinding away down the gulch until he appeared to be no more than another little old shrub or stone on the floodplain. He had said he was getting us ready for the winter. By and large it was much the same as any other day out there. When he came back he was toting a mangled badger by the tail. The poor animal was old and drooling blood from a withered gray snout. I pulled some cattails to stew with it.

That night the sun set earlier than it had yet out there and I recall remarking that fall was sure deep upon us now. The man cleaned the badger outside the hut by the light of the pine-knot lantern and I built up the fire in the stove and listened to the poor creature's innards falling and sticking in the grass. I peeked out from behind the old sheet we used for a door as he worked the animal with the spey blade. A gust kicked up and filled his long hair and blue coat such that he looked like a man from an older time, out of an age past when the wind blew from uncharted territories and languages had fewer words.

He brought in the cleaned badger and set about cutting it up. He said: Do you know what I was just thinking about out there?

No, I said. What was it? I had not wanted to seem too eager, but it was unusual for him to offer any conversation.

I was thinking it'd be great if I could change my appearance whenever I wanted. I could be somebody else. I could have a different life every day. One day I'd turn into a beautiful woman and head out in the big city and see what that was like. Or another day I'd turn into just a regular guy in high school and go to a school dance. Or I'd be a child and go see a movie and meet some people there. Another day I could be a white man with green eyes on the beach, another I could be a black woman with brown eyes. Could be anything.

I had some questions. Would only your appearance change? I asked him. Would you change? Would you be obliged to act differently, being that I suppose you would not truly be any of these people?

Once you look a certain way, he said, you don't have to act too much to be what everybody else tells you you already are.

I asked him why he wanted this shape-shifting ability.

He quit cutting up the badger. He got a scrap of cloth and wiped the blood from his hands and said: Some people're granted access to experiences others aren't. I want to experience as many of them as I can. And I kind of always just thought that whatever I was, I was too many things for anybody to accept that they could all belong in one person. Do you know what I mean? For example, I knew a man back home who said sometimes he felt like he was a woman. Most people just want you to be one thing and won't allow you to be anything else. I guess it's easier that way for them.

We had our supper and went to sleep. In the night the wind came up again and blew in cold through the chinks in the hut and woke me. The man slept curled up on his pallet. I tucked Erasmus's fur around my neck and turned to the stove and built up the fire. I warmed myself, listening to the wind, and soon I was back asleep.

I woke up again in the night, this time not for the cold but for the intense heat. Gracious, it was like the Texas sun on my face. I opened my eyes and above me churned an immense vortex of smoke and flame!

Fire! I mean to tell you I could not see a thing past it. I coughed like a steam engine and covered my face with my hands. I endeavored to holler out for my friend but all I could manage to do was cough.

I heard him hollering my name over the noise of the conflagration. Mrs. Waldrip! Mrs. Waldrip!

I spun about and looked for him in the chaos. My dear, I could not see him!

Suddenly he burst from the fire, swaddled in flame and smoking like some birth of damnation, hollering out in pain. He rolled me in Terry's coat and a blanket and swept me up in his arms, then he carried me out like a child. Cool air was on my face and the wind blew away the heat.

With my eyes closed I lay on my back in the grass. I had a tough time catching my breath.

There was a thud. I opened my eyes, still coughing something terrible. The hut was swallowed up in an enormous fire and great licks of flame jumped all around it like the mad worship of the Pentecostal. The white pine, also ablaze, burned amid the dark like a great bright hand of fire, at once so terrifically beautiful and awful it was like it were the authentic hand of God. I suppose that is the fantasy of a guilty mind. I worry that if I had not put more wood in the stove that night, the conflagration might not have caught and some things might be different now. However I have come to understand that a mighty good deal of life is learning how to abstract guilt to some other notion that will not bother you so much you cannot go on.

I put my hands over my body. Miraculously I seemed to be unhurt. I looked for my friend. He was on his back next to me. His face was black and bunched up in a terrible grimace like an old plum. His clothes smoked and a leg of his blue jeans had burned away and lines of embers yet chased the cloth. This exposed the burnt-black flesh below his knee, which brought to mind the way Mr. Waldrip used to enjoy his bacon.

I jumped up and put out the embers on him with my hands.

He groaned. His eyes were still shut when he asked if I was all right.

I told him that I was fine and asked how he felt.

Not so good, he said.

Your leg is badly burned.

That's what it feels like.

I told him that I would return. He only grunted. I hurried to the creek and felt around in the dark for the old plastic bucket we kept there. When I found it I filled it up and brought it back to him and I poured the water out over his legs and then his face and washed away the soot. He moaned again and then he was unconscious. I put my head to his chest and listened to his breathing and the slow pump of his heart. I lay awake like that the rest of the night until sunrise, listening to him breathe, and was kept warm by the hut and the white pine burning all around me, hot as the hinges of hell.

The fire burned on into morning. I remember well the paling of it as the sun rose over the mountains and touched the gray ash and the column of smoke. The five-fingered white pine reached up, black and smoking and cracked with veins of dying fire like a piece leftover of a storybook giant's cremains. The grass was dewed that morning and it was mighty cold, and I huddled up with the man close as I dared to the dwindling fire. Both of us were white with ash like a pair of spirits. I kept a finger on his pulse.

When he finally regained consciousness he sat up to look at his leg. It was a gruesome mess. The flesh was bubbled up with welts and sores and crystalline polyps and it glittered and glowed such as a kind of rare rock formation I had seen with Mr. Waldrip at the Panhandle Plains Museum. The man shook his head and lay back in the grass.

I asked how he was feeling and he said that he would be all right.

I recalled that Grandma Blackmore used to make a poultice of dryweed and mallow root when Davy would scrape up his knees. I told the man that I would go into the woods and find some to make my own.

You'll just get lost, and then where would we be? After all this. No, I'll just take some water, please.

I went to the creek and filled the bucket again and brought it back. He grabbed ahold of it and I helped him drink.

I told him that he had saved me again. He said nothing.

Well, not to worry, I said. I am going to get you fixed up.

I went to the smoldering heap under the pine, where there remained only heat and scarcely any flames, and I turned up a stick and skimmed through the ash with it where I assumed his pallet had been. The ash blew up in my face. Finally I turned up what I was looking for and kicked the knife from the fire. The fine oak handle had burned away and the blade and ornamented scabbard were all that was left. Once the blade had cooled enough I used it to cut away the man's blue jeans. His was the first male sex organ to which I had been exposed since I had seen those of Mr. Waldrip and the vulgar homeless man who hides in the crates by the grocery store. At the time I did not think much on it, but I suppose it is only fitting that I should have seen my friend naked being that he had seen me in my birthday suit too. I covered him with the blanket we had saved from the fire.

The rest of that day I spent giving him drinks of water and watching what was left of the pine burn down. When it had, I set about tossing on any wood I could find to keep the fire going for nightfall.

The grim figure of a small man strolled bandylegged on the side of the road. Lewis's headlights reached him in the falling murk and she saw that it was Pete. The video camera hung from his neck and he was capped still with the bloodstained coif. He waved his arms. Lewis pulled the Wagoneer over to the shoulder of asphalt at the overlook where he had stopped. She cranked down her window. Coin-operated viewers leaned bent and vandalized with crude symbols and female nudity beyond a shot-up wooden sign which hardly yet read *US Forest Service Black Grass Vista.* The mountain range blazed red in sundown.

Evenin, Ranger Lewis. I was lookin for you.

What is it, Pete?

Officer Bloor leavin this mornin got me to thinkin. I've decided I'll be goin back home end of the week.

Had enough?

Heart's on the mend and I reckon it's just about time to get back to normal.

Best of luck.

Thank you, Ranger Lewis.

She looked at the man, waiting. There anything else? I'm supposed to be pickin up some cigarettes for Jill before the Penguin closes.

I just wanted to give you somethin. Now, I'll be honest with you, at first I thought about turnin this over to the authorities, or to Officer Bloor. I weren't sure if it were rightful or not. Koojee.

Don't use that goddamn word, Pete. It's not a real word.

It's not?

Goddamn it, Pete, it's been a long day.

Pete brought out from the back of his belt a video cassette. That night we were out in that shelter I got spooked, so I was up takin pictures, waitin for Claudey's one-eyed sex ghost to show her face. But this camera seems to harbor a mind of its own. Pete held out the cassette to the open window.

Lewis turned the engine off and took the cassette. She held it and turned it over. What d'you mean?

You and Jill cuddlin together in that bottom bunk.

I don't know what you're talkin about.

I got it on tape. It looked like you guys have somethin more between you than what an average fella's likely to notice. Couldn't see much on the tape cause it was dark, but I got enough. I got you givin her a kiss while she was sleepin.

Lewis looked hard at the small man. What in the hell're you suggestin?

Pete shook his head. I've been workin real hard to be honest with my heart up here. It's the reason I came up to stay with old Claudey, even if he's popped his noodle a bit. You got to work on yourself and find out who you are to know what you want, or else you're liable to end up a real scary example of yourself and do somethin bad to yourself or somebody else just happens to be there. Ain't no need to pretend to be somebody else with me, Ranger Lewis. I ain't no judge.

Lewis grabbed the thermos from the passenger's seat and drank. Goddamn it, what do you want from me, you goddamn goofball?

Don't get me wrong, Ranger Lewis, Pete said. I don't want nothin. Didn't get any footage of any special rare sex ghost or anythin like that while I been up here but I got this, and it sure seems rare enough. And like I said, I didn't know what to make of it at first. You both bein female and bein she's only seventeen and a subordinate in your volunteer program.

She's eighteen.

Ain't she just turned it yesterday?

Yes.

Still there's got to be a kind of power imbalance there. Anyway, then I watched the tape over a few more times and I got to thinkin you guys didn't look all that bad. Like it weren't wrong you were touchin her and you were both female and she was young and in your care. And there's always some power thing, ain't there? Don't matter who it is. Don't matter when it is. Don't matter how old anybody is. Somebody's got the upper hand.

I've never had the upper hand, Lewis said.

Point is, this sure didn't look like somethin bad was goin on, or somethin without heart. Hell, if you got some pictures of the way me and my wife used to look together you'd say better stone those two dead fore there's another second shared between them, fore they ail the rest of us with their ignorance of love. Watchin you guys in the station today, I can tell you got her best interest at heart. So what I'm tryin to say is thank you, Ranger Lewis. Thank you for showin me somethin real nice.

Lewis looked down at the cassette and turned it over again. She shook it. Did you show this to Claude?

No, ma'am.

Tell him about it? Tell anybody about it?

No, ma'am, I reckoned it weren't my place.

She looked at Pete through the open window. He hunched with his hands in his coat pockets. Lewis shook her head. Leave it to a goddamn man to think he's surrounded by lesbians.

Pete smiled and put a hand to his pigeon chest. I sure do appreciate you lettin me in the volunteer program, Ranger Lewis. It's been a few months of the best therapy a man like me could ask for. Turns out I'm sexually frustrated and I hate women. That's only cause I don't have any real respect for myself, but I'd like to think there's hope for me yet. I know I'm a strange bird, but I'm pretty sure I ain't a bad one.

No, you're not a bad one, Pete.

Their headlights lit up the rotted wood sign at the trailhead: *Egyptian Point*. Lewis put the Wagoneer into park and stopped the engine. She cut off the headlights and all was dark. From the passenger's seat Jill's smoke scattered blue under the moon. The girl opened the door and climbed out and took with her a bottle of merlot from the backseat.

They made the trail to Egyptian Point. Lewis passed uneven before them a flashlight and spat to the wayside. They came to the clearing and there was no fire in the pit. There was no wind and it was quiet. All they could see was the moon above and the outlines of tall figures made of candle wax and merlot bottles with long wrists of electrical wire and soup bowls for breasts. One of the figures wore an old campaign hat Lewis recognized and the other held a karaoke microphone plugged into its rectum.

Goddamn it, Maggie.

Jill sat on one of the logs angled around the pit. She smoked another cigarette and held the bottle of merlot between her small knees and uncorked it with a corkscrew she had brought from the Wagoneer. Lewis dragged to the center of the pit some cordwood from a nearby stack. She took a squeeze bottle of lighter fluid from her coat pocket and doused the logs. She dropped a match in them and caught her trouser leg on fire and stamped it out in the dirt. Firelight fell about and lit the scarred face of the girl where she sat, watching.

Lewis sat next to her and took the bottle of merlot. She drank and said, I'm goddamn sorry.

Why?

I expect your dad leavin this mornin was difficult.

Jill took back the bottle and drank. No relationship is a citadel. They're all tents.

Lewis studied the girl. Goddamn it, your dad really has you figured all wrong.

Together they drank off the bottle of merlot and Lewis drank what was left in the thermos. She took from a coat pocket the cassette Pete had given her. She shook it once and tossed it on the fire.

What was that? Jill said.

Nothin, Lewis said.

They watched the cassette melt down through the logs under an acrid smoke.

From the trail came the racket of hikers and Lewis laid a hand on the butt of the revolver at her hip. There came the three young men they had seen before in front of the Crystal Penguin. One of them wore a turtleneck and cradled a box of beer. The skinny mohawked boy led the group into the light of the fire, his round glasses as opaque as two silver coins.

You ladies enjoyin your evenin? he said. The jewelry in his tongue flashed.

Lewis stood and brushed off her trousers. You boys aren't allowed up here. I figure you know that.

What about you?

I'm a goddamn ranger in the United States Forest Service.

The one in the turtleneck nodded at Jill. Well who's she? She ain't no tree cop.

You don't need to know who she is, Lewis said. If you don't head back, I'll write some goddamn tickets.

The mohawked boy slunk to the other side of the fire and perched on a log. The two other boys joined him on either side. The fire was the only sound and light, and the wind was calm and the wood burned slow. The boys opened cans of beer from the box. The mohawked boy unzipped a large bag and took from it a sandwich bag and a mantel clock of dark wood inlaid with gold.

My mom's clock, said the boy.

She died, another said, and he held up the sandwich bag. We're comin up here, to this place, to sprankle out her ashes in honor of her memories.

The mohawked boy placed the clock on a stump next to him and all of them went quiet for a moment to listen to the loud tick and tock count the whip of the fire. When my dad and her were my age, he said, they'd scratched their names on that big junky rock right over there looks like a vulva. I knowed her clock'd be better off up here in that spot right there than back in my trailer. It'd look out of place with me in my trailer.

The weather'll ruin it up here, Lewis said.

That's all right. Everything ruins everything else, don't it?

Lewis spat in the fire. I'm sorry about your goddamn mom, she said, then she told them that she would allow them to scatter the ashes and have a brief memorial, but then they would need to be on their way.

The boys mumbled to each other and rose from the logs with their cans of beer like they were marionettes strung on the moon. The mohawked boy took the sandwich bag and stood out on a far ledge over the expanse below and opened it and shook it out by the corners into the windless dark. He strolled back to his companions, his shirt and trousers grayly dusted and his eyes unseen for the reflections in his glasses. Each of the other two boys touched a shoulder of his and sucked from their cans.

All right, Lewis said.

The mohawked boy nodded and took up the clock from the stump and placed it high in the hollow of a wide rock face under his parents' names. He turned back and hung the empty bag off a shoulder and went away down the path. The other boys were slow to follow and the one in the turtleneck knelt to get the box of beer.

You're goin to have to leave those, Lewis said.

Why's that?

Can't have alcohol on goddamn state property. I ought to give you goofballs tickets. Just let them be. I'll dispose of them.

I bet you dispose of them, all right, the other one said. Like you're disposin of that wine.

You're a real dirty tree cop, I hope you know that, said the other. Abusin your power and takin advantage of us cause we don't have the heart to argue with a shitty old woman.

She's thirty-seven, Jill said.

A really dirty tree cop, a real sad old lesbo, said the one in the turtleneck. I hope that hermaphrodite ghost gums you to death and steals your soul to Neptune.

Lewis told them again to get and they looked at each other and then at Jill and they set off dragging their feet down the trail after their mohawked companion.

Lewis stood and stumbled at an angle to the box of beer and hauled it over to where Jill sat on the other side of the fire. She opened a can and handed it to the girl, then opened one for herself and raised it. To us, she said.

She sat beside Jill on the log and they drank can after can.

Don't believe that nonsense about Cornelia, Lewis said. Goddamn people're hell of a lot scarier than stories. I'll keep you safe from it all.

You want to keep me safe?

Course I do.

Why?

Lewis slid from the log and lay in the warm dirt before the fire. She lifted her boot from where she lay and crushed an empty can and chucked it drunkenly to the pit. I figure I'd like to find out what kind of woman you grow up to be, she said.

I'll be this size until I die.

You're not goin to die. By the time you're my age they'll have a goddamn pill to help with that.

With dying?

Maybe it'll even make you young again. We'll just have a country full of immortal teenagers.

Jill crawled from the log and lay down beside Lewis. I do not want to die.

I won't let you, Lewis said. I won't let you stop callin, stop keepin in touch. And I won't let you die. We're goin to always know each other.

Jill made a sound and Lewis figured it was a laugh. We will do our best, Jill said.

Lewis rolled over onto her side and looked at the girl. She put a hand to her cheek and traced a thumb over the scars that mapped the girl's face. Jill leaned in and touched her lips to Lewis's chin. Lewis moved and brought their lips together. The clock in the rock face knocked out a rhythm and the two of them lay together close to the fire under their coats.

Lewis awoke in the dark. The fire pit smoldered under blackened cans and the wine bottle. The mantel clock chimed 5:00 a.m. The wax figures stood over her. From the trees came a moaning that then died away. Lewis leaned up on her elbows in the dirt and squinted at her hands by the glow of the embers. Red ants scaled her fingers. A fat one stung her and she flicked it away. The moaning started again and the trees swayed in shadow. Black nightbirds flew against them and the blacker mountains.

Goddamn it. Who's there?

Lewis pushed herself up slowly to her feet and stood there undulating as if she were in a canoe. She reached for the revolver and unbuttoned the holster. The moaning grew louder and a rock flew out from the trees and missed her. She drew the revolver and aimed at the trees and fell over.

The moaning stopped. She waited. Nothing followed.

She heard the girl crying and looked around. Jill's head was out from under the gray coat covering her and she shivered in the dirt. Ants roamed her face and struggled in her curls. Lewis holstered the revolver and leaned over her. She brushed the ants away and touched the girl on the shoulder and shook her awake.

The girl quit crying and sat up. Red welts had spread across her cheeks and lips. She blinked wearily and wiped her swollen mouth. What is this?

We dozed off on a goddamn anthill.

Jill said she was cold and did not feel good and asked if they could leave.

Lewis flashlit the way and they staggered down to the trailhead and found the Wagoneer. Keyed into the driver's side door were the letters *L E Z*.

Lewis snaked down the mountain road, leaning forward and squeezing the wheel. She pulled over on the way and Jill vomited from the open passenger's door into wildflowers growing from the pavement. Lewis vomited from the driver's side.

Half an hour later they got to the pinewood cabin and Jill had fallen back asleep. Lewis parked and went around to the passenger's door and opened it and hoisted the girl into her arms. She lumbered with her across the driveway and nearly tripped over the nose of the doe head she had buried there. Its worn face peered glassily up at her from between her boots, partly unearthed in the gravel. She went on and caught with one finger the door handle and carried the girl inside. The living room was dark and Lewis lowered Jill onto the couch. The girl stirred but did not wake. Lewis watched her sleep by the new light of dawn coming in the kitchen window.

Soon the girl woke and sat up and cried into her palms.

What's wrong?

I want to go home.

I thought you wanted to stay with me.

Can I call my dad and have him come get me?

Lewis knelt before her. I thought you wanted to stay here.

The girl quit crying and dried her eyes with the sleeve of her sweatshirt. She tipped up her marked and scarred face and looked at Lewis and said in her bizarre way of speaking: Do you think we all victimize each other without even knowing it?

Goddamn it. I don't know.

I kept hearing that clock last night and I thought about the old lady.

Cloris Waldrip?

She lost her husband. I think it would take another lifetime to get over someone that you had already spent a lifetime with. She never had enough time. Do you think it's cruel to make yourself stay with someone for that long?

I don't know, Jill. I don't want you to go.

I think it's cruel for me to stay with you on this mountain.

We can go somewhere else, Lewis said. Let's go to Tokyo.

Jill swatted at nothing and placed her small hands on Lewis's cheeks and squeezed her face and held it there. I want you to understand me, she said. You were my age when I was born. I'll be your age in the year 2005. Things will be different then.

I know that.

Some people the years don't weather them, but they have weathered you.

It's the age difference. You think of me as a mother.

I guess I've lived a sheltered life. And I'm still young. I'll be someone else in a few years' time. I want to be someone else in a few years' time.

I expect that's only natural, Lewis said between the girl's hands. But I don't know what you want me to do. What do you want me to do?

My parents told me I was born with my face like this, the girl said. But I know what really happened. Everyone gets changed from the very beginning. We're all changing each other all the time. You have concerns that are beyond my experience. I'm not desperate yet. I haven't found desperation like you have. And I'm glad for that. But when I do find it, and I know someday that I will, I hope to have the decency to be afraid of what it will do to others.

Lewis took the girl's hands from her face and held them by the wrists. Goddamn it, Jill. Your goddamn dad sure doesn't give you enough credit.

Jill moved from the couch to the floor and wrapped her arms around Lewis's waist. Lewis put her arms around the girl and smelled the top of her head and they held each other there until the sun was up.

I do not allow that anyone can truly know another person through and through. I knew Mr. Waldrip better than anyone, but did you know that after my ordeal in the Bitterroot I discovered that he had been writing letters to a woman in Little Rock, Arkansas? Our will and testament had provided for our belongings and remaining assets to go to First Methodist, and when Mr. Waldrip and myself were declared dead in absentia, my dear friend Sara Mae Davis volunteered to take a hand in the great effort of sorting through it all. Not only that, but I understand she and her nephew were kind enough to lay a final resting place for our poor cat Trixie, under the crabapple tree in our backyard. As I had feared, Trixie did not survive our absence. I was told she was found atop the credenza. Anyhow, while Sara Mae was clearing out Mr. Waldrip's desk in his study these letters from Arkansas turned up and once she had read them she decided to keep them. I will not put the Arkansas woman's name down here. I see no reason to draw her out into the light for this, for I believe she is a married woman if she is still living as I write.

From what I can tell Mr. Waldrip must have come across her advertisement in the classifieds in the back of a Little Rock newspaper after having gone there to look at some cattle in 1965. He would have been fifty-three then. I know some young people have pen pals in the Internet these days. Back then we used paper. Some of you may not believe me, but I tell you the letters did not upset me. I believe I have read them all and I cannot be certain if they ever did meet in person or not. That does not matter much to me. But there it was. Mr. Waldrip wrote to another woman and by the way she wrote him back it would appear that he had great affection for her. He would have been mighty embarrassed to know Sara Mae had read them.

At the heart of it I suppose I knew Mr. Waldrip well enough to know that he was the kindest, most decent man I could ever have hoped to marry. I love him and miss him very much. He was a powerful sweet man and this woman must have done something to earn these affections from him and I hold no ill will for her.

I understand now that most of us are much more complicated people than we care to let on. We all have our separate lives and I do not allow that there is a person alive out there who does not have at least one secret they will endeavor to take with them to the grave. I imagine most everyone has at least one locked door in their heart to which they alone keep the key. Perhaps we are all our own lonely bedrooms. And as thoroughly as I have bared myself in this account, I know there are some things I will just have to keep to myself.

The day after the hut burned down I poked around through the ashes and turned up the old olive can to boil water in. I took an hour or so and built up the makings for a fire and set it with embers dug up from the debris. I boiled water from the creek and gave it to the man. He drank it and did not speak. He had his back to a boulder under a big tree. Most of the time he just watched the sky.

We spent two nights out in the open like that. Thank goodness it did not rain. We were both mighty hungry and I did not sleep much at all on account of the cold and I had to be vigilant about the fire so that it would not go out.

The man's leg worsened. It changed colors and gave off an odor like that of Catherine Drewer's horrible mushroom casseroles. Gracious, that woman never could discern sugar from salt or etiquette from honesty. In time it also seemed she could not tell perfume from cat urine.

The man's traps and snares were set a considerable distance away and I did not dare find them on my own, being disguised as they were, and being that I had not heard the cry of any poor critter, I imagined they were empty anyway. On the second day I endeavored to catch some fish for us. His tackle box had burnt up in the fire, so I fastened the spey blade of his knife to the end of a branch and set about using it for a spear. The man kept watch over me from under his tree, out of the sun. I jabbed at fish after fish in the creek for a good couple of hours and believe it or not at last I stuck a slow and backwards-looking mudfish plumb through the middle and flung it from the water! I was mighty proud of myself. I cleaned and cooked that mudfish over the fire. The innards hissed and burned up in a black smoke. We had our supper in the late afternoon. My friend did not eat much. We also had some cattails.

Often in the night when he thought I was asleep I would hear him groan and sit up and drag himself out behind the big boulder to relieve himself. On the second night I heard him trying to bawl quietly. It is no common sound to hear a man bawl to himself in the dark when he imagines no one can hear him. It is an awful sound of misery and I do not rightly know what to compare it with. I did not let on that I was awake or get up to comfort him. I suppose I knew it would embarrass him too greatly and make matters worse than they already were.

On the third day after the fire, on what I believe would be the 8th of November, the man started a fever. He glowed all over with sweat and he did not speak and often partly shut his eyes. He had a bad pond-water color to his face and his lips split and bled. I knew that I had to do something or he was going to meet the end in no time at all.

That sundown, as purple snow blew from the tallest peak in the range, I got it into my mind that I would get him down that mountain myself and get him to a doctor. I did not know how I was going to do it yet, but I had decided that would not stop me. I went to him before dark while his eyes were shut and whispered in his ear: I am going to get you to safety, Garland.

Lewis goose-stepped over hedges and a low bulwark of schist out to the forest behind her pinewood cabin. For ballast she swung waistlevel a heavy bottle of merlot and murmured angrily to herself about a mousy-voiced girl who had phoned into *Ask Dr. Howe How* about dreams she had been having of her grandfather's knees. Her mouth was darkly smeared like a jester's and her hair was tangled under a sideways campaign hat. She soon came to an overlook of granite above the gray wilderness and she sat there and watched the night fall. When it was dark and she had finished the bottle she chucked it off the mountain and could not see where it broke.

She felt her coat for a flashlight, but she must have left it back at the cabin. She sat in the dark and pouted and whimpered, and she lay back on the granite slab and figured she would never again hear from Jill Bloor. She recalled the way Jill had looked getting in her father's black truck the previous afternoon when he had picked her up in front of the pinewood cabin. Bloor had not gotten out. The last thing Lewis saw of the girl was the cigarette smoke blowing out the passenger's window as they drove off.

She sat up now and started back for the cabin. Clouds covered the moon. Small and dim through the trees she could just make out the deck light she had left on. She had not taken but a couple of steps when there sounded a sourceless and low tone and she stopped. It recalled to her an old oscillating belt fan that had sat on her father's desk for years issuing a dissonance only he could tolerate.

The tone stopped all at once and the forest was silent again and then came the moaning she had heard before, plaintive and sexual. To her left there was the shuffling of feet. Lewis twitched and unbuttoned the holster she wore and drew the revolver and braced her back to a tree. She raised the revolver and shook it outheld.

Who's there?

There was no answer and something neared.

Who's there, goddamn it? I am a Forest Ranger. I'm armed.

No answer.

If you're anybody but goddamn Cloris Waldrip, you step back and go on.

The body in the trees quickened its pace and Lewis lined up the front sight with a dark place between two pines. A tiny globe glinted there like a lone eye. She began to sob in a manner she had not since she was a child.

Goddamn it, get it over with and have me, you goddamn goofball.

From the trees the dark figure came bounding. Lewis bellowed the Lord's name in vain and fired all five rounds in the cylinder.

The forest was darkest after the muzzle flash. Her ears buzzed.

She sat down deaf and blind and caught her breath in the powder smoke. She lowered the revolver. She sat a minute and pushed herself from the ground and steadied herself by the bough of a pine. The clouds had blown off and the moon stuck in the fog and the powder smoke.

Lewis wiped her eyes with a sleeve and said hello to the dark place.

No answer.

When she flipped open the cylinder it burned her thumb. She jammed the ejector with her palm and let the casings fall over her boots. She reached around and punched free from her belt five cartridges and loaded them and closed the wheel against her trouser leg. She crept forward and let her eyes adjust to the moonlight. She watched the ground.

She stopped.

The dog was sprawled on its side, a pink tongue unraveled from its mouth. Black blood slicked the pine needles and pooled low places in the mud.

Goddamn it, she said. She knelt down and nudged the dog with the barrel of the pistol. She squinted and saw its skull was opened. Goddamn it. She took hold of the collar and turned it around the neck and angled the bloodwet heart-shaped tag to the moonlight. The light glanced across the name *Charlie.*

Lewis shook her head and slumped back to the ground. She wiped on a trouser leg the blood and hair from her hand.

Every fall the ladies at First Methodist would get together once a week in the basement of the church house and sew quilts for the indigent and discuss scripture and the weekly gossip. During that time I learned to quilt very well. I will also tell you that I know how to fix a strong plait.

I used to plait the dark hair of a nervous little girl I had in my class prior to taking the position of librarian. Plaiting her hair was the only way to get her to hold still long enough for me to read aloud from *Little Women* or *The Adventures of Huckleberry Finn*. She was a gorgeous fidgety thing. Gracious, how envious I was of her dodo-bird mother when the awful woman would collect her at the end of the day, smoking a nasty cigarette and scowling at her children like they were incalculable evil. I took the position of librarian in part because students like this little girl had become an unfortunate reminder that I could not have children of my own and, as I have mentioned here before, I was mighty disappointed about that at the time. We once took it in our minds to adopt, but it was not a common practice then in Clarendon and the process was overly difficult and required much more money than we had at the time.

All of which is to say that when I woke up out there in the Bitterroot on what I count to be the 9th of November I was up with an idea. I salvaged all that I could that had not burned up in the fire and I set about building a raft. I plaited reeds and cattails and used them to cinch together odd lengths of pine into a lattice about the size of a large mattress. Then I used the reeds and the spey blade and quilted together charred pieces of blankets and covered the topside of my strange vessel. It was most troublesome and awkward work but I stayed after it and by sunset I had finished. The raft did not look nice, but I hoped it would float. I imagine that many of you will not find it likely that a little old woman could hope to get a fully grown man onto a crude raft and paddle him down a mountain creek to safety. But that is what I meant to do.

I will tell you about one summer when a heifer broke her hind legs in a cattle guard. Our ranch manager, Joe Flud, found her in the pasture. Joe was a diminutive man, but he was also clever and managed to fashion a makeshift hoist out of a fence post and a tarpaulin he had kept in the bed of his truck. He got the heifer back to the pens at headquarters by himself and made splints for the poor creature from a ladle and a spatula he had taken from his wife's kitchen. Cassidy was away visiting her folks at the time and Joe said she threw a fit when she came home to find her cutlery plastered to the hind legs of that heifer. But Joe saved that heifer and she eventually calved and brought a fair price at the feedlot. My thought was that if little Joe could rescue a heifer by himself with some ingenuity and steadfastness, I ought to be able to rescue this injured man who had done the same for me on so many occasions.

The man did not say much that day save to ask for water. He had gone from green to a terrible shade of orange and his breathing was like that of Judith Ellery, a lifelong smoker who had sat in the pew behind me at First Methodist for many years rattling like gravel caught in the wheel well of a truck. Then her breathing worsened and worsened until one Sunday she did not come to service. She was discovered by her deaf boy facedown in her parsley garden.

Before it was too dark I tugged the raft down a slope of slick mud and into the creek to see if it would float. It did, thank goodness! However I was not certain it would float the both of us. I pulled it back up onto the mud and collected all that I had salvaged. This included a lighter and one fire-starter stick and the ornate spey blade. I bundled it all up in a sheet and tied it down to the raft. I also tied down the long pine branch I had found to use for a kind of punting pole. I decided that we would leave the following morning.

That night I lay close to my friend with my back against him, watching the fire. I did not sleep much. Dawn came fast and cold and I zipped up Terry's coat and wrapped my hands with strips from a half-burned blanket so that I could better grip the pole in the chill. The sky was gray with skinny clouds and the birds did not want to sing.

By this pale light of dawn I woke him. We have to move you now, I said. We needed to get him onto the raft, I told him, and that I would support his weight and we could take it one step at a time to the creek.

He opened his eyes some but did not utter a word in response. I had left the raft only some yards from us on the side of the creek. He looked at it without moving his head and then used the spruce he was under to pull himself upright onto his good leg. He hollered out an awfully vile word and bunched up his face in pain. I was mighty sorry for him, but I never see a call for nasty language. He leaned on me and my walking stick and I counted out loud each step and bit by bit we hopped him over. He collapsed to the raft and cursed again. Pitiful tears ran off his cheeks. Once he had settled on his back and shut his eyes he was quiet again.

I got a good deep breath and with all my might I pushed that raft down the slope of mud. It took off with less effort than I had expected. I had not accounted for the man's weight. My gracious, did it take off! I chased after it best as an old woman could but it reached the water without me. He was pulled out to the current and I was not on the raft! I worried I had just sent this injured man on a lonesome boat ride for which he had not bargained. I took a couple of steps back and holding my walking stick I ran and made a jump for it. I flew and landed right on his leg and he gave a big yell! I slung my walking stick over and climbed aboard.

The weight was uneven and cold water sloshed over us. He fussed a bit and held his eyes shut. Out of breath, I told him that I was very sorry I had landed on his bad leg but that he should not worry and we would get him to a doctor in one piece. I situated myself between his legs and forward on the little raft until it balanced and was more or less level above the water.

At first the current was not strong and the raft went slow and was often stuck in the shallows. Often I had to nudge it free with the pole. After a spell the creek turned into a river and the gulch opened up into a great colorful valley of limestone and outcrops of pink granite. We had been blessed with an unusually warm day and the sun was out. We sailed along quicker then and the man slept and after a while we passed a place I recognized, the grave marker I had carved into the stump.

By and by the river wound down into the conifer woods. After going along peacefully through the pines for some time the current turned white and quick and roared over a bevy of jagged rocks. The little raft spun around! We were faced backwards and a pine log broke free from the starboard side. The man partly sank into the cold water and he grimaced and fussed but did not open his eyes. I feared we would capsize and drown. The water splashed in my face and got in my eyes. I wiped them and turned around and endeavored to see ahead. I was shivering something terrible. A little fall appeared ahead in the river. I was sure it would destroy our raft to go over it. I used my pole like a rudder to steer away to the riverbank.

I mean to tell you I maneuvered that little raft with all the strength I could muster. Suddenly I was not exhausted. My arthritis was gone. I have heard stories of women who perform incredible feats of strength beyond their abilities to protect their children. Not to suggest that I took the man for a son, but I had grown mighty fond of him. The physician here at River Bend Assisted Living, a kind and fastidious Oriental Indian man by the name of Dr. Laghari, has told me that I was using my adrenal glands in overtime. So, bless you, I was able to get us angled just right, and gritting my teeth, I sent us careening into the riverbank.

The pitiful little raft ran aground and I dug my heels in and with a last gift of strength I heaved the man up onto the bank of mud and rock and collapsed beside him. We lay there for a time shivering and soaked through, letting the warm sun dry us. We did not speak.

Dark was soon to be upon us, and I urged myself to get up. I set about building a fire. My hands shook so much it looked like I was endeavoring to play some difficult music on a make-believe piano. I got the fire going with the last fire-starter stick we had and the flip lighter. The night settled in cold and I cuddled up close by the man. His fever put out heat like a stove.

Morning came and I found my friend upright with his back to a pine and his legs stretched out. Poor dear, he had messed himself in the night and his blue jeans were black. I pretended not to notice. He was awake and his eyes were on the mountains.

I bade him good morning and sat up. How are you feeling? I asked him.

Better, he said.

Oh my, that is wonderful, I said. And I got up and started for the riverbank. I told him I would boil some cattails for our breakfast and have our trusty vessel fixed in no time. We should be sailing out of this place by the afternoon, I said. I will have you to a doctor quicker than chain lightning with a tailwind.

I'm not going, he said.

Stop being silly. We must get you to a doctor.

I don't want one, he said.

I told him that was foolishness.

I can't go to a hospital.

Why not? I said.

I'll be all right, he said.

Now, look, you are badly hurt, I told him. You require a doctor.

He looked ahead to the river. I can't go to a hospital, he said. I'm wanted by the FBI.

I did not say a word for what seemed like a good long while. Finally, being that no conversation I had ever had before had prepared me for this one, I asked him a silly question. I asked him if he was a fugitive.

He said: I'd just like you to know I didn't do what they say I did.

What are you accused of having done?

They say I kidnapped a ten-year-old girl.

What makes them say a silly thing like that?

A misunderstanding, he said.

What misunderstanding?

He looked to sink some into the dirt under that pine. I fell in love with a younger girl, he said. The police got involved. I wasn't charged with anything, but they know about it. After that I was staying in a house down the street from where this other girl was supposed to have disappeared. I can't understand why they'd think I did it other than that. I woke up one morning and a drawing of my face was on the news, but they didn't know my name or who I was. I still don't know how my face got there.

I told him that I did not understand, then I asked him how old was the girl he had fallen in love with.

Twelve years old, he said, and gripped his thigh. I'd never hurt anybody, he said.

Again I did not have word one to say for some time. I recall folding my muddy hands in my lap and watching the water run in the river. What did you do to her?

Who?

The twelve-year-old girl.

I didn't do anything to her, he said. I met her at the mall. I worked at the movie theater in there. She'd come in, see a movie, and talk to me. We'd go to the food court and get Chinese food.

Did you touch her?

What do you mean?

Did you touch her inappropriately?

One day we were in a movie and we kissed. We started doing that. We held each other and kissed and that's all we ever did. I only ever saw her at the movie theater. I loved her, I'd never have hurt her.

I was quiet again for a spell. I thought back now to what I had seen of this man. The elastic undergarment bands he had worn around his wrists and the women's undergarment I had found in his coat pocket. The old key that looked like it had gone to an old padlock. The glittery stockings and pink shirt I was wearing, which he had given me. Where had they come from? My heart was jumping like a loosed bird dog. I realized I had backed away from him.

Finally I said: Why would you want to do that with a twelve-year-old girl?

He exhaled and slumped a little in pain. I don't see myself when I look at people my age, he said. They look older. I think, that person can't be my age.

I told him again that I did not understand.

I'm not attracted to them, he said. It's hard when you're different inside than what you are on the outside. People don't accept someone when they're not what they're supposed to be.

We will go to the doctor and then we will go to the police station and sort all this out. You do not have to be out here if you are innocent.

Yes I do, the man said. Innocent or not.

I said to him, Now, listen, Garland—

My name's not Garland.

Tell me the truth, please. I would like to know, and be honest, for whatever God may or may not be anymore, and I do not know, whatever He is He is telling you to be honest right this minute. Did you take that little girl?

No, the man said. I did not.

I watched him for a spell.

He said: You want to know why I'm here in this place, like this? I'm out here because I can't help the way I am or what I like. I don't think I'm very different from anybody else that way.

He sat there shrunken against that pine glistening white as stone. The flesh on his leg had grown porous and was welted with colorful polyps. He trembled something terrible and would not look me in the eyes. I was not sure what to think. But I mean to tell you I have hardly ever experienced more compassion for someone in all my now ninety-two years on this earth. I do not doubt but that many of you will hold that I am an amoral old witch to have compassion for a man like that. However most of you have not lived past the end of your life to claw your way back to a world where its inhabitants and all the things which they have created seem small and ridiculous and beyond concern or consequence. Without you having lived through something like that, I do not believe you will ever understand. I do not believe that I can describe it. What I will put down here is that I have found that morality is not the anchor of goodness, and that a person is too many things to be the one thing that we all want them to be for our convenience. Whatever else this man was, he was right about that.

I took his filthy hand in mine and held it. He turned and I imagine that he saw something in my face which comforted him for he squeezed my hand and let out a good long sigh.

I told him that I would go and pull up some cattails and get water to boil before we set out again, because whatever he had done or had not done I was not going to leave him there. He shut his eyes and put his head back to the pine.

I had gone upriver to fill the tin in some calm water. I was hoping to catch some minnows and tadpoles with it too. A cool breeze was blowing. It almost sounded like it did back in Texas. Gracious, did it sound good! I shut my eyes and I saw the rippling plains of yellow grass and all the country roads smoking up with dust and I saw our little house and the water tower above turning shade around it like an enormous gnomon, measuring out the days until that first Sunday morning of that strange and terrible season of Kingdomtide when I would board a little airplane in Missoula and fall out of the clear blue sky into the Bitterroot Mountains.

I opened up my eyes and took the tin from the river. I studied it for a minnow or a crawfish or some other unfortunate critter I might have caught. But the only thing in that tin was an odd little feather floating on top of the water. When I looked up, great pulpy tufts of them were blowing around me, maelstromed in the breeze, twisting and curling and alighting on the river like white and gray mayflies. It was a mighty strange but beautiful sight to behold.

I looked around to see if I could know where they were coming from and I peeked on down through the trees to where I had left the man. He was some ten yards or so downriver and I could just see his boots between the boles. Those little feathers clouded the whole place, frothy white like the burp of the sea.

I made my way back to him with the tin of water under my arm, righting myself with my walking stick. More and more of these little feathers came with each gentle gust of wind. They festooned the trees and the granite and stuck in the grass and sure enough it got to where it looked as if a weird and otherworldly snow had fallen.

I hollered to the man: Do you see this?

I rounded a tree and found him on his side in a place of sun. His down coat was partly snagged on a branch, making for a posture that held his arms up an inch above the ground in the manner of an orchestra conductor. His coat was tore open and the down of it spilled out and the wind was carrying it off in great big dollops. I dropped my walking stick and went to his side quick as I could. I knelt there by him and unhitched him from the branch. Then I rolled him on his back and brushed the feathers from his face.

I have heard it said before that often as not when people pass away they look as if they have only gone to sleep. I do not believe that anyone who says this has ever truly seen a dead person. If you know the face at all you can see death in it by the way the face settles or looks stopped on some unknown eternal thought. When Davy passed away there was an open casket at the wake. I was only a young girl but I recall looking at my little brother embalmed and rigid there in his little coffin and believing that someone was meaning to trick me. He did not look like the little boy I knew and cared for. I was certain he was an effigy in wax, fabricated by some nitwit who had not known him at all.

I have corresponded with a kind physician in Michigan, Dr. Rebecca Alcott, and what she believes happened was that the man had endeavored to stand and this had put too much strain on his already septic and traumatized system and caused cardiac arrest. He had fallen to the ground dead, but not before catching his coat on a low pointy branch and spilling the stuffing to the breeze.

I sat there for a spell with his body in the sun and the gleaming goose down and the wind. When I got up again I gathered from it what I could use and left it behind.

VIII

The carcass of an elk swung from an eyebolt screwed into the eave of a hunting shack. It was half-flayed like a man with one arm in his coat. Lewis cut the engine, honked the horn, and leaned across the passenger's seat to crank down the window. She called out a name.

A black head cocked wildly from behind the shack, then came the rest of the large man. He bounded shoeless to the Wagoneer in a tuxedo too small for him. His wiry hair was pulled back into pigtails and he wore his mustaches old-fashioned and curled with lard. Ranger Lewis, he said as he reached the Wagoneer and rested a forearm on the open window of the passenger's door. Workin on a Sunday?

Almost didn't recognize you, Eric.

Yap, tryin out somethin for this woman I met down the mountain last week. I bought this here money suit off a destitute ombudsman in Missoula.

Looks nice.

Thank you, Ranger Lewis. You look nice too.

Feel like hell. I quit drinkin this weekend. Got another call in about you, Eric.

What'd I do this time? T'weren't somebody in one of those tents I fell all over last week, was it? They got to put them suckers up in the tent area. If I go to the spigot for some potable in the night, which is my unassailable right, I cain't see them tents just the way I cain't see a hat on a flea.

No, wasn't them. Somebody made a report you were swimmin in the nude close to the campgrounds.

Which area?

Goddamn Clover, I think it was.

So you're tellin me I cain't swim in the buff up here? What century'd the nekkid body get to be so offensive? If you cain't get nekkid up here what's all this for?

There're rules of common decency, Lewis said. Bylaws and codes, nationwide for all parks and recreational zones. Especially if there're children around. Goddamn decency.

Eric shook his head and twirled in his fingers the end of a mustache. My great litterbox, he said. Why's one silly offense mean more than another? I cain't no longer see the beginnin to the sense and the end to the nonsense.

Just stay away from the campgrounds. That's all you got to do, goddamn it. All right?

All right, all right, Eric said. Hey, you guys ever find that old lady you was lookin for?

No. She never materialized.

Now that is sad. Old ones love a spot named for their bones so their kids can visit.

Lewis leaned back and started up the engine and spat out the driver's side window. Could you tell me somethin?

Hope so.

Why're you livin out here like this?

Well, Ranger Lewis, people generally don't like me.

Lewis nodded. Let me ask you, you seen anythin at all out of the ordinary recently?

Eric turned his greased face to the sky and squinted at the cold fall sun. His dark eyes watered. I seen so many things out the ordinary, I just cain't tell what the ordinary is anymore.

But what about smoke, you see any more over there on the Old Pass?

There's been a lot more smoke comin from up that way than there used to be. Almost like you got campers like it was back in the sixties when people wasn't afeared to lose sight of a radio tower. One night I saw what I surmise was a big stinky fire goin. I'll say, look.

Lewis looked to where the man pointed. There were peaks high in the clouds and the snow there turned off them into the sun, and the trees formed a meniscus below tunneling out into oblivion and there she spied a cut of white near lost in the daylight.

That goddamn smoke?

Yap. Must be.

Lewis shook her head. She shifted out of park and clasped together her hands and leaned on the wheel. Who knows who's up there, she said.

The next day she went into the station early and turned on the space heater and the coffee percolator and as dawn came in the wide window she read the *Missoulian* under the weak bulb at her desk. The newspaper was a day old, dated Sunday, November 9, 1986. On the front page next to an article about Iran was a newsprint picture of the missing girl. *Sarah Hovett still missing, authorities assume the worst.*

Lewis finished the newspaper and dropped it in the wastebasket at her feet. She brought in a cardboard box from the Wagoneer and cleared out her desk. She filled a plastic sack with the empty wine bottles she had hidden in the space between the desk and the wall and she went to the sink in the kitchenette and emptied the thermos of merlot. The merlot circled the drain and she recalled how it was to help her father wash the bone saws and lancets after surgery at the clinic.

It was 9:05 a.m. by the wall clock when Claude came through the station door. He stopped in the doorway. I'd say we usually do that in the spring, don't we?

Lewis was wiping down the desk with a damp rag. She dropped it. Claude, you've been a real goddamn good colleague, she said. But I can't find the joy in this job anymore.

Joy?

I'm movin to a big city. Someplace like Seattle or Boston.

I'd say this'll be leavin this station undermanned.

Pete already leave?

Left before the weekend, Claude said, looking out the window behind her. I'd say he's back in Big Timber by now. Claude touched the scraggly scarf he wore around his neck. Left me this goofy thing he'd been knittin.

He's a nice man, Lewis said.

I'd say he's all right.

A strange bird.

He's that too.

John said he'd be sendin my replacement up on Thursday, Lewis said. A man by the name of Sokolov.

Sokolov? I'd say he's Russian.

I expect so.

I guess I can't say I'm surprised you're leavin.

You'll be all right, Lewis said. Eric Coolidge and goddamn Silk Foot Maggie can't get into too much trouble in three days. Then you'll have Sokolov.

What'll you do in Boston?

I don't know if it'll be Boston. Goddamn, I don't know. I figure I can find a job in the city park service.

Claude took the campaign hat from his head and smoothed his neat black hair. You know someone shot Charlie?

What's that?

Yeah. Few days ago. Shot her to pieces.

Her?

Charlie was a bitch.

Lewis looked out the window at a flock of geese shadowing the valley. I'd forgot.

Found her out back a ways. Her bowels were irregular, you remember. I let her go off by herself for some privacy. Shot to pieces. I'd say someone with a lot of hate had to do a thing like that.

You didn't hear anythin?

I was in the shower.

I'm sorry, Claude.

Thought you might've, Claude said.

What?

Heard somethin at your place.

No. Sorry.

Well, it's goin to get pretty lonely up here, I'd say. Claude thumbed the blue end of his nose.

Lewis unpinned the badge from her chest and set it on the clean desk, where only the holstered revolver and the receiver to the radio remained. The light from the window gave clouds to the lacquer there. Lewis touched her fingertips to the desk, paused a moment, then swung the plastic sack of wine bottles over a shoulder and went clinking to the door. Grab that box?

Claude replaced the campaign hat on his head and lifted the box and followed her out to the Wagoneer. He set the box in the backseat and folded his arms and watched Lewis drop the plastic sack in the back.

Thunderclouds rolled over them and they both looked up. I'm sorry you still haven't got any proof of Cornelia Åkersson, Lewis said.

I saw her, Debs. I don't need anybody else to believe me. I know I saw her and the glyptodont. I'd say that's all that really matters.

All right. That's fine.

Claude nodded down the road. I'm sorry it didn't work out between you and Officer Bloor.

Goddamn it, Lewis said. It just wasn't right.

Nope, didn't seem right to me neither.

No?

No, said Claude. Talk about a strange bird.

Lewis came around to the front of the Wagoneer and leaned on the hood. I'll be lookin forward to a visit whenever I get where I'm goin.

I'd say you don't know me very well if you think I'm goin to go to Boston.

Been eleven years, Claude.

Claude clicked his tongue and looked off. Well, people come and go, I'd say. You can do nothin for it. He looked at his boots. Blood stained the hems of his trousers. I'd say it's when you try and hold on to somethin, that's when you get into the real trouble. I think you've got to keep a loose grip on everything you love.

I figure that's probably right, Lewis said. You're my best friend, Claude. Want you to know that.

Thank you.

I meant it. Never had a better goddamn friend. I'm sorry I've not always been a good one back.

Claude shook his head. He pulled taut his uniform and straightened his back and saluted over the brim of his campaign hat. To care for the land and serve the people, he said.

Lewis returned the salute. To care for the land and serve the people.

Claude smiled and reached up and put a hand to her arm. So long.

Lewis nodded and climbed into the Wagoneer and Claude headed back to the station. She waited a moment and honked the horn. Claude turned at the station door. She leaned over and cranked down the passenger's window. I shot your dog, Claude, she called out. I'm goddamn sorry about it.

Claude stood there and looked up to the brim of his campaign hat. I figured, he called back. It's all right. So long, he said, and turned back to the station.

Lewis watched the screen door clack shut behind him and pulled out onto the road.

Thunder shook the night mountains and rain lashed the windshield. Lewis, clear eyes ahead, brought the Wagoneer down the winding alpine road and buffed with the end of a finger the surface of her teeth. When she rounded a bend she passed a beat-up towncar heading the other direction up the mountain. In the dark a ghoulish woman behind the wheel was briefly lit up by the instrumentation, her lime-colored face like that of a corpse, mouth wide and abyssal, hair in a big bouffant. At that moment the two strangers were the most important people in each other's lives, for all that separated them from certain death, Lewis figured, was a painted yellow line and faith in the system.

Lewis turned on the radio and listened to a woman with throat cancer and a voice like a jaw harp phone in to ask Dr. Howe about the nature of grief and why had her sister wanted everyone at their mother's funeral to see her cry. For the vast majority of people, Dr. Howe said, grief is what you do to remind everyone that you are a person. That you have inside you an entire universe of emotion and thought, a universe that only you can truly know and access.

Before long Lewis reached the bottom of the mountain and pulled out onto Florida Avenue and the flat land. She drove north and arrived in Missoula in little over an hour, steering under the warm streetlights and listening yet to the radio show and the rain. A man with a deep voice soon phoned in, and he asked Dr. Howe about love, and how could he ever know for certain when he had it. Love is a wonderful and elusive state of being, Dr. Howe said. By its very nature it is difficult to explain to someone who has not found themselves in a position to know it. Love is something that you will know when you feel it, and when you are in love you will know.

Lewis shook her head and turned down a small street lined with closed shops and darkened alleyways. Dr. Howe went on defining love for the man with the deep voice. Lewis spotted a rain-swept pay phone bolted to a brick building next to a bus stop, orange under a streetlight. She swung the Wagoneer to the side of the street and halfway up onto the sidewalk in front of the pay phone. She scooted across the seats and turned up the radio and climbed out the passenger's door into the rain.

She fished two quarters from her pocket and pushed them into the pay phone slot. Already she was soaked through and her dark hair was matted down over her head like a straw hat with a frayed brim. Lewis dialed the number she knew by heart and gave the squeaky voice on the other end her maiden name. The voice told her that hers would be the next call on air.

Over the pummeling rain Lewis listened to the radio blaring from the Wagoneer. Love is something worth hoping for, waiting for, Dr. Howe said. It is the salve to all trouble and fear, only it is hard to discover and even harder to sustain. I hope you find it. Thank you for calling in, Mr. Hopscotch, and good luck. And now we have our next caller, Miss Silvernail. You're on the air, Miss Silvernail, how can I help?

I don't think you've got any of that right about love, Dr. Howe, Lewis said.

Do you want to tell me why you feel that way?

Yes. I was sure I was fallin in love with a girl much younger than me. She's eighteen. I'm older than that.

Do you identify as a lesbian, Miss Silvernail?

That's not important. But I'll tell you what I figured out about fallin in love with this goddamn girl. It wasn't hardly anythin to do with her. I enjoyed her company and I was attracted to her. For a little while I couldn't figure if I was like a mother or somethin else. Didn't know what she thought of me either. And I started to get the urge to squeeze her and kiss her and show her all kinds of affection and protection. I thought that was love.

What was it if not love?

Lewis sighed. Rain traced her face and her hand on the handset. Well, I don't know, goddamn it. That's the point. Desperation, maybe. I've never been good about carin for people. But I just decided I'm not goin to give names to things I don't understand. Names like love. The joy of love. The joy of sex. Right or wrong, good or bad. I don't figure anybody should be doin that anymore.

How should we talk about anything like love if we do not have a word to use to signify it?

We don't know what it is, Dr. Howe. That's the point, goddamn it. How're we ever goin to talk about it no matter what we call it? It's all the same behind all those goddamn words.

Watch your language if you can, Miss Silvernail.

I just decided I'm goin to live without them. Is that all right with everybody out there? Cause of people like you sayin that shit you've been sayin over and over again, usin all those old meaningless words, there's still goin to be a whole lot of people gettin together just cause it feels good to get to say them to someone else. They're in love, they'll say. Then they get all worked up over who they think they are and they don't have to be alone anymore with all the thoughts about who they aren't. Goddamn it. We're not a true goddamn social animal out here, Dr. Howe, much as we try and convince ourselves otherwise.

Perhaps you are simply expressing your own antisocial feelings.

No. Somehow this eighteen-year-old girl understood all that. She might be a genius, even though her goddamn dad thinks she's retarded. I'd like to figure her generation or the generation after's goin to do a better job than we ever did with words like love. And Mr.

Hopscotch, if you're still listenin, I'm sorry, but I don't figure there is love the way you want it, so you're not goin to find it in anythin but stories. I figure love bein a real thing is just one of those lies we'll never admit to. Something phony to keep us occupied and entertained and lookin for nothin. Just another stupid goddamn ghost story.

It sounds like you must really be hurting, Miss Silvernail.

Down the street an old woman carrying an umbrella walked alone, stooped and deformed, moving away into the rain made visible by the streetlights. No, not yet, Lewis said. I'm just gettin ready for it.

Lewis hung up the pay phone and went farther into the rain after the old woman. The garbled radio show faded behind her as she made her way down the dark and quiet street: *So on that rather disheartening note, we must close our show for this evening, wishing Miss Silvernail all the love in the world...*

Excuse me, Lewis called to the old woman. Excuse me, ma'am.

The old woman turned. She had no face that Lewis recognized.

I'm sorry. Goddamn it. I thought you were somebody else.

There are all manner of uncommon perversions. The first and only time I got into that Internet without our dear grandniece there to shepherd me I read an article about a young man, a Daniel Plant, who claims to have had sexual intercourse with 2,367 cats and dogs and 112 even-toed ungulates. Apparently he takes great pride in his efforts, as he had requested inclusion in the *Guinness Book of World Records*. I understand he was denied. Now, what is a person, let alone a person my age, supposed to make of a thing like that? I have now spent some time reading about the sexual customs of different cultures throughout history, and there are certain practices I have learned about that have upset and confused me tremendously. Those of Ancient Greece, in particular, and how even now on some islands in the Pacific women have more than one husband while on other islands the elderly are known to bed children, all of it acceptable to them. But I suppose we are all for better or worse deviants of one kind or another to someone somewhere in the world. Depending on the way things are at the time, some of us stand out more than the rest.

When you give it any thought, it sure is funny how we decide what ought and ought not to be tolerated in the civilized world as time goes on. I cannot always find the reasoning in it. We all desire one thing or another. I suppose we just have to find the decent way to go about getting it, without causing misery to those who do not want the same things we do. The problem with Mr. Plant is that we do not know whether or not any of these animals consented. I am inclined to think they did not. I do not know Mr. Plant but I have not heard of any man who could talk a pig into having sexual intercourse with him.

However here is the problem with passing judgment on Mr. Plant: we do not give a pig much say about anything else a pig does. I do not believe pigs volunteer themselves up for bacon duty. Yet most people in this country are mighty happy to play a part in that. What I have come to understand now is that judgment is often passed as a matter of convenience. And I am inclined to believe that the savage satisfaction most of us get in casting the first stone will be the eventual undoing of civilization. For this reason I fear there is no remedy to the problems we have understanding one another, and I dare not venture a guess as to how any of it is going to end. The only solace that I can find in any of this is that I do not expect to be around much longer to see how bad it all gets.

An Agent Derek Ellery at the Federal Bureau of Investigation spoke with me in the weeks following my return to civilization. I told him about my friend out in the Bitterroot. After that, I never heard anything more from Agent Ellery. He was a curt and dismissive young man and I do not know that he believed me. Years later, while doing my research for this account, I was directed to a now retired FBI Special Agent named James Polite. He has been mighty gracious to answer the very many questions of a very persistent and very old woman. I have told him my story and he believes the man who came to my aid out in the Bitterroot may have been a man by the name of Benjamin Merbecke.

The FBI hold that on Friday, June 27, 1986, at approximately 1:35 a.m., Merbecke entered the Phoenix home of Michael and Paula Hovett through an unlocked backdoor. They will tell you that Merbecke ascended the stairs to the second story, where he crept into the bedroom of the Hovetts' only child. He is thought to have rendered ten-year-old Sarah Hovett unconscious with a rag soaked in a fast-acting paralytic and to have removed her from the premises to some unknown location, likely someplace in the Idaho wilderness. As I put down this account in the year 2006, some twenty years later, it is my terrible duty here to include that they have not yet found poor Sarah Hovett. May God keep her wherever she might be. There is little else as cruel as a missing child.

For several months into the investigation of the abduction they could not identify the suspect. Eventually the FBI put Merbecke's name to the individual they and the newspapers had been calling the Arizona Kisser. His description matched that of an adult male who had been going around kissing young girls, and a man matching his description was also spotted buying girls' undergarments at various outfitters.

Special Agent Polite lives up to his name and was kind enough to visit me (in an unofficial capacity) here at River Bend Assisted Living in Brattleboro, Vermont. He showed me one of the composite drawings they do at the FBI. It seems it is the only image of Benjamin Merbecke that has turned up. The FBI has not been able to locate any photography of him. There were no images at the Department of Motor Vehicles, and apparently his mother told them that she had lost the family photo album in a flooded basement. The composite drawing was developed from the testimony of a woman who reported that she had seen a suspicious man circling a middle school near the Hovetts' neighborhood the evening of June 26th. My goodness, I mean to tell you the drawing was the spitting image of my gallant friend. If the drawing had been in color, I imagine it would have had emerald-green eyes. Therefore, I accept that it is likely that this Merbecke and my friend in the Bitterroot are one and the same man.

Many people believe that Merbecke took Sarah Hovett. However, twenty years later, the investigation into the abduction is as yet ongoing. As such, Special Agent Polite could not tell me everything they had in the way of evidence against Merbecke, but from what I understand it is flimsy and circumstantial. Special Agent Polite has said as much. It is a considerable shame they do not have any of that DNA evidence that is popular today. I believe that it would show Merbecke is innocent of the abduction, however guilty he may be of his other behavior. But Merbecke has quit the earth, and his body has never been recovered. Still some crazy folk do not want to believe me on the fact that he is deceased. No doubt some people believe that I am making all this up.

I will put down what is generally known.

Merbecke lived in a carriage house down the road from the Hovett household. He punched tickets at the Cine Desert picture house frequented by Sarah and her friends. It is unclear if Sarah knew him or not. He had been let go from a position at a summer camp some years prior for having an inappropriate relationship with a twelve-year-old girl there, and again from the picture house under similar circumstances. He never was arrested nor charged with any crime, but some lawmen did speak with him and made note of it. He was also known to buy girls' undergarments. I will put down here too for good measure that I asked Special Agent Polite about the silly clothes Merbecke had given me to wear and if they had been Sarah Hovett's. He could not provide me with an answer.

I cannot say to a certainty whether or not Benjamin Merbecke kidnapped that poor girl. There are very few subjects anymore which I can speak to with certainty. However, I do not believe he did. Some of you will slam this book shut and holler that I am a silly old woman warped and rattled by the awful privation of my ordeal and the loss of my husband and that I am without the sense God gave a pig. You get to decide for yourself what you want to believe.

Still, no, I do not entirely know what to make of it all. But I do not allow that this man was too terribly different from the rest of us. As far as I can tell, we sure do all cause a good deal of trouble trying to get what we want. We are all of us the benefactors of someone else's disadvantage some way or another, whether we would call it that or not. We take turns being bound to secret altars, and we take turns wielding the sacrificial knife. I do not now shy away from the truth that I am a part of that and that Mr. Waldrip might could have married himself a better wife. I have taken more than I can ever hope to give back, and just by going for a little ole walk outside I set new roads for the wind.

There is no great question that the flinty moralists out there who know this story will find nothing in their hearts for Benjamin Merbecke. I surely cannot fault them. Prior to my adventure I would have stood with them in contempt of that pitiful man. Yet whatever uncommon perversion was in him, he had some stroke of heroism in him too, periling his life for me as he did. I cannot be sure that Catherine Drewer would have done any of what he did for me out there in the Bitterroot. I expect she would have thumped me on the head and devoured me over a low flame.

All I am certain of is that Merbecke was not evil. The only authentic evil I can see in people begins with calling other people evil. Nothing quite makes the sense we would like it to. There are those who just do not fit with the way we have it all set up here nowadays, and that is just the way it is. I suppose I sympathize with Merbecke a little bit about that.

I fear that misfits like Merbecke may be the least of our worries. I see a dead emptiness in young folk today. Sometimes I worry that there is little left in a person these days save the desire to participate in a mighty strange collective fever dream of fakery and grand-scale mischief. Perhaps I am just too old and do not know how to play along. Maybe those leaving the world always bemoan its being left worse off for those to follow. The good old days have gone, we say. Maybe I just cannot see what the young people see today with their clear eyes shining against all those impossible lights.

That night after Merbecke passed on, it began to rain. I took shelter leeward a limestone outcrop and used the flip lighter to set a fire in some dry wood I turned up there. I put out the tin to catch water and then slept poorly, curled up to the limestone and wrapped in Terry's coat.

In the dark I woke to enormous footfalls in the trees like those of a fairy-tale giant. A bull elk the size of Mr. Waldrip's truck came along. He was a mangy old thing and had antlers that looked as if they had grown too heavy for him. They were chipped and scarred like an old table in need of a good varnishing. I would imagine that he was my age in elk years, howsoever those tally. And gracious, he was big!

I did not move. He settled by me against the outcrop not two yards away. I could have reached out and touched him. I sat up until sunrise listening to the old beast struggle to breathe and to the pluck of the rain on his hide. Then I got up slowly and as quietly as I could I took the tin and sallied forth again into that gentle storm. Downstream I followed the little river. The sun came out in the rain. Mr. Waldrip used to say that meant the Devil was spanking his wife.

The nights were dark and damp and cold and it poured some through all of them. Thank goodness it did not snow. I did not sleep much. When I did sleep it was to dream of hot baths and hollow glass people filling up with hot water. Still I pulled on downriver each morning, hammering the earth with the end of my walking stick. I ate anything I could. Mostly I suppered on tubers and once a handful of worms from a rotted beehive. I did not often stop to fish. I understood I had to keep moving.

By my count I was by my lonesome making my way downriver for five days and four nights until I came to a dewy little cedar brake. Although the rain had let up that day, clouds still covered the sky, but it was not very cold. I sat to rest on a small sickly variety of juniper. I dropped my walking stick to the ground and sipped water from the tin and watched the mountains.

When I would come to find my way out of that wilderness I made big headlines in the newspapers and was met with a good deal of fame and celebrity. I have encountered many remarkable people in the twenty years since. One such person was a lively and charismatic woman with curly brown hair cut short and peculiar scars on her face almost like chicken wire. Her name was Jillian, if I recall aright. She had an unusual accent, as if she had emigrated from a country that may not exist. I met her earlier this year while I was making a talk at the Explorers Club in New York City about an article I had written for a magazine on the twentieth anniversary of my ordeal. The article was titled "Kingdomtide: A Seventy-Two-Year-Old Woman's and a Masked Man's Journey Through the Bitterroot Wilderness." Anyhow this Jillian approached me as I was leaving and told me that she had known all about my story back at the time. When she was seventeen years old she had been a volunteer with the Forest Service in Montana during the time of my ordeal. Her father had led the search party that had gone after me and she made mention of a park ranger there, a woman named Debra Lewis, who had persisted in the search after everyone else had abandoned it. Jillian said that she had not thought much about that time for many years, and had not kept in touch with this park ranger, but her story and description of this woman have left a lasting impression on me.

I made an effort to track down Ranger Debra Lewis but have so far not had any luck. There were two leads, a ranger named Claude Paulson whom she had worked with, and a ranger chief named John

Gaskell. The former was sorry to say he had not heard from her after she had left, and the latter has unfortunately passed. Debra Lewis remains as yet a stranger to me, although I think on her from time to time. It is hard work to know what difference she had in my adventure. Perhaps her efforts remain unproven and without purpose. Perhaps, in the end, they are the same as Benjamin Merbecke's. Same as mine. I never had any good reason to live these twenty more years after I crawled out of that little airplane. I suppose the terrible truth of it is that not an earthly creature ever has any good reason to live at all. But we do it anyhow, even when we have all the good reason in the world not to. And just take a gander at all the harm we do. All the which of it is to say that if Ranger Lewis has occasion to read this account, I hope she would find that I have done the story justice.

I was mighty tired as the sun went down on what by my count was my seventy-seventh night out there in the Bitterroot. I looked through the trees to the world-old mountains behind me. I picked out the one I knew to be where the little airplane had gone down, where I imagined that Mr. Waldrip's body yet dangled. The entire place looked smaller to me now. Through a break in the clouds the red sunset rolled down the mountain and turned it blue with night.

Over the bowed and sickly juniper I draped a filthy piece of the blanket I had preserved from the hut and made a tent to keep the spitting rain off. I did not build a fire that night. I wrapped myself in Terry's coat and pulled my legs into a ball as much as I could and I slept.

I woke to the sound of the ocean and the sun on my face. Somewhere waves were breaking on a beach. I had not heard that sound in thirty-two years. The last time was just after my fortieth birthday. We had paid a visit to Mr. Waldrip's brother in Florida to watch him pass away in a hospital near the water. After he did, Mr. Waldrip and I walked down to the beach and we sat out in the sun with our eyes shut. I recall listening to the waves and opening up my eyes to find Mr. Waldrip's alligator-skin boots nearby with his socks balled up in them. He had gone and trotted off to wade out in the water with his blue jeans rolled up to his knees. He played there in the waves like a little boy and I recall thinking just how terribly much I loved him and how I sure did not look forward to the day when we would have to part ways.

I opened up my eyes to the sun. The blanket had blown off in the night and I could not find it anywhere. The rain had quit and so had the wind. I looked to where I had heard the waves and I heard the sound again. It was a peaceful swooshing behind the trees. The notion struck me that perhaps I had lost track of time and had traveled for months and had followed that river clear to the ocean.

I set my walking stick and pushed myself to my feet. The swooshing had gone again as quickly as it had come, but my eye caught something different through the trees. I pushed forward in my tore-up shoes, ducked under a spruce, and stepped out into the bright sunlight. My hair was longer than I had worn it since I was a young woman, my getup as strange as a city person's and considerably tattered and now the color of earth. But bless you, I was standing on the side of a two-lane paved road!

I dropped my walking stick and went to my knees. I pressed the palm of my hand to the warm asphalt. All was dead quiet. There were no cars on the road that I could tell in either direction. It went on straight in both ways, cleaving a timbered valley until it could not be seen. I stood up again but had no use for my walking stick. I looked from one end of the road to the other.

It was not but ten minutes before a blurry element appeared in the far haze off to my left. I could not take my eyes from it. They stung and tears ran off my cheeks. The object drew closer and closer and by and by I could see it was a station wagon. Even now I can shut my eyes and conjure it, growing larger on the road until it slowed and halted just a couple yards from me.

A young woman got out. She had on a green bowler hat and a black leather coat such as I have seen worn by noisy motorcyclists. She looked at me like I was a polka-dotted cow. She said: Are you all right, ma'am?

I could do with a ride to the nearest town, I told her.

This dear young lady, whom I would later know by the name of Sidney Wygant, was a mighty kind and earnest young woman. She had been away at school in Spokane, Washington, for some curious thing called urbanology and was driving home to Colorado. She had decided to take the scenic route through the mountains.

Sidney approached me and gave me her arm.

She walked me to her station wagon and opened the door and helped me inside, then got in on the other side and set us off down that paved road away from the wilderness. I looked ahead out the windshield and waited for the buildings and power lines to rise on the thin horizon beyond the little pine-tree-shaped air freshener swinging from Sidney's rearview mirror.

When I later made my return to Clarendon, Sheriff Daugharty had to let me into our dear little house under the water tower. By that time the locks had been replaced, being that the sheriff had been obliged to knock down our front door. Not a soul had been privy to the key Mr. Waldrip kept hid under the rock shaped like a steer. The house was dark and empty. About the only thing left in it were the furniture marks in the carpeting, and someone had missed the First Methodist calendar of 1986 pasted on the pantry door. The pantry light switch was left up and the bulb had gone out, and the calendar pages stirred in the breeze blowing in from the front, where the sheriff stood waiting for me. The pages were still flipped to August. I was overcome with sentiment then and I ran my finger over that little circle Mr. Waldrip had drawn around the 31st, the first Sunday of Kingdomtide. I myself have since circled on that calendar the last Sunday of that desperate season, the 16th of November 1986, the day I escaped the fearsome Bitterroot.

However nothing escapes the hands of the clock. And nothing of life comes to mean exactly what you expect it will, and neither is it often simple nor easy, particularly when you get to be my age. Though I do not care for the language, I am here reminded of something that Colonel Goodnight, the father of the Texas Panhandle and inventor of the chuck wagon, once said: Old age hath its honors, but it is damned inconvenient.

It is winter now of the year 2006 as I close this account and I mean to tell you I am not the same woman I was. Whatever strange parts here remain of me will soon be returned to Clarendon. I am having my body flown back. While I do not care to live another day in Texas, I will not mind being buried there. My body will be interred at the Clarendon Citizens' Cemetery, there under the drifting seeds of a little ole cottonwood beside my dear Mr. Waldrip.

Acknowledgments

The author would like to thank: James Hannaham, Doug Stewart, Ben George, Helen Garnons-Williams, Reagan Arthur, Craig Young, Ben Allen, Liz Garriga, Szilvia Molnar, Danielle Bukowski, Caspian Dennis, Ashley Marudas, Gregg Kulick, Oliver Gallmeister, Liv Marsden, Philippe Beyvin, Evan Hansen-Bundy, Alice Lawson, Joe Veltre, Amanda Lowe, Clarinda Mac Low, Don T. Curtis, Diane F. Curtis, Shanna Peeples, Deidre F. Schoolcraft, Rhonda LeGate, Madison David, Blair Pfander, Bob LeGate, Jessy Lanza, Winston Case, Ayse Hassan, Ahbra Perry, Taylor Higgins, Emma L. Beren, Penny Nicholes, Madeline and Lester Farrington, the author's family and friends, the Diamond Tail Ranch, and Emily "Mimi" LeGate.

About the Author

Rye Curtis is originally from Amarillo, Texas. He is a graduate of Columbia University and now lives in Queens. This is his first novel.